SOMETHING TO HOLD
ONTO

Something to Hold Onto

Silver Series Book Two

MELISSA K. MORGAN

Contents

Published by Melissa K. Morgan, Edited by Cameron Yaeger, (Aurora Publicity), Cover by Melody Barber, (Aurora Publicity)
First Printing, 2020
Imprint: Independently Published

For Mickey Silver
You're the loudest voice in my head.

Chapter 1

Mick

There's a saying in life that good things come to those who wait. That doesn't work for me since I'm one of the most impatient people on the planet. Don't mistake that for not having *good* things. I've got more than my fair share of desirable assets and then some. Patience may be a virtue, but I've never been known for my morality.

Do you know why good things happen for me? It isn't luck or fate or some random philosophical bullshit. I make it happen. I work my ass off for what I want. That's how it's always been.

Being the prodigal son of Jack Silver, lead drug kingpin for the Pacific Northwest since 1985, I had no other choice. He was my father, my teacher, my boss. If I didn't strive to reach his level of success, I'd be useless. That's why I take what I want or die trying, and I'm not dead yet, so I'd say I'm a success.

People call me a workaholic or an asshole who's selfish and ruthless. They're probably right, so I'll take it. Just like I take everything else I want. I don't give a damn what anyone thinks of me because I've soared higher than most people, including all the druggies I know.

There's only one person who's ever been able to slow me down and she's sitting in the chair opposite my desk ringing her fingers together so tightly I'm afraid she'll break them. She's been my best friend for years, almost like a sister to me.

I frowned as I crossed my arms over my chest. It's been a long time since I've seen her this quiet.

"Mackaela, talk to me," I urged softly.

Her amber eyes flicked up to mine with the faintest smile ghosting her lips. It's nice to see her smile after all these years. She's been doing that a lot more lately thanks to my brother, Simon. He had a way of bringing her out of the depths of brokenness. A way that I didn't because as much as I loved this woman, she needed someone stable, someone comfortable enough to walk away from this business without glancing back.

I was working on that myself, although there were still a few loose ends to tie up.

She inhaled a deep breath her shoulders rising. "Okay, here it goes ... " I arched a brow at her. "Mickey, I have something to tell you. I don't want you to freak out. I was talking to Sadie yesterday and she mentioned Ricky Delgado. I know you've been looking for him since ... well, since what happened with Simon. There's a rumor he's picking some of your guys off."

Freak out? Nah that wasn't my style. Blood boil with pent up rage? Hell yeah. I wasn't sure what to say that didn't result in several expletives, so I kept my mouth shut, biting back on my molars as she continued.

"I think Simon would look into it himself even though he's not really interested. You know he doesn't want to get involved if he doesn't have to." I did know that. I helped him get out of this brutal life right along with Mackaela. "She heard his name and another at work the other day. Some strung out junkie came into the ER. She overheard a call he made to Cory Wilson."

I uncrossed my arms, gripping the edge of my desk, nearly splintering the wood. "So we have a traitor do we?" My voice was hard as steel. "In fact, I haven't seen him in a few days."

Mackaela's eyes widened. "You think he's working for Ricky?"

"Possibly. It was clear nearly a year ago that he was trying to steal clients, so why not employees? Who's this junkie, did Sadie get a name?"

Her dark brows crumpled. "Sadie said the guy took off after a while refusing treatment. He was yelling at Cory, claiming he got screwed on some molly he'd bought and that it was laced with meth or something. He then mentioned Ricky's name, accusing him of mixing product."

A dull ache formed behind my eyes. I probably shouldn't have drank so much last night. I didn't think Cory Wilson was capable of going behind my back, but at this point, I was running low on information so any lead was a hot one when it came to Delgado. He'd been caught down in Portland months ago yet managed to get away and hide like the coward he was.

Wilson was a decent dealer for me, although I'd always pegged him as an opportunist. It was possible he was offered a new position. While normally that wouldn't bother me, if he were working for an enemy on top of stealing my merchandise he'd be in big trouble. I didn't lace our product and certainly didn't sell anything apart from the purest forms. The fact something else was being sold in my territory meant all signs pointed to disloyalty.

"Sounds like I need to find this guy and pay him a visit," I said. "There shouldn't be anyone else in town or surrounding areas manufacturing or selling."

She nodded. "That's what I thought. I'm trying to stay out of this as much as I can, however you needed to know. Sadie refuses to communicate with anyone other than me and Dom since the baby's been born."

"I appreciate the info. It'd be pretty ballsy for Ricky Delgado to come back on my turf. I'll get in touch with Hawks to see if he's heard anything. Is there something else you wanted to talk to me about?" I zeroed in on the big ass diamond ring that sat on her left finger.

My fucking brother. He'd fallen for Mackaela so hard and fast that at first I was worried it wouldn't last. Yet seeing them together, how much better they both were now, made me believe he really loved her. He did take a bullet for her after all.

Her cheeks turned a shade of pink as she tucked her hair behind her ear. "Simon proposed."

I couldn't help the grin that spread across my lips. "I'm happy for you."

I noticed tears threatening to escape as she nodded. "It's weird though. I mean a year ago I was ... so different."

"Yeah, you're not the same person. None of us are. That's a good thing, Mackaela. You deserve to be happy."

She blew out a breath as she stood. "I should get going. Simon wants to go out to dinner to celebrate," she said, wrapping her arms around my waist in a hug.

I pulled her into me, dipping my chin to kiss her forehead. "Don't worry about Ricky. I'll take care of him. It's the last thing I have to do before walking away."

She stepped back. "I know. Mickey?"

"Yeah?"

"Be safe, please. I'm going to need you to walk me down the aisle."

I chuckled. "Deal."

She punched my arm. "I love you, Mickey Silver."

"I know."

As soon as Mackaela was gone, I called up Randall Hawks, my new business associate who'd be taking over my side of the business. I'd sold my half of the business to him already but was still very much involved until I got Delgado. Hawks was now part owner of Silver Enterprises. Why my father was still running things at his age was beyond me. Most people would be retired by now, living on a beach somewhere. Truth be told, I wasn't sure he'd ever be able to do anything else with his life. He'd been supplying and running drugs longer than I'd been alive.

"Hey, Silver, what's up?"

"Heard any news lately regarding Ricky the snake Delgado?" I plopped down in my desk chair rubbing my forehead.

"Not a thing. Why, have you?"

"I just had someone inform me a junkie called our boy Cory Wilson to bitch him out over some laced MDMA. As far as I know we're still selling pure product."

He grunted. "Damn right we are. We have a monopoly of the entire coast from here through Oregon. If he got bad stuff it wasn't from us."

"You think that stupid fuck would sell on our turf?" I asked, undoing the top two buttons of my shirt.

"I thought I gave him a good enough warning down south last year before he ran. Scared the piss out of him with the business end of my Glock. It sounds like he's trying to start up his own business or something."

"That's never going to happen. Whether it's him or someone else, we need to get to the bottom of it. Have you heard from Wilson lately?"

"Negative, Mick. Last I saw him was a week ago when he brought cash in from dealing."

I let out a breath. "See if you can't figure out where he is or someone who might know. I'm gonna track down this junkie to get some answers."

"You've got it, boss."

I scoffed. "Not for much longer, man. Once Ricky's dealt with I'm out." I ended the call, tossing my phone on top of the desk.

A lot of people thought Seattle was a big city. However, when you knew the streets like I did and a good majority of the people, tracking someone wasn't extremely hard. Questioning a guy to get information would be like taking candy from a baby, and if my fists didn't convince him, my 9mm would.

Claire

Seriously fuck Friday night traffic. I was so sick of living in Seattle, Washington. Besides, the traffic, the noise, and the amount of people squeezed together in tight spaces like the monorail drove me crazy. The only reason I hadn't left yet was because up until a week ago, I thought I'd stick around awhile.

I hailed from an incredibly small town in Washington state on the other side of the Cascades called Winthrop. There was literally nothing other than farmland with open fields as far as the eye could see. Sure, we had a cute little Main Street area chock-full of tourist attractions along with camping and cute little hotels. However, for a twenty-one year old woman it didn't offer much in the way of adventure or social interaction.

My mom and step-dad were less than thrilled to let me go. I tried to explain to them that I was growing restless at home, that I was tired of living a simple life. I'd always felt more like an outsider. I was sure I got that trait from my father. He was long gone now, but that didn't mean I didn't inherit certain qualities from him.

I was definitely jaded when I first got here nearly two years ago. The cost of living turned out to be a lot higher than I expected, forcing me to have a roommate. I'd found an ad on Craigslist seeking a tenant to rent a room which is how I met Bianca Rogers.

Bianca was successful with a good paying career and a ton of friends because she'd grown up in Seattle her whole life. Not only did she rectify my housing situation, she got me a job where she worked. Thanks to my temporary career, I was well on my way to a decent savings account.

While I normally appreciated my newfound friend, I was sorry I'd met her at the moment. She was the one who introduced me to Cory Wilson who was my least favorite person in the world as of last Friday. When I first met him, I thought he was cute, funny, charming, the total package. What a nice package he had, too, which made staying with him worth it for a while. That was up until he started caring more about slinging drugs than he did me. The occupation didn't bother me at first, but I got tired of being second to his constant "working" and running errands for his boss.

He worked for Mickey Silver who I hated almost as much as Cory. We met a few times when Cory begged me to come to some of the parties with him. When Cory said we were going to a party at his boss's house, a man who ran the Seattle underground drug ring, I expected some sleazy looking guy who lived in a bad part of town.

Imagine my surprise when I was introduced to a perfectly sculpted twenty-something with eyes that reminded me of the rolling fields back home and a square jaw that looked like it could cut glass. His hair was the color of honey, falling almost to his chin. It irritated me that he was always brushing it back with his long fingers. Most of all I hated the arrogance that exuded from him like he was God's gift. It was obvious the world totally revolved around him, that he took what he wanted without having to ask. After a handful of times, I'd opted out of attending the parties.

The last time I saw Cory was a week ago because he'd received a job offer in Portland, Oregon from another guy starting up his own business. He supposedly couldn't pass up the opportunity for more money. He asked me to go, claiming he'd be making double what he was now, but I declined. I may be a little off my rocker to pack up and leave home by myself for the big city, but I wasn't naïve enough to travel to another new city with a man who I'd recently found out cheated on me. That information revealed a series of escapades he'd had which solidified my decision. After over a year together, we'd finally called it quits.

I really hoped I wouldn't get fired for being late tonight. It was ten minutes to seven and I still had a few blocks to get through before I made it to the parking lot of *Rosie's*, which was one of Seattle's top strip clubs. Initially I was apprehensive about being a stripper. I had years of dance experience from middle school and high school though, plus Bianca promised good money.

This particular establishment catered to high-end clientele, so most of them were prominent members of the city. There were business owners, politicians, and also musicians. We always had larger crowds on the weekends, which was my favorite time to work because of the tips. That was precisely why I was driving like a mad woman to get there on time.

Growing impatient, I cut a guy off by merging my gently used Volkswagen Jetta in front of him with ease. He blared on his horn and I lifted my middle finger in the rear view mirror.

"Speed limit's thirty, asshole," I shouted though he'd never hear me.

My gaze darted between the car ahead of me to the stoplights and the clock on my dash. Time was passing way too quickly right now. I was able to get through two yellow lights before coming to a dead stop one block from the club. I could see the flashing crimson sign ahead beckoning me closer. Situated just outside the downtown area, *Rosie's* was an ideal location for its patrons. For tardy employees it was absolute hell.

Growling, I rode the ass end of the truck in front of me, barely making it through yet another light. At exactly seven I was pulling into a parking spot at the back of the building. I grabbed the over-sized bag in the passenger seat, slinging it over my shoulder as I slammed my car door shut and bolted to the side of the otherwise non-de-script navy colored building. Harvey was standing at the door with massive arms crossed against his broad chest making the white t-shirt he wore stretch like it'd tear off at any moment.

"Just in time." He winked as I flew past him.

"Hey, Harvey, thanks," I mumbled before racing down the narrow hall toward the staging room.

I slowed my pace as I casually strolled into the room, brushing by a couple newbies to my assigned vanity. Bianca was sitting at the one next to mine applying a heavy amount of eyeliner to showcase her whisky colored eyes.

"You're late, *Harlow*." She smirked at me.

Huffing out a breath, I pulled out my stage outfit before placing it on the couch behind me. "Yeah, damn traffic."

"Where'd you come from? You weren't home this afternoon."

I pulled out my makeup bag, placing all my items on the small space in front of the mirror before plugging in my curling iron. "I had a doctor's appointment." After pulling my hair up into a top knot, I began applying my makeup.

"That's right, how'd it go?" she asked, puckering her glossed up cherry lips in the mirror.

"As good as it can when a guy has his fingers all up in your vagina." I rolled my eyes.

Bianca threw her head back in laughter. "Girl, you are too much. You sure don't sugar coat, do you?"

Shrugging, I said, "What's the point in stifling the truth?"

"True." She stripped off her sweater and bra before grabbing the skimpy lingerie on the back of her chair. "What time are you on tonight?"

Now that my face looked totally flawless, I undid my hair to curl the ends. "Eight."

"Did you eat something?"

"No."

Exhaling soundly, Bianca began digging in her bag, tossing a package of peanut butter crackers in my lap. "Eat something, please. If you faint on stage Clint's going to flip out."

"Thanks," I muttered. Bianca was a good friend, always making sure I ate properly or had enough water.

"Jade, you're on in ten!" Kiley, our stage manager, hollered from the doorway.

"Coming!" Bianca said, fastening the tiny bra that barely covered her chest.

We never used our real names when in the building. It was an anonymity we maintained for our protection. I choked down the crackers then grabbed a bottled water from the mini fridge across the room. After donning my stage outfit, I painted my lips up a dark shade of burgundy and inspected myself in the mirror.

I was no longer Claire Evans, newly twenty-three year old woman from a small town. I was Harlow the dominating temptress. Like every other night I was working, I'd zone out, play nice, and earn my money. I'd do my dance, flirt with clients, and daydream about a different life where I could finally be content. Where I wouldn't struggle with chasing something I couldn't even see.

Chapter 2

Mick

The junkie kid from the hospital ended up being Roy Smith, an eighteen year old who liked to party more than work. He still lived with his parents in their basement, getting high most nights and sleeping all day. It wasn't challenging to track him down. I got the information I needed and learned it was definitely Cory Wilson that sold him the drugs. The kid still had some of it left so I was able to do an inspection. Lo and behold, it wasn't my supply. No shocker there. However, that meant my fear of someone stepping in on our territory was true. I was able to confirm Delgado's name from him as well, so just like that I was on my way to vengeance and freedom.

I was so close to being out of the business that I could taste it. I hadn't really thought much about what I'd do after all was said and done but was more than ready to walk away. The line of work simply didn't have the same appeal now that I had my brother in my life again. Seeing my best friend take back her life while also finding companionship in Simon gave me hope for a better future. I grew more attached to the idea of separating myself from illegal activities and becoming a law-abiding citizen. For the most part.

The moment I had my information, I dialed up Hawks to find out what he'd learned about Cory's disappearance. Unfortunately, a lot of Cory's acquaintances didn't get too personal. However, there was one woman who might know his whereabouts. Claire Evans, his girlfriend, as well as the only person he'd trust enough to tell all of his deep dark secrets to. It'd been a while since I'd seen her around with him. I wasn't entirely certain she'd be willing to chat. Nevertheless, we had to try.

He'd received word that she worked at *Rosie's* downtown as a dancer, so he suggested we pay her a visit at work in hopes of getting her to talk. Initially, I wasn't down for disrupting a place of business. However, the only other option was showing up at her home and something told me that wouldn't go over well. I wasn't in the mood to add breaking and entering to my résumé, which would likely happen if she slammed the door in my face.

We found a small round table with two chairs in a dark corner to wait for the right moment. Hawks stared at the stage where a curvy brunette was finishing her set. I got the feeling he'd wanted to come here for reasons other than work. I cleared my throat. "So what's the plan here?"

"As soon as she's available we'll invite her to talk. Worst case scenario I ask for a VIP room with her." He shrugged.

Irritation took root in my gut. Typical Hawks to turn an interrogation into a reason to chase pussy. Dude had women around him all the damn time. Not that I could really speak against it considering I had my own track record of hookups. I wasn't mixing business with pleasure tonight. In fact, lately I'd cut back on women because I was busy cutting ties with the business and helping things run smoothly at the shop with Simon. It's not like I'd taken up a vow of celibacy or anything. Although it had been about two weeks since I'd slept with a woman. That had to be some kind of record for me.

"You think she'll talk to us?" I asked, taking a sip of scotch.

He took a long pull of his beer. "Probably not. Although for the right amount of money ... " He trailed off as he reached into his pocket before producing a large wad of cash.

"You're going to bribe her to tell us what she knows." It honestly wasn't too bad of a plan. She was most likely working here because she needed the money. With a stack of bills taunting her she may just spill.

Hawks smiled. "Your dad's not an idiot, Mick. I'm a great negotiator."

"I don't doubt that."

I'd heard he ran his old business in Olympia similar to ours here in Seattle. Our personalities as well as work ethic weren't far off from each other, either. It was the reason I trusted him to take over the business for me, although we hadn't gotten off on the best foot last year when I heard about him.

I thought he was trying to impede on my turf because Delgado had gone behind my back to sell for him here. Kind of like what the asshole was doing now with Cory. It turned out that Delgado had stolen a decent supply from Hawks who didn't realize it until after the fact. Or at least that's what he claimed. I had no reason not to believe it knowing what Ricky Delgado was capable of. We kind of bonded after that so I figured with his northern territory added to ours we'd make a much larger profit. It was a win for all of us. It also hadn't taken much to convince him.

The rock music the brunette was dancing to faded out as the MC guy stepped up to the stage.

"Give it up for our girl Kitten. Awesome job as always, right?" There was a series of catcalls. "Now you're in for a real treat. Say hello to a crowd favorite, our dirty little dominatrix, the blonde bombshell Harlow!"

The lights on the stage dimmed again as loud rock music began playing through the speakers.

"This is our girl," Hawks said, knocking back his beer.

She sauntered out into the spotlight swaying her narrow hips to the music. The first thing I noticed was her pale creamy skin peeking through thigh high fishnet stockings that covered her long legs. My gaze wandered up to the black leather mini skirt that did little to hide the red panties underneath.

"She's drop dead gorgeous if you ask me. I don't know what she's doing with a simple dealer like Cory Wilson."

Her flat stomach was bare and a black bra covered her perfectly round tits. I took a swig of my scotch, totally fascinated by this woman. Her long blonde hair was curled at the ends adding to the tantalizing getup. I licked my lips, watching her mouth the lyrics to the song playing as she scanned the crowd with those piercing violet eyes.

She turned around and bent over showcasing her fine ass before removing the skirt. I thought I remembered her from a year ago, yet the girl from the past was more innocent looking than this. This version was like a sexy little fantasy I'd somehow conjured up. She was unreal, working that stage like she owned it.

Her tall black heels clacked off the platform as she worked the pole in the center, flipping her hair while stalking the crowd with bedroom eyes. I shifted in my seat, taking another drink.

"Dude, you look uncomfortable. What's the deal?" Hawks asked, glancing at me.

I rolled the glass between my hands, staring at the tabletop. "It's weird seeing her up there. Any time I ever saw her before she seemed like the good girl type."

He winked with a sly grin. "Everyone has their secrets, Mick. You of all people know that."

I grunted in agreement before shifting my attention back to the stage. She wrapped her hands around the pole as she slithered up higher. Once she was close to the top, she released her grip before leaning back using only her legs to hold herself up.

Fuck Mme.

She expertly removed the bra as she hung there showing off her full chest. Claire grabbed the pole again, sliding down slowly. She knelt down in front of the crowd moving to the music as she scanned the room again, running her hands down her body. My gaze drifted up her face to those stunning eyes that were now locked on me.

Her brow crumpled briefly before turning her attention elsewhere. Claire didn't look at me again as she exited the stage to the back once the song ended. There was no doubt she remembered me. Based on the glare she'd given me I knew she wasn't going to answer our questions easily.

The room erupted in applause as the MC encouraged them before introducing yet another dancer. I finished off my scotch.

"She'll be making the rounds in about ten minutes. When she comes over I'll see what info we can get."

A waitress came by to drop off two new drinks for us. I handed her some money, waiting until she walked away before speaking.

"I think she recognized me. What if she refuses to talk? She could be protecting Cory."

Hawks placed his elbow on the table leaning forward. "She can't refuse a paying customer." A devilish smirk appeared across his face.

I glared at him. The thought of him touching her made my skin crawl. I liked the guy well enough but the look on his face told me he'd use whatever means possible to get her to talk. Knowing what he was capable of might have me leaving this place in the back of a cop car if he laid a single finger on her. Rumor had it he "*trained*" his girls in Olympia personally and he liked it rough. Not really my style. Besides, the women in my business weren't dainty damsels. They certainly didn't need training so I never got into that. I didn't need to sample the merchandise when I had a line of women willing to give themselves to me.

"Maybe you just tell her why we're here. We can gauge her reaction first. Scaring her isn't going to work," I bit out.

Hawks barked out a laugh, shaking his head. "Sounds like you've got a soft spot for the little tramp, Silver."

"I told you she seemed like the innocent type the few times I was around her. Maybe we should tread lightly instead of going in for the kill. Patience is important in business," I said, giving him a hard look. "Make waves and you can kiss your stake in Silver Enterprises goodbye."

He grimaced. "All right, Mick, we'll try it your way first. If she doesn't comply I'm moving on to my idea."

Sure enough, about ten minutes later Claire appeared on the floor, making rounds to the patrons. Her long blonde hair was pulled back now and she wore a low cut purple tank top with the shortest denim shorts I'd ever seen. She was still wearing those high heels that looked like they could do some damage if she stepped on you.

I studied her as she moved around the dimly lit seating area talking with different men. As she drew closer to our table, I turned my attention back to Hawks.

"Be cool," I reminded him with a hard stare.

"Yeah, Mick. Got it," he growled.

For all we knew Cory was lurking in the shadows or Claire would run off to tell him we'd tried to get information from her later. It's not that I was worried about Cory Wilson. The guy was as stacked as Dom, but I was sure I could take him down if necessary. I simply didn't want to risk losing my chance at revenge on Ricky Delgado.

I glanced at her as she approached. Her eyes quickly shifted to Hawks instead of me. "How's it going handsome?" she asked in a sultry tone, angling her body toward him as he took in every inch of her.

"Better now." He shot her a wink. I clenched my hand into a fist under the table.

"Can I do anything for you?"

He raised a brow at her then flicked his gaze to me. "Yeah. Actually you can do something for *us*."

Her shoulders tensed. Those violet eyes full of fury gave me a once over. "What do you want?" she gritted out.

"Easy, tigress." I pointed my finger at Hawks. "Seems he's having a little trouble with something that your boy might be in the middle of." I didn't care about the supply being tainted. I just wanted info on Delgado.

Claire pinned me with a look of contempt. "I don't know what you're talking about."

I arched a brow keeping my focus on her. "Come on, *Harlow*, you and I both know Cory likes trouble."

She shook her head. "I don't know what Cory's gotten himself into. Both of you need to leave. Now." She turned to walk away. Hawks grabbed her wrist.

Holding up a stack of bills, he shot her an expectant look. "I'm not done." He spoke calmly. "There's a lot of money here. Besides, you're the perfect little piece for me tonight."

She yanked her wrist free. "I'm not doing a damn thing for you and I don't need your money," she seethed.

"You'll give me a private dance and tell me what you know about your boyfriend working for Ricky Delgado."

"I told you, I wouldn't know anything about that."

"You better quit playing us, girl, or you're going to be sorry."

I shot my arm out gripping his shoulder. "Ease up, man. She said she doesn't know."

He turned his glare to me. "She's full of shit, Mick."

"I am not, asshole. Who are *you* anyway?" Claire asked, taking a step toward him.

I glanced up toward the bouncer who was staked out near the bar watching the crowd. "Best we don't make a scene," I gritted out through clenched teeth.

Hawks was turning this around to go bad for us. I wasn't totally sure if Claire had been telling the truth. However, if we had any chance of getting answers I'd need to take matters into my own hands. Being kicked out would kill the opportunity which he was close to making happen.

"I'm the guy running things now. Cory works for me." His lips pulled back in a sneer. "As if you didn't know that, *slut*."

"That's it." I growled as I stood abruptly nearly knocking the table over. I laid my hands flat on the table.

Claire took a step back while Hawks snapped his attention to me. I tried to suppress my anger as I glanced between the both of them.

"You're being a dick which isn't helping so now you can shut the hell up," I said to Hawks before pinning Claire with a hard look. "You're going to take me back to the VIP room. I've got a lot of cash on me. I intend to use every bit of it while I'm in there with you."

Claire opened her mouth to object. I cut her off. "No. This isn't a negotiation. I'm two seconds away from punching this fucker's lights out followed by getting you fired. You want that, darlin'?" I raised a brow at her.

Gaping at me, she shook her head.

Turning back to Hawks, I said, "Stay here. Be cool or I'll make sure your ass is out. You act like a dick you can kiss your promotion goodbye. Got it?"

He tipped his beer toward me before taking a long tug. "Got it, Mick," he said with a cocky grin.

I straightened, meeting her eyes again. As I swept my arm in front of me, I said, "Lead the way."

"I hate you," she muttered before heading for the private area toward the back of the club.

I didn't need her to like me anyway. All I wanted was whatever answers she could give me then I'd never have to speak to her or see her again.

Claire

First I was late for work and now I'm taking Mickey Silver to the VIP room for a private dance. Clearly, I'd pissed off the gods to be dealt such a fate. Clint had been watching me from the bar during the little exchange so there was no doubt he'd seen the stack of cash that idiot flashed at me. Turning down a paying customer was likely to get me fired. I couldn't afford that yet.

I didn't know anything about Cory's current whereabouts or who he worked for. It pissed me off that barely a week had gone by, yet here I was still dealing with his baggage. I'd never even heard the name Ricky Delgado before. It might have been the guy he'd been going to work for, but I had no specifics and I sure as hell didn't want to be involved.

The VIP rooms were down a long hallway tucked near the back of the building. There were four of them total. The time spent in here could be as quick as five minutes or last hours depending on the girl. I'd heard rumors that some girls actually had sex with the clients which was something I'd never done, nor did I want to. I'd been a crowd favorite since I started, however no amount of money was worth selling my body like that. Bianca always said that's what made me appealing to the customers. They thought I was a tease when in reality I simply had standards.

I chose the furthest room at the end of the hall deciding to play it safe in the event I ended up screaming at Mick. Hopefully, no one would hear me over the loud music out in the main area. The space wasn't excessively big, more like a large closet with one oversized leather chair in the center. As I wandered in I glanced back to see Mick standing just inside the entryway. He was completely stoic with arms crossed over his broad chest, pinning me with those hazel eyes that I hated. I nodded my head toward the chair.

"Have a seat," I said in an overly sweet voice, the one I used on normal customers.

He wanted to bring me back here? I'd play the perfect little part of accommodating hostess. Maybe I'd even have a little fun at his expense by giving him blue balls. I knew he wasn't bluffing about getting me fired. I needed this job for just a little while longer. I'd be damned if he ruined that for me over something dumbass Cory did.

His throat rolled in a swallow as he glanced at the chair before approaching, all the while studying me as if I might attack him. When he brushed by me I caught his scent. It was like cinnamon mixed with whatever distinct musk that was all him. I hated the way my body responded to it.

Once in the chair he spread his arms before placing his hands at the end of each armrest. I found myself wondering if he'd been in a room like this before based on how easily he'd sat down. It wasn't a secret that he liked to sample different girls. Most of the women at his parties flocked to him like flies to a dead carcass. He'd probably gotten more lap dances than any other man in Seattle.

I took in his athletic build and the length of his fingers as they curled over the leather chair. He was wearing dark jeans with a white button down that showcased what was likely a full sleeve tattoo on his left arm. Multiple designs began on the back of his hand before traveling up into a rolled up sleeve.

Mick kept his gaze glued to mine. I bit down on the inside of my cheek as I sauntered over, placing my hands on his thighs as I bent forward. My face was mere inches from his with my lips at his ear. I could feel the heat emanating off him. His breath on my bare shoulder gave me goosebumps.

"You have five minutes to ask me whatever it is you want, Mick," I whispered in his ear.

He angled his head slightly so that his cheek was against mine. Heat flooded my belly. "How does Cory know Ricky?"

Sliding my hands to his chest, I said, "I really don't know. I've never heard the name before."

I stepped away from him, turning around while swinging my hips as I played with the hem of my tank top. I glanced back over my shoulder noting the way his eyes slowly lifted from my ass to my face. Typical, he was already becoming distracted. Giving him a coy smile, I removed my top before facing him again.

"Jesus," he murmured, staring at my naked chest. "Where's Cory right now?"

I stalked forward, lowering myself to his lap before grinding my ass against him. I tensed when I felt his hard length against me, snapping my gaze to his. He raised a brow.

"Surprised?" he asked with the hint of a smirk ghosting his lips.

I narrowed my eyes. "I thought you came in to talk."

He widened the smirk, chuckling softly. "You're a beautiful woman. I can't really help the reaction when you're grinding on me right now."

I didn't like the way his eyes sparkled in the dim room. Letting out an exasperated sigh, I said, "I don't know where Cory is."

Mick glowered at me. "You're lying."

This was the last place I wanted to be right now which had me growing angrier by the second. Who did he think he was to come to my work and start demanding things of me? I needed to get him to leave.

Pinning him with a glare, I continued shimmying against his lap. His hips lifted slightly taking me by surprise yet again. With any other client, it was common to have that reaction. However never in a million years did I think I'd be giving Mickey Silver a lap dance that he'd be enjoying it this much. Glancing back at him over my shoulder, I met his stare. "I'm not lying. All I know is he moved to Oregon for a new job."

I turned in his lap, placing my knee between his legs hovering above him. I ran my hands over my chest down to my hips noticing how he followed the movement. I couldn't help my smile as I stared down at him, watching that square jaw pulse. The muscles in his arms flexed as he held tight to the armrests. Did he want to touch me?

His head fell back against the chair as he looked up at me with hooded eyes and his lips parted slightly. "Oregon. Did he say who he was working for?" he asked in a husky voice.

I slid my hand over his shoulder behind his neck as I angled forward until my breasts lingered inches from his face. His eyes closed and I felt him tense. When he opened them again, he pinned me with a dark look.

"Answer me, *Harlow*," he demanded.

His breath warmed my skin, sending a current of electricity through me. I bit my bottom lip as I leaned back, running my other hand along his chest, gliding it down to where I felt a strong solid set of abs.

"He didn't tell me anything." My voice was weaker than I anticipated. "Why are you doing this?"

My fingers inched closer to the bulge in his jeans. A spark of curiosity got the better of me and I slid my palm over him causing him to suck in a sharp breath.

"Why are you doing *that*?" he asked through gritted teeth.

"This?" I asked innocently as I continued moving my hand.

I wasn't answering any more questions. The only way to get him to stop talking was to continue my diversion tactic. My head grew cloudy as each second passed. Licking my lips, I studied his face as I stroked him through his jeans. His chin dipped to watch me as I worked him. Okay, that was pretty hot.

Mickey let out a low groan before muttering a curse. His head snapped up, nostrils flaring.

"Claire ... Stop," he growled. "*Please*, stop." Inhaling a shaky breath, I stood on wobbling legs.

God, what was I doing? I couldn't stand him, yet I was touching him like ... like I didn't hate him at all. Irritation prickled my scalp. I needed to get away from him.

"I have no idea where Cory is, that's the truth. If you want more information, go ask one of the other dealers. Your five minutes are up, *Mick*. Don't come back here ever again." I didn't give him a chance to question me anymore after that. Grabbing my discarded top, I marched out of the room.

I kept my composure as I walked out to the floor, away from the other customers, and into the back room. As soon as I reached the staging area, I sunk down on the couch in front of my vanity, covering my face with my hands. I didn't like that I enjoyed touching Mickey Silver. It was so stupid. I was so stupid. Embarrassment rushed through me for acting like I wanted him when I knew I could never have him. Hopefully, I'd never have to see him again.

Chapter 3

Mick

"I'm going down to Portland." I tucked my gun into the side of my duffel bag before zipping it up.

"Can't you have Jack look out for Ricky?" Simon asked. He was bent over the front of a '72' Chevelle installing the battery.

"Nah, he's out of town. Besides Ricky got away from him and Hawks last time. I question their ability to capture deadbeats. Plus I'm not looking for Ricky anyway."

Simon lifted his head to look at me. "Mackaela mentioned your dealer Cory might be double timing. He down there, too?"

"According to his girlfriend he bounced just over a week ago. She claims she doesn't know who he's working for though all signs point to Delgado. I don't know why anyone else would suddenly mess with us."

He nodded. "Just be careful. Things are really busy here so I don't have time to drive down there to avenge your ass." His lips kicked up.

Scoffing, I said, "I'm invincible, bro." I slung the duffel bag over my shoulder. "I'll check in later tonight."

I'd tried pressing some of the other dealers for information on Cory or Ricky yet came up empty. If anyone else knew anything they weren't talking which would be a massive mistake on their part if I found out they'd lied to me. I was known for being a fairly reasonable guy, although anyone who'd witnessed my bad side would strongly disagree.

The drive to Portland was just over two hours so I'd decided to leave early, hoping to catch Cory off guard. That was *if* I could track him down. I wasn't positive he was in the city. However, I had no other leads right now other than what Claire told me. I was an hour into the trip when the music cut off on my stereo as my phone started ringing through the speakers. I frowned at the unknown number that flashed on the screen. Pressing the answer button, I started to speak but was immediately cut off.

"I hear you're looking for me." Cory's voice boomed through the cab.

"Well, well, well, if it isn't yet another traitor. How much is he paying you?"

He chuckled darkly. "More than you, Mick. There won't be anything left once we're done with you."

In spite of myself, I laughed. "That's a nice little dream you have, prick. Too bad you don't have the manpower or resources to make it a reality."

"That's what you think. I've got something you want, something you'd do *anything* for."

Clenching my jaw, I asked, "What would that be?"

"Freedom. I've got an in with your guy Ken Watson. You know the one you manipulated into steering clear from Ricky because your stupid skank has a big mouth."

I gripped the steering wheel inhaling through my nose. "What are you talking about?"

"He's going to give you up to the feds, Mick. Your freedom depends on how much you're willing to help us out here in Oregon. Back off or Watson's gonna turn you over just like that."

That stupid fucking lawyer. I knew I shouldn't have trusted he'd keep his mouth shut, to ride off into the sunset after Simon kicked his ass. He'd been distant over the last year and I figured it was due to the fact he couldn't have Mackaela anymore as his mistress. I had video evidence of his favorite past time so screwing with me wasn't in his best interest. Wilson had to be bluffing.

"I'm not signing my business over to you or Delgado. I'm not giving you a single thing!"

I glanced in the rear view mirror, spying an inconspicuous black sedan with tinted windows coming up fast on me. The second the red and blues flashed, I knew I'd underestimated their capabilities.

"We've got important people on the inside, too, Silver. Had a little favor called in so you'd think twice about pursuing this. Do you see our surprise yet?"

"What did you do?" I growled.

Cory laughed now, the sound sending a sinking feeling to the pit of my stomach. "Had to buy ourselves a little bit of time."

Did Claire tell him I'd questioned her? I started veering off the highway toward an exit.

"They won't hold me long," I said, knowing full well the cops had nothing on me to keep me in jail. I had a clean record thanks to hiring multiple guys to do the dirty work for me. Money as well as power could make you damn near invincible with the law.

"Not this time," Cory replied. "It'll slow you down for sure though. Perhaps it will give you time to figure out if you want to help us out or not."

"What do you want?" I rolled into a near empty parking lot putting my car in park. I sent a quick text to Simon letting him know where to pick up my car. The undercover cop pulled to a stop behind me.

"The south. We've got men preparing to deal down here already. Your dear old dad's getting older so he'll be gone soon. Rumor has it you're out the door anyway."

"You want the whole state of Oregon?" I snorted. "Good luck with that, dipshit."

"Clock's ticking, Mick. Next time I call you, you better have an answer for me. If I don't like what you have to say, Watson's just itching to turn you in to the feds." The call disconnected.

Dragging a hand through my hair, I muttered a curse as I rolled down my window for the officer approaching.

It was a routine traffic stop up until the guy told me to step out of the vehicle before patting me down. After that, he claimed an excuse to search my car. I could have fought back or ran but it wouldn't matter. He found the gun which was clean because I had a concealed weapons permit. Somehow, he still needed to detain me "just to be sure." I didn't know who the prick was that pulled me over. He looked younger than me. Probably new on the payroll or trying to get an in as a dirty cop. Poor kid didn't realize the people I dealt with were much higher up so this little incident was nothing for me.

I'd been cuffed before. Dom had family in the local precinct which basically gave me immunity as well as kept my name off records. I also had a top-notch lawyer that made every ounce of wrongdoing disappear. I'd never been arrested for something as trivial as a traffic stop though which fucking irritated me. Usually it was for something like fighting or pistol-whipping a degenerate when I was out with one of my girls or mouthing off to the wrong guy while threatening to kill him.

Once we were at the station, I let them do the whole intake thing while sitting in a chair across from the officer as he asked me questions. This was all unnecessary since I'd be out in a few hours so he was wasting his time.

"All right, I've got all the info I need. You get one call before I take you to a cell."

"Yeah I'd like to take advantage of that."

He tipped his head toward the far wall. "Phone's over there. Make it quick."

Oh I'd make it quick. I knew exactly who I was calling. She'd better answer. Cory Wilson and Ricky Delgado thought they could back me into a corner, thought they could blackmail *me*? That they could take my freedom in order to sway my decisions?

Well two could play at that game.

Claire

After the awkward lap dance and composing myself, I mustered up the courage to get back out on the floor to do my job. Each night since then when I was working, I'd grow anxious, afraid they'd come back or try to talk to me again. I hadn't heard anything from Cory since the incident. I also decided to refrain from contacting him about it. The less I was involved in whatever situation this was the better.

Today was my day off so I'd been able to relax a little bit. I was sitting poolside with Bianca, soaking up some sun while trying to let whatever was going on with Cory go. I'd told her about what happened with Mick because I needed to talk to someone and she'd found me in the staging area that night. Bianca said not to worry about it, that he'd probably move on to questioning other people. I hoped that was true because I never wanted to see him again.

Although my stupid mind wasn't helping alleviate my stresses. I found myself playing back what happened in that VIP room. The way his raspy voice sent a blazing fire of awareness through me when I realized how turned on he was. How he'd felt beneath my palm as I touched him. Instead of being repulsed by his attention, I enjoyed it. That didn't sit well with me. Even now, my skin buzzed and I felt a warmth pooling between my legs at the memory. I had serious issues to be crushing on Mickey Silver.

Thankfully, the shrill sound of my phone snapped me out of my ridiculous thoughts. I grabbed it off the small table between us, frowning.

"Are you going to answer that?" Bianca asked as she got up to grab a drink.

I thought about letting the unknown number go to voicemail as the ringing continued, but then it might be my mom. She'd mentioned looking into getting a new phone when I talked to her last weekend.

"Hello?"

"Afternoon darlin'." My throat tightened at the sound of Mick's deep voice.

"How'd you get my number?" My voice squeaked. Clearing my throat, I tried again. "Why are you calling me?"

A low chuckle sounded on the other end. "I'm a resourceful man, sweet Claire. Now tell me, why did you lie?"

Shaking my head, I released an unsteady breath. "What are you talking about?"

"I don't have much time so stop being evasive." He growled. "You told your boyfriend I was asking after him." I opened my mouth to speak, yet nothing came out. Was he for real? "You're working with him to screw me over. Ringing any bells yet?"

"I told you we don't speak," I snapped.

"It's a shame that pretty mouth of yours spits fabrications."

I bit back on my molars. "I don't know anything."

He released a breath into the phone. "Yeah? Prove it."

Bianca came back to sit down, staring at me with a questioning brow. I lifted my hand before letting it fall to slap against my bare thigh. "How am I supposed to do that?"

"You're going to help me—-"

"Like Hell—"

"Do. Not. Interrupt me again." His voice was ominous, frighteningly low. "You're going to help me take down your piece of shit boyfriend."

"How ... I ... What can *I* do?" I stammered as my heart thumped against my ribs.

"I have to go. I'll be in touch soon. Oh by the way, Claire?"

"Yeah?" I tried to swallow the lump in my throat.

"Breathe a word of this to anyone and I'll cut that lovely tongue out."

Some sort of strangled squeak escaped my throat as the line disconnected. A shudder of fear rolled through me when I set my phone down on the side table.

"Who was that?" Bianca asked, placing a hand on my shoulder. "Claire, you look like you're going to have a heart attack or something."

I rested my palm against my chest as I inhaled a deep breath before letting it out slowly. *"Breathe a word of this to anyone and I'll cut that lovely tongue out."* Would he really do that? I didn't know Mick well, but something told me he didn't have a single problem with bringing harm to others. Especially snitches. Raking my fingers through my hair, I felt sweat gather at my temples.

"Nothing," I managed in a low voice. "Just um ... my brother. He wants me to come back home."

Bianca frowned. "You sure?"

Nodding, I took another steadying breath. "Yeah, it's nothing. I'm fine."

I wasn't sure if she believed me or not but she didn't press it. I wandered to the edge of the pool staring at the serene blue water. I didn't want to be involved in this and here I was getting drawn in unwillingly.

One thing was certain, if I ever saw Cory Wilson again I'd punch his lights out before kicking him in the junk. The punch for wasting my time the last year, followed by the kick for introducing me to the biggest asshole on the planet. I wasn't sure what Mick had planned or how he thought I'd help. I only knew I wasn't going to make it easy for him. Powerful or not, nobody talked to me that way. Nobody told me what to do.

*

I had no idea when Mick would be getting in touch with me. Three days went by without hearing anything. It was beginning to make me paranoid. I was constantly glancing over my shoulder whenever I was out in public or at work. Thursday nights I worked the mid shift at *Rosie's,* which meant I was off at nine instead of working until midnight. I was looking forward to getting home to hopefully relax for the rest of the night.

I threw my hair up in a messy bun before wiping my face clean of the dark makeup I'd donned for the evening. Bianca wandered into the staging room as I packed up my bag, her brows tilting down as she let out a soft sigh.

"You out of here?" she asked.

I heaved my bag over my shoulder. "Yeah."

She'd picked up on my mood the last few days, asking again what the phone call was about. I told her the same thing I had before, that it was nothing, although my cautious attitude was more than a little obvious. Especially when I'd double check the doors and windows in our apartment because I had this irrational fear that Mick would barge in demanding more answers.

"You sure you're okay? You seem off."

"Yeah, I'm fine." I shrugged. "I'm tired. Maybe I'm coming down with something."

Nodding, Bianca pulled me in for a hug. "I'll be home around one. You should take it easy tonight. I got these new lavender bath bombs you can try."

I plastered a smile on my face as I pulled away from her. "That sounds good. I'll see you later." I gave her a small wave as I left, heading toward the back door that led to the parking lot.

Harvey wished me a good night after I pushed the door open. I barely glanced at him as I booked it to my car which was parked around the corner. Pulling my keys from my bag, I peeked up at my car, freezing in place. I blinked at the man leaning against the trunk with his arms crossed. There was a light on the side of the building that cast a soft buttery glow on his too handsome face, making his hazel eyes sparkle as they narrowed at me. A small smile played on full lips.

"Shit," I muttered.

"Told you I'd be in touch," Mick said, pushing off the back of the car before stopping within a foot of me. "How was work?"

"Um, what?"

His head cocked to the side, scanning the length of me. "Work. How was it tonight? Did you have a good day?"

"Sure," I replied, my brows inching up my forehead.

He dragged his bottom lip between his teeth, searching my face. My attention drifted to his mouth. "Are you ready to tell me where your boyfriend is?"

God, he just wouldn't let up! I heaved an exasperated sigh. "Are you stupid? Honestly, for a supposed businessman I thought you'd be a bit more intelligent."

His jaw muscle twitched as he glowered at me. "Careful now, darlin'."

"I told you I don't know *anything*. I don't know why you think I'm lying, why you think I care about you or your stupid business."

"The only other person I've been able to question besides you is a strung out tweaker. I talked to him already. Guess what? He had zero information so that leaves you and you alone," he seethed, stepping closer to me. His chest brushed mine and I inhaled a sharp breath. "You don't care? Great. Then you're going to help me out."

I stood straighter not wanting him to think he could intimidate me. "What if I don't want to?"

His lips curled up in a sneer. "You'll do what I say."

I snorted. "Or?" I countered. "Are you going to make me? Force me against my will? Is that how you've had so many women?" I gave him a once over.

A low growl rumbled from his chest. "What do you know about Wilson?" His hands fell to his sides, clenching into fists.

"What are you gonna do to me, Mick?" So over his harassment and empty threats I leaned forward invading his space. "Bring it on. I *dare* you."

His nostrils flared which told me I hit a nerve. Good.

"You're making this incredibly difficult." He scowled.

Shrugging, I played it cool even though I was totally afraid he might actually hurt me. Although I wouldn't let him know that.

"Go ahead, do your worst. Just so you know, I'm enrolled in box-ing classes for fun." I shook my head with a smirk. "I'm sure I can take you."

Before I could register what was happening his fingers curled around my biceps. His chest bumped mine, forcing me backward until my back smacked against the side of the building. His head lowered, lips hovering dangerously close to mine stealing the air from my lungs.

"You sure about that?" He pinned me with a dark look that made my knees weak. "Want me to show you exactly how *I'd* take you?"

Chapter 4

Mick

Never in my entire life had I ever met a more infuriating woman. She was fearless, headstrong, irritating, and incredibly sexy when she back talked. I was so close to kissing that intoxicating mouth of hers while running my hands all over her incredible body. I wanted to beg her to touch me like she had in the VIP room, give her free reign to use me however she deemed fit. I wasn't used to a female standing up to me this way. I liked it way more than I should.

I didn't care if she noticed how hard I was as I pressed against her hip, turned on by the way she challenged me. Her lips parted in a gasp, her eyes closing halfway as her head fell back against the wall. I skimmed my nose against her throat, inhaling deep. She smelled like cotton candy.

"I'd enjoy every single minute taking you," I murmured before shoving away from her, leaving her rattled.

Her chest rose with a sharp breath, pinning me with a frustrated glare. I couldn't help the grin that appeared. I thoroughly enjoyed the fact she was unsteady around me.

"I'd rather drill a stake through both my eyes," she retorted.

Quirking a brow, I said, "Ouch. You're violent."

"You don't know the half of it." She crossed her arms over her chest. "Listen, I'm tired. I was on my way home. Can't you bother me tomorrow?"

Shrugging, I stuffed my hands into the pockets of my jeans. "Yeah, I could do that." Relief shown in her violet eyes. "However, I'm going to need your word that you'll work with me."

Her lips turned down. "I already told you I don't know where exactly Cory is or who he's working with. I didn't speak to him."

"I have the information I was seeking the other night. I had to spend a night in jail to get it, but whatever."

Her brow furrowed. "You went to jail?"

"Wasn't the first time," I muttered. "Anyway, they're trying to blackmail me into giving up our territory. That's where you come in."

Shaking her head, she said, "I don't understand why you need me at all. Can't you get someone else to help you?"

Cocking my head to the side, I studied the blonde hair pulled up high on her head to the incredibly long legs and painted toes in the sandals she was wearing. "Something tells me you're the best thing that ever happened to Cory Wilson."

She snorted which I found incredibly adorable for some reason. "You're probably right, though I still don't understand what you need *me* for."

My lips tilted up slowly as I held her stare. "I'm going to hold you for ransom." Her breath caught as I stepped close to her again, placing a small card in her palm. "You have twelve hours to contact me with your response. If you ghost me, I'll come find you and, darlin', trust me, you don't want that."

I headed for my car, glancing back at her before I got in. She was still against the wall observing me cautiously. Shooting her a wink, I slid into the leather driver's seat of my classic Camaro. If I actually heard from her before the twelve hours were up, I'd be surprised. That'd be fine by me though. She had no idea how much I loved the chase.

*

"You can't hold someone against their will." Mackaela shook her head.

Shrugging, I tipped back my beer. "*Shouldn't,* however I most definitely *can.*"

She whipped her head to Simon who was giving me a questioning if not slightly amused look. "Tell him this isn't okay," she demanded. He let out a sigh, his gaze shifting to hers.

"I mean he's not wrong. It's not like he's kidnapping her for real."

A slow grin crept up my lips. "You get it, bro. See, this is why I love having you around."

Rolling her eyes, Mackaela took a healthy sip of her rum and diet. "You're both idiots," she mumbled. I chose to ignore her.

"Look, I'm simply trying to gain leverage. If Wilson thinks I've got his girl he'll second guess choosing Ricky's side. I'll split their little rag tag army up before going after Delgado, getting my revenge, and walking away for good."

"Mickey, I love you, really I do, but this is insane. Not only that, what happens if this girl won't go for it. Will you actually kidnap her?"

I pursed my lips. "Maybe."

"Mick," Simon said, frowning at me. "You need to be careful. You're so close to being out of the business. I know you want Delgado, hell, I want him, too, but you've got to tread lightly for your safety as well as hers. How much have you thought this through?"

"Enough to know it's a brilliant idea." Mackaela scoffed and I glared at her. "She's safe with me. It's not like I'm going to lock her in a dungeon. However, she's not going to be able to work anymore, then there's also her needing to agree to my terms." I'd need to draw up a contract. Make her an offer she couldn't refuse.

"Where does she work?" Simon asked.

"*Rosie's.* She's got a roommate who is also her coworker, Bianca Rogers. I'm not sure I can trust her because she had a brief relationship with Delgado a few years back. I've got Dom and Kyle doing some digging on her."

"I don't like this. Mickey, if this comes back to bite you in the ass, I don't know if I can be sympathetic."

I nodded, placing my hand on Mackaela's knee.

"I get it. I'm not asking you for anything. I just ... I need you guys to trust me. I want a life outside of slinging drugs. I'm tired of dealing with the chaos and violence." I glanced at Simon. "I've got to get Delgado though. I want to murder him for what he did to you both, however I'll settle for a hard prison sentence."

"I never talked to the cops," Simon said. "You think he'd get locked up?"

I grinned at my half-brother. "Come on, it's me. I have a plan."

I divulged what I had in store for Ricky Delgado as well as Cory Wilson. Of course, all of it depended on whether or not Claire would agree to letting me keep her for a while. If she did, I'd then need Wilson to dip out on Ricky. It was risky, a little dangerous, and probably borderline crazy. That didn't matter. Delgado needed to know he messed with the wrong guy. He was going to pay for his sins. I wouldn't rest until I had the justice both my brother and best friend deserved.

Claire

Mickey Silver wanted to use me as a pawn in whatever deranged game he was playing. Lucky me. Nothing about this was what I had planned since Cory had left. I was hoping to work for another month or so, pad my savings and leave town. I toyed with the idea of running now even though I knew I wouldn't get far. If I refused him I was certain he'd come find me. With the power he had and the connections, it probably wouldn't take a lot of effort on his part.

I stared at my cell phone which was sitting on the coffee table in our living room as I chewed my thumbnail, pacing the length of the hardwood floor. He didn't give me much of a choice. I'd had a nice quiet breakfast with Bianca an hour ago. We discussed our plans for the day which I hated because I had to be vague. I had no clue what was going to happen now with Mick. I didn't want her wrapped up in my sudden mess, although a part of me wondered if she had any idea what was going on.

She was the one who introduced me to Cory when I'd went with her to some party, so I knew she had friends that worked for Mick. I should have never gone to that party, should have never gotten tipsy and taken Cory home. This was my fault because I made stupid decisions, kind of like the one I was about to make.

Inhaling a deep breath, I squinted at my cell phone. I had fifteen minutes to make the call before the twelve hours were up. For all I knew he was waiting for me outside this apartment. The last thing I wanted was for him to storm in here.

There were so many questions running through my head. Like what did holding me for ransom entail? If I complied with his request, what happened afterward? I'd have a target on my back for working with the enemy. While I wasn't totally sure of what Cory got himself into, I knew he had a hatred for Mickey Silver that ran deep. What if he retaliated against him, harming me in the process?

I grabbed the phone, digging the card he'd given me last night with his contact info from the back pocket of my jeans. My fingers were trembling as I dialed his number, my heart beating wildly in my chest. This was insanity. Taking another breath, I hit the 'call' button, bringing the phone to my ear.

"Cutting it close, darlin'." Mick's gruff voice made my stomach dip. "You've made your decision?"

"I have questions," I said.

"Understandable."

"What are your intentions with me? Also, what happens after?"

"I intend to use you to soften your boyfriend, to turn him from the dark side."

"Aren't *you* the dark side?"

A low chuckle sounded and my heart skipped a beat. "Oh, sweet Claire, you have no idea."

I wasn't about to get into specifics with him. Instead, I asked, "What happens after?"

I heard rustling in the background like he was shuffling papers or something. "After services are rendered you can go on with your life. Of course, you'll have to stay silent about our arrangement. There will be paperwork to fill out, an NDA, as well as a few other safety precautions. Whatever you want to do once I'm done with you is your business not mine."

I frowned. "Paperwork?"

"Yes. I need to cover all the bases, go about this the right way. You'll be staying with me at an undisclosed location. I'll be keeping you until I get Cory to fold. Once that's accomplished I'll release you."

"What location? What about my job?"

"Details I'll share at our meeting. Are you available this morning, say around eleven?"

I swallowed my racing heart, closing my eyes as nausea swept through me. "What if I don't want to do this?" I asked, suddenly feeling breathless. This was all happening so fast.

"Then you tell me no which will force me to find another way. Although that wouldn't be wise—"

"No, I don't want to do this," I replied quickly. Was it really that simple that he'd leave me alone? "Find another way."

"You didn't let me finish." He growled and my spine straightened. His angry voice was intimidating as hell and also a little arousing. God, what was wrong with me? "I'll pay you. Quite well, too. It wouldn't be wise to say no."

That got my attention. "How much?"

He chuckled again. "Ah, there's the enthusiasm I was hoping for. Besides living rent free for however long this endeavor takes, I'm willing to pay you for your time. How does twenty thousand dollars sound?"

My mouth popped open. Holy shit that was a lot of money. More than I'd ever seen at once in my life and plenty enough to get me out of town. I could start over some place new, somewhere I could get away from my small town and this big city that gave me nothing except grief.

"That's a lot of money."

"Not really. I mean, I single handedly run the drug game in this state. Manufacturing, supplying, dealing. It's a lucrative business."

I smiled to myself thinking if he's going to keep me for a while, I'd make him pay for it both literally and figuratively. "Make it fifty, then maybe I'll consider your offer." I was surprised when he didn't miss a beat.

"Done."

"What?!" I shrieked.

"Fifty thousand dollars, Claire. Asking for more shows an initiative I wasn't sure you had in you. It's kind of hot actually." I ignored that statement. "You get twenty-five up front, the rest once our deal is over. Does that sound reasonable?"

"Um ... yeah that's fair," I mumbled.

"Excellent. Meet me at my office downtown at eleven. I'll text you the address and, Claire?"

"Yeah?"

"Welcome to the *darker* side." With that, he disconnected the call, leaving me blinking at the wall with the phone still to my ear.

*

I sat in a waiting room type area in a non-de-script building downtown that was apparently Mick's office. It had floor to ceiling windows with ducts exposed in an industrial style on the ceiling. The red brick walls were plain with no artwork or logos. Of course, why would there be any of that in a drug lord's office? The woman at the pseudo front desk which was more of a narrow writing desk with a laptop, smiled at me.

She had dark hair with skin so pale she reminded me of the Disney character Snow White. Her dark eyes crinkled slightly in the corners when she'd told me her name was Shelly, before asking me to have a seat in one of the high back cream colored chairs. I'd been waiting ten minutes so far. There was a dark wooden door behind her as well as one across the room that had a small plaque on it reading *Employees Only*.

I checked the time on my phone, growing anxious as the seconds ticked on. I had to be at work in a couple of hours. I hoped whatever stupid meeting Mick and I were having was short and ended with a large sum of money making its way to my bank account. Another five minutes went by before the door behind Shelly opened and Mick appeared in the doorway.

His hazel eyes landed on mine as a slow smile formed on his full lips. His hair was slicked back, the length of it curving behind his ears. He was dressed in a pair of charcoal gray slacks that fit him well. They matched his tie and suit jacket over a dark blue button down shirt. Jesus, Mary, and Joseph he looked good which wasn't doing the disdain I had for him any favors. For being in the line of work he was in, I figured he'd dress a little more casual. Seeing him in professional attire on a weekday threw me off balance.

"Claire Evans, my favorite new employee," Mick said as he sauntered toward me.

I took a cleansing breath as I stood to my feet, running my clammy palms over my denim-clad thighs. His gaze swept the length of me and I hated how my pulse kicked up at his perusal.

"Do you make a habit of being late for the meetings you schedule?" I asked. "Not really good business practice."

The smile left his face. "Sorry to keep you waiting. Shall we?" He turned slightly, sweeping his hand toward what I assumed was his office.

With a brief nod I drifted by him toward the room. A large mahogany desk sat in front of a black wall. There was a yellow couch to the right of me on the opposite wall of the desk. The left wall was like the waiting area with floor to ceiling windows. It was like corporate meets uncoordinated. A mini fridge sat near the couch. How dorm chic.

"Have a seat," Mick said politely as he closed the door behind him.

I lowered myself to one of the black chairs in front of his desk. He moved around the desk to take his own seat. Leaning forward with his elbows resting on top of the desk, he steepled his fingers under his chin.

"You have a receptionist," I said.

He raised a brow at my observation. "Of course I do. I can't be everywhere at once. She helps keep things organized."

"You sell and manufacture drugs. It isn't legal."

"I pay Shelly a higher wage than some other office would. She's a family friend." I nodded. "So you're here which I'm assuming means you're still on board for this arrangement."

"*Ransom* as you so eloquently put it."

His brows raised. "True, I did say that. That's what we'll call it when speaking to Cory or anyone else. Between the two of us it's simply a ... business agreement." He searched my face.

"Whatever."

Straightening, he reached into one of the desk drawers, producing a small stack of papers. He slid them across the top toward me, grabbing a pen and placing it on the stack.

"You're welcome to read through our contract. It basically states that you'll be accompanying me South, close to Oregon while staying in my father's home. During your stay, you'll be given access to the entire house including food, water, toiletries, clothing, electricity, and heat. You know, the essentials."

Panic began to take root. "I'm not moving to another city with you!"

"Yes, you are. We need to be close in order to act quickly once the opportunity arrives."

"What about my apartment, my job?"

He leaned back in his chair resting an elbow on the arm. "I'm paying you far more than you'd make in a year. You're really worried about your job?" I opened my mouth before closing it. He had a point. "As far as your apartment, tell Bianca you've decided to move on or don't say anything at all." He waved his hand flippantly. "It doesn't matter as long as you leave any mention of me out of it."

I frowned. "How do you know her name?"

His smile resurfaced. "I know a lot, darlin'. She can afford the place on her own, right? I'm sure it won't be difficult to find another roommate."

"You've got it all figured out," I seethed.

He shrugged. "Think of it as a vacation."

I scoffed. "Except I have to do as you say, right? Be *used* by you." I glared at him.

"The only thing I plan to use you for is to get Cory to change his mind." He leaned forward again, pinning me with an intense stare. "I need you with me to make it believable. I'm not sure what you think of me but—"

"You're no saint," I interrupted. "You're in the drug business, not an ideal or law abiding profession. I *think* you're a cocky asshole with power, money, and the world at your fingertips."

"You're not far off base, although I'd never force you to do anything dangerous that might put your life at risk. I'd never personally bring you harm."

"You expect me to believe that?"

His jaw muscle twitched. "I expect you to accept my word. To trust me."

I shook my head. "Not gonna happen."

"Sign the paperwork or don't. I have little time for this." He growled. "Although where else are you going to make the kind of money I'm offering you so quickly?"

It was a lot of money, true. Yet I'd be giving up my entire life here. Not that it was that great to begin with. I was planning on leaving anyway, but was I ready to move on now that the situation presented itself?

"How long will you need my help?" If I was going to agree to this, I needed a timeline.

Mick bit down on his bottom lip. "I can't say for sure. How much does your boyfriend value your life, value you?"

I snorted. "He left me here. Told me if I wasn't going with him, it was over. I was fine with it since I'd learned that he cheated on me."

"What?"

A small smile formed. "We've been having issues for a long time. He's an asshole, kind of like you. We're not together anymore."

Mick frowned, his gaze falling to the top of the desk. Minutes ticked by before he spoke again. He lifted his head to look at me. "Will he care at all if I have you?"

"Yes," I answered automatically. It was the truth. "If he knows I'm with you, it'll anger him. He doesn't like you."

He only nodded, unfazed by the fact that Cory disliked him. "Perfect." He placed a long index finger on the stack of papers, sliding them closer. "Sign on the dotted line, Claire. I think this is the start of a beautiful alliance."

Chapter 5

Claire

The next few days were going to be a total nightmare. After agreeing to Mick's deal I was expected to pack as much as I needed for who knows how long. I'd also decided to tell Bianca I was leaving. I might not have said anything at all but she'd wonder why I was packing. Anything like my bed or random belongings were to be left behind because the "ransom" needed to look believable. I wasn't sure what plan Mick was going to execute to kidnap me which made me a nervous wreck since leaving his office. It was official, I was certifiably insane. Although tell me, if you were offered double your annual salary for what was expected to be a quick job, would you take it?

I didn't trust him. However, I knew the money was good because I already had the first half sitting in my bank account. He'd wired the money before I left his office, assuring me there was more where that came from. I could have ran with twenty-five thousand sitting in my account, however being the cunning businessman he was, he'd thought of everything. Namely confiscating my social security card to make sure I stayed right where he wanted me. I'd get it back once our arrangement was secured.

I texted Bianca to make sure she was home, telling her we needed to talk. Her response was simple with an "okay." The fact that Mick knew my roommate by name, said he'd known a lot of things, worried me. I really hoped she wouldn't need to be involved in any of this. I'd grown fond of her over the last year and a half. I hoped we could still remain friends after all of this was over.

I came up with a good enough story saying I was missing my family so I was planning to go back to Winthrop for a while to clear my head. It would coincide with my lie about my brother calling a few days ago. She didn't know that he'd moved East to pursue a career in journalism. I hadn't spoken much about my family at all since moving here. Part of being a wanderer was not allowing people in fully. I'd never found myself to be an open book and Bianca never asked too many questions.

When I entered our apartment, she was sitting on the couch filing her nails while watching some cheesy early nineties sit-com.

"Hey, where you been?" she asked as I set my purse on the kitchen counter before plopping onto the couch next to her.

"Eye appointment," I lied. I didn't have time to beat around the bush so I decided on getting right into it. "I'm going back home for a while. My family needs me there right now."

She dropped her hands to her lap, staring at me. "What? I thought you hated small town living."

Shrugging, I pulled my knees to my chest, curling my arms around my legs. "I do, or I did. I don't know. After Cory left I'm beginning to wonder if he was the only thing keeping me here. I need some time to clear my head."

Her brow crumpled. "Are you coming back?"

"Yeah," I said. "I think I just need to step back for a minute."

Shaking her head, Bianca muttered, "I guess that makes sense." Giving me a small smile, she added, "I'm going to miss you."

Smiling, I nodded. "Me, too. I don't think I'll be gone long. I'm leaving the day after tomorrow."

"So soon?"

"Yeah, I already let Clint know. I think it's for the best."

"I understand," she said. "Family's important."

I was surprised at how easy going she was being about this. Standing, I stretched. "I guess I should start packing."

Bianca stood, too. "I'll help you."

*

I ended up packing two suitcases with enough clothing to last for a month just in case. As Bianca helped me, I thought about the fact that I'd be leaving this place for an unknown amount of time which brought on a level of sadness I hadn't expected. Not because I was disappointed to be leaving, it was more because I wasn't. The thought of never coming back didn't bother me like I thought it would. That was a little scary because I was afraid I'd never be happy anywhere. Would I ever want to lay down roots at some point?

Bianca took my mind off the anxiety of my new adventure by offering to take me out one last time. She claimed a proper sendoff was in order since she wasn't sure when she'd see me again. She seemed genuinely concerned that I wouldn't be coming back. I felt bad that I was lying to her, that I was unable to give a timeline. I didn't have a lot of friends, let alone a best friend. Bianca was as close as it got.

We started the night by going to our favorite restaurant downtown followed by dancing and drinks at one of the higher end nightclubs. She knew the bouncer there so he let us in without having to wait in line. I was already a little tipsy on the five-inch multi-colored heels I was rocking with my strapless black leather dress.

Bianca held my hand as we navigated through the throng of people rubbing their bodies together to the loud music in the club. She ordered us each a fruity cocktail before we made our way to one of the small tables near the dance floor.

I sipped my drink, swaying to the music in my seat as I scanned the crowd.

"I'm going to miss you so much!" Bianca shouted over the heavy bass remix that was blaring through the speakers.

"I know! I promise to come back."

"Maybe I'll come over there to visit. You can show me what farm living is like." I smiled, head buzzing with the alcohol and music. "Woah," She stared behind me, her eyes widening. "Oh my god, Claire."

"What?" I began to turn, stopping when she grabbed my wrist to capture my attention again.

"Mickey Silver just walked in. Didn't you give him a private dance last weekend?"

My stomach knotted. What was he doing here? "Yeah, when he was asking me about Cory." I rolled my eyes, trying to play it cool.

She shook her head, still gazing beyond me. "He's with some hot hunk of man. Never seen him before." She licked her lips before dragging her teeth along the bottom one.

I pivoted in my seat, scanning the club. Sure enough, Mick was standing toward the far corner of the dance floor with that other guy who'd been at *Rosie's*. I thought his name was Hawks.

Great.

"I think that's his business associate," I said, gaining her attention. A slow smile spread across her cherry red lips.

"I like the sound of that. We should go say hi."

"No," I argued immediately. "No way. I hate that guy."

Bianca raised a brow at me questioningly. "That doesn't mean we can't have fun." Her face fell, bottom lip sticking out in a pout. "Come on, *Harlow*, I just want to say hi. Dude is freaking gorgeous."

"Then go for it." I grabbed my drink, taking a healthy sip. "I'm staying here."

Bianca stood as she downed the rest of her cocktail. "Fine, then *you* dance with me." She held her hand out for me to take.

I emptied my glass as well, shuddering at the overly sweet drink. Interlacing our fingers, I let her lead me to the dance floor while glancing over to where Mick still stood. His hazel eyes found mine, narrowing slightly. I matched his glare, flipping him off quickly before joining Bianca in the crowd of people.

Mick

"You really think she needs a babysitter?" Hawks grumbled.

"She's practically drunk. She could spill her guts any moment. I've got to protect my investment." It was more than that. I didn't trust Bianca Rogers one bit since I'd learned of her little side business.

"The chick she's with keeps eye fucking me."

"You say that like it's a bad thing."

"Is this outing business or pleasure, Mick? Last time you were a total prick about me mixing the two. If I can't act on the gorgeous woman tempting me, it's a horrible thing."

We were here to watch Claire, to make sure she didn't divulge the new business arrangement. As much as I'd hoped she was trustworthy, I wouldn't risk my ultimate goal. I also wanted to water the seed I'd planted about having a sudden interest in her. There would be no doubt who took her when the time came.

I knew she was here thanks to the power of social media. Bianca couldn't go a minute without snapping a photo or updating her status. The second I saw Claire tagged in a post with them at dinner and Bianca mentioning going out someplace special, I knew I needed to act. This was the only nightclub in town with a bouncer that Bianca knew. Jeremy was a trusted employee of mine as well as a personal friend of Bianca's. After reaching out to him to confirm my suspicions, I decided to pay a visit to my new employee.

I watched Claire dance to the music. She was almost as enticing as she had been on stage at *Rosie's*. If she weren't so important to the end game, I'd likely be trying to spend some one on one time with her that concluded with both of us in various positions on my mattress. However, this was business. She was an employee for all intents and purposes. Knowing she wasn't with Cory anymore, something that stopped me from acting out some very wicked fantasies in the past, had my mind racing with possibilities.

Don't judge me. I never claimed to be a good guy. Just because I didn't act on my attraction didn't mean I wouldn't think about it.

Bianca's gaze locked with mine. She smiled at me before shifting her attention to Hawks. Placing a hand on Claire's bare shoulder, she whispered something in her ear. Claire glanced back at me, those stunning violet eyes burning with what I assumed was pure hatred. She never seemed happy to see me. Tragic.

"Let's get a drink," I said as I headed for the bar.

Once we had our drinks we made our way to the table the girls had vacated minutes before. I sat down, nodding my head in their direction. "Go dance with the girl." Hawks' eyebrows shot up. "I need a moment of Claire's time."

With a swift nod, he took a healthy gulp of his drink before heading for Bianca. I crossed my ankles, sliding my glass of scotch along the tabletop. It didn't take long before Claire was standing beside me. I caught her sweet scent, cotton candy. Jesus, I'd never be able to think of it the same ever again.

"What are you doing here?" she demanded.

I twisted slightly in my seat to glance up at her. "Behaving yourself?"

I noticed her lips were painted an interesting shade of purple when they fell open. The color nearly matched those intoxicating eyes of hers.

"I haven't said anything if that's what you're worried about. I'm not going to."

"Well, you've been drinking so ... " I trailed off, my gaze sweeping over that skin tight dress down to the high heels that made her legs seem longer. "Have to keep an eye on my assets."

Her lips curled up in a sneer. "I am *not* your asset. Never in a million years would I ever—"

I stood abruptly which caused her to stumble slightly. Gripping her forearm, I lowered my lips to her ear.

"Never say never, darlin'." Stepping back, I grinned at her. "Please, sit with me a moment."

"I hate you," she complained yet took the seat across from me.

I took a sip of my drink as I studied her carefully. "You're not drinking anymore tonight. I'm not risking you blowing up my plan before it starts."

She grimaced. "You're not the boss of me."

Raising a brow, I said, "No? The money in your bank account says otherwise." She had nothing to say to that. Instead, she lowered her eyes to the table in defeat. A waitress came by to drop a glass of water in front of her. I'd ordered it before leaving the bar. "Drink."

Grabbing the glass, she took a decent tug off the iced water. "Are you always an asshole?"

I chuckled. "When I have to be, yes. Always?" I shrugged. "I think I can be quite nice, considerate in fact."

She snorted. "Why don't I believe you? You're incredibly arrogant and way too good looking."

Ah, a moment of weakness. She found me attractive whether she wanted to admit it or not. That didn't surprise me. I worked hard to maintain a good physique. "Can't I be all of those things while still maintaining some semblance of politeness?"

"Maybe. I still think you're an asshole."

"It's probably better that way." She shot me a questioning look. "Wouldn't want you to fall in love with me." I winked at her. My gaze shifted to Hawks who was probing Bianca's mouth with his tongue like he was searching for the holy fucking grail.

"Your roommate's a bit promiscuous."

Claire followed my line of sight, shaking her head slightly as she drank more water. "Bianca takes what she wants. She doesn't care what anyone thinks of her."

I frowned as I shifted to look at the woman in front of me again. "Why didn't you go to Oregon with Cory?"

Slowly, she looked at me over the rim of her glass. It was nearly empty now which was good. I needed her sober for the plans I had later.

"Like I said before, I found out he'd been cheating on me. While it hurt, I sort of realized I didn't genuinely love him. Plus I don't want to be a part of your guys' world."

I couldn't fault her there. I didn't even want to be a part of it anymore despite the fact it was all I'd ever known. "Why were you with him?"

"He was fun at first, someone to pass time with. I'm not a nun. I ... enjoyed his company."

I hadn't quite expected that response. She was gorgeous, seemingly smart, and definitely headstrong. Was she really just with him for the sex and company? Perhaps we weren't that different in seeking companionship strictly for the sake of something or someone to do.

"Did he love you?" My voice was deeper, my jaw twitching as I awaited her response. If all they had was casual, I was worried my strategy would be full of holes already.

Claire shrugged. "Whether he did or didn't doesn't matter. He hates you, Mick. That's enough to get him where you want him."

I rubbed a finger against my forehead before finishing off my drink. Setting the glass back on the table, I folded my hands next to it, pinning her with a hard look. "I want him to walk away from this new job opportunity. I also want him to bleed for betraying me." She needed to know that I'd do whatever it took to end Ricky. That if Cory Wilson was caught in the crossfire, so be it. "You okay with that?"

Her tongue slid along her lips slowly. God, she was sexy, and I was a bad man for entertaining this idea. Those violet eyes held mine with a similar edge. This woman was tougher than anyone gave her credit for, of that I was sure.

"If I never see Cory Wilson again, it'll be too soon. Is that an acceptable answer?"

With a swift nod, I stood, ready to get out of there before I did something stupid like continue to enjoy our conversation. "Yeah, see you *soon*."

I didn't give her a chance to respond. Grabbing Hawks by the scruff of his shirt, I hauled him off Bianca who growled at me like a hungry lioness who just lost her meal. Ignoring her, I shoved him toward the door. It was time to go home, to finish preparing for what I hoped was a simple extraction. I would use Claire as collateral, back Cory off, ease Ricky out of hiding, exact revenge, and walk away for good. Shouldn't be too difficult, right?

Claire

Bianca fumed about Mick's abrupt exit the entire cab ride home. She was upset that he'd ruined her plan to take Hawks into the ladies' room to show him a good time. Even as we entered the apartment, she was still griping about it. I had the urge to slap some sense into her. Honestly, it's not like she couldn't have found another guy. Although I'm sure it didn't help that the minute Mick left, I was ready to get out of there, too. He'd thoroughly ruined my evening with his presence and I realized in that moment, Bianca was right. He was a dick who deserved to be punched in the face. Maybe I'd get the opportunity when I saw him next.

After saying goodnight to Bianca, I decided to turn in for the night. She was going to call one of the guys she had on speed dial to invite him over and continue her fun. As I lay there exhausted and anxious, I thought about how it was one of my last nights in the apartment. I'd miss Bianca, miss our morning ritual of coffee and listening to her escapades with whomever.

I still wasn't sure where I wanted to go after this job for Mick was completed. I wondered how long it would take, how quickly Cory would be roped into backing down once he found out I was with Mick. *If* he complied. I wasn't certain he'd care enough to leave whatever new thing he had going. He was notorious for choosing money over everyone else, so it wouldn't surprise me if Mick had to find another angle. I secretly hoped that would be the case. Then I'd be able to dip out without ever having to see either one of them again.

Knowing I was with Mickey Silver would piss him off enough to take notice though. I didn't care about Mick's vendetta against

Ricky Delgado or Cory. All I cared about was the money he was offering so I could get out of dodge. I wanted to go somewhere far away where I'd have the opportunity to finally feel satisfied in life.

Now if I could just figure out where exactly that was, I'd be set.

*

The loud banging of the front door woke me up. The crack of wood splintering had me darting out of bed to my closet. Crashing to my knees, I pulled the trim away from the wall as my heart hammered wildly in my throat.

"Get on the fucking ground!" a distant booming voice ordered to who I could only assume was Bianca or maybe whoever came over after I went to sleep.

"Don't shoot!" a male voice begged as Bianca shrieked.

I stuck my arm into the void behind the trim feeling for the cool steel of the handgun Cory used to keep hidden here. I really hoped he hadn't taken it with him. As soon as I felt the rectangular barrel, I let out a relieved sigh, yanking the gun out. Heavy footsteps sounded on the hardwood floor in the hall. My fingers trembled as I tucked myself against the wall outside my closet aiming at the doorway.

It was early morning, the sun just beginning to rise through the window in my room. I tried to regulate my breathing when the footsteps stopped. A faint shadow filled the space at the bottom of my bedroom door.

"There's no one else here!" Bianca cried out.

"Oh no? Why's this door closed then?" a male voice asked in a surprisingly calm tone.

"Please, we don't have anything. You need to leave," her friend said.

"Shut the fuck up!" another distant voice demanded.

Inhaling a deep breath, I held it as my finger slid over the trigger. I'd only shot a gun one other time in my life. That was just messing around with Cory last summer when we went camping. I really didn't like the idea of using a firearm on a living person. Although whoever this was wouldn't take me down without a fight. Maybe I could scare them off.

I could make out rustling noises from the living room, along with the soft whimpers of Bianca. Suddenly my door swung open as a tall figure dressed in black jeans and a black hoodie stood before me. I could tell it was a man by his build. Unfortunately, his face was covered with a ski mask so I had no idea who he was. All I could scarcely make out were his eyes, but the sun hadn't risen enough for me to see the color.

Cocking his head to the side, the intruder chuckled. "Look at you with your little pistol. You know how to use that thing, sweetheart?" His gaze roamed over my body as bile rose in my throat.

I was glad I'd decided to sleep in a long t-shirt that fell to my knees to cover my underwear, although I really wished I'd put some pants on after grabbing the gun.

"Stay back!" I tried to shout. My voice came out in a whine with the lump of fear in my throat. I lifted the gun aiming for the intruder's chest.

"You're shakin' like a leaf. Not sure your aim will stay true."

"Doesn't matter," I bit out as tears pooled. "I can still do some damage."

That earned a full on laugh from the guy. I glared at him.

"You're adorable," he said before rushing me.

Before I could squeeze the trigger, he grabbed my wrist roughly which caused the gun to crash to the floor in a loud thud. I swung my leg out, kicking at the man as he captured my other wrist and yanked me forward.

"You're a fighter," his muffled voice said as he let go of one wrist to lock an arm around my waist. I continued thrashing even as he lifted me into the air, marching out of my room and down the hall. "No wonder the boss likes you. You've got some fire."

I struggled in his hold, trying and failing to get free.

"Claire!" Bianca screamed. My head snapped toward the living room where she was tied up in one of our kitchen chairs next to a guy I knew as Matt. "Please don't hurt her!"

There was another man dressed identical to the one holding me, standing with his arms crossed next to Matt.

"The girl comes with us," the man said.

"No!" Bianca and I yelled at the same time. "Don't take me. Please, please don't take me." Tears streamed down my cheeks as Bianca's solemn face became a blur.

"Don't take you?" the man next to Matt said. He pulled a gun from the back of his pants before aiming at Bianca's head. "How about I shoot her instead?"

Bianca paled. Her panicked expression was a punch to my chest. "No!" I sobbed. "Please, leave us alone."

"You're coming with us, sweetheart. Either that or this bitch gets to meet her maker."

In a last ditch effort to battle, I kicked my leg out in front of me before swinging it back with enough force that my heel connected with the intruder's knee. He doubled over as I slipped out of his hold.

A loud growl rumbled from him which I ignored as I shot toward the shattered front door. I wasn't sure where to go. Maybe the neighbor's downstairs? Someone had to have heard us by now.

"Help!" I screamed as I darted for the stairs. "Somebody ple—" A large hand covered my mouth. I was pulled back into a hard body.

The guy snarled in my ear. "Don't make a sound, don't struggle. If you do, I'll shoot you in that pretty face of yours. Understand?"

I tried again, which only made his arm around me tighten more to the point it was difficult to breathe. I gave a swift nod hoping he'd ease up a bit. He didn't.

"We gotta roll, man. Someone's probably called the cops by now," the other intruder said from behind us.

"You got the stuff?" my captor asked.

"Yep."

What *stuff*? I tried to speak yet couldn't form words with the meaty hand pressed against my lips. The guy basically dragged me down the stairs, around the building, then toward an awaiting black car that was idling across the street. I was tossed into the back harshly before being followed in by one abductor. The trunk slammed closed before the other guy slid in the passenger seat. I scrambled for the driver's side of the car trying to open the door. It wouldn't budge.

"Child safety locks are one of the best inventions," the intruder in the passenger seat mused. "You're not going anywhere."

The man beside me closed his door so I sunk against the opposite side trying to get as far away from him as possible. The driver was the only one without a mask, but all I could see of him was the back of his head. I could tell he was tall, making the seat of the sedan look smaller than normal. His hair was black and shaved close to his scalp, his shoulders broad like he could win a strong man competition or something.

"Who are you and what do you want?" I asked as the car pulled away.

"Who we are isn't important," the man beside me said. "It's who *you* are that is. The boss needs to make sure everything looks legit."

Not knowing what that meant because my mind was on overdrive, I let my head fall against the window as I stared out at the ever-brightening morning sky.

*

I spent forty-five agonizingly silent minutes in that car with three men who were kidnapping me. Forty-five minutes of fear trying to figure out how to get out of this situation. We pulled off the highway, traveling down a long winding road toward some sort of industrial type area that looked abandoned. I noticed an SUV parked beside a metal structure.

As the car came to a stop, the driver of the other vehicle opened their door to step out. The purest form of rage festered inside of me when I saw *his* face. Those stupid full lips, those damn hazel colored eyes, and the golden blond hair that was slicked back perfectly made my blood boil. He was wearing a white t-shirt with faded blue jeans that hung low on his hips. The black converse on his feet looked well worn. I'd never seen him so casual before which surprised me. It didn't matter.

No. What mattered was my plan to punch that face as hard as I could the second they let me out of this vehicle. Then I was going to kick Mickey Silver in the balls for putting me through this turmoil. For *actually* kidnapping me without notice.

The driver of the car I was in got out, making his way to Mick. The other two removed their masks before exiting as well. I didn't recognize either of them. However, the driver I realized was a man named Dom that I'd seen a few times at Mick's parties.

Dom said something to Mick who glanced at the car with a grin. I glared at him between the two front seats hoping he could see me. After whatever little debrief the four had, Dom came back to the car and opened my door. I was ready to scratch Mick's eyes out. I wasted no time gunning for him the second my bare feet hit the gravel. I didn't care that the soles of my feet were being torn up, he was going to pay.

Mick looked genuinely surprised as I rushed him, my fist preparing to hopefully break his nose. Instead of connecting with his face, his palm shot up to take the impact. Growling in frustration, I shoved him instead which didn't work at all. He barely moved, and that only pissed me off further.

"What the hell is your problem?!" I stepped up to him, shoving him again a little harder this time. He backed up so I did it again until he was against the front of the SUV. "How could you send people to actually take me? They had guns!"

Mick's jaw ticked as he scowled at me. Grabbing the front of his shirt, I cocked my fist back again. This time when I swung, he grabbed my wrist to pin my arm behind my back. Leaning forward, he dipped his chin which brought his lips close to mine. Tension rippled off of him in waves as butterflies took flight in my belly.

"I had to make it look real. If you go for my face again, I'm going to tie your hands behind your back."

I scoffed. "Fine." Lifting my knee, I decided I'd go for another part of him instead. Wrong move. He shifted suddenly, somehow spinning us around so now my back was to the vehicle. He gripped each of my wrists in his hands between us, squeezing tightly.

His brows raised. "Really? Low blow, darlin'."

"Fuck. You," I seethed.

He chuckled darkly. "That'll be hard to do if you go for my balls again."

I tried to move my leg again and that resulted in him pressing his hips against mine. My brain short-circuited like I'd stuck my finger in a light socket. I could feel every inch of him against me including the part of him I was trying to injure. My breath caught in my throat, my eyes widening.

"Heard you almost shot one of my men."

"I wish I'd pulled the trigger," I snapped.

"Oh, sweet Claire." His breath was warm against my lips. "While I find your strength incredibly sexy, we both know you never would have shot him."

I pinned him with a dark look. "You don't know a thing about me."

"Yet," he said, pulling back slightly. "We need to get on the road. Are you going to play nice?"

My nostrils flared. "No."

His lips kicked up on one side. "Good. Neither am I." He stepped back completely then, calling out to one of the guys. "Get her bags loaded and call Simon to let him know we're rolling out." He curled his fingers around my bicep, leading me to the passenger side.

He opened the door before gently shoving me toward the seat. "Get in on your own or I'll put you in myself."

Huffing out an exasperated breath, I climbed into the seat. While I was absolutely irrevocably angry, I had agreed to going with him. Just because I was being easy now didn't mean I would be the entire time. I'm not sure why I felt compelled to prove to Mick that I could hold my own. Maybe it was because I desperately wanted to knock him down a peg or two.

"Can I at least put on some pants?" I asked as I buckled myself in. Mick leaned against the open door while fixating on the bare skin of my thighs.

"Eventually." His eyes flicked up to mine. There was a darkness in them that sent a jolt of awareness through me. The look was fleeting though as his jaw went rigid. When he spoke again ice replaced the warmth. "Don't ever provoke me like that in front of my men again." He closed the door before wandering over to where Dom stood. He'd been watching our entire exchange.

Chapter 6

Mick

"You picked a fierce one." Dom chuckled.

"Yeah," I replied with clenched teeth. I wasn't happy about Claire trying to fight me in front of my guys. Normally I'd stay calm, cool, and collected. Not with her. She elicited some primal response in me that made me want to slap some sense into her before bending her over the seat and fucking her senseless. I was messed up with her around. "Listen, I'll be in touch when I can. I want to lie low for a couple days. Make this all seem real."

Dom nodded. "Got it. I stuck two burner phones in the glove box. The only people that have the numbers are me and Simon."

I clapped his bicep. "Thanks, man." I made my way back to the SUV. Thankfully, Claire was still in her seat. "Take it easy if you can. Mack said Sadie's off this weekend so you should be, too."

"Yeah, I will. Good luck."

I gave him a quick wave before sliding into the driver's seat. We had an almost four-hour drive ahead of us before reaching my father's private house high in the hills of southern Washington. Claire was silent in the passenger seat, refusing to look anywhere but straight ahead. I headed toward another building on the other side of the industrial park.

"I'm sure you need to freshen up or whatever," I said as I came to a stop in front of a trailer. "We don't have time for a shower. You can do whatever else you need to do though. It's a long trip so I don't want to stop constantly."

Claire rolled her eyes before opening her door. "Whatever," she snapped before slamming it.

"Lord grant me patience," I muttered before going around back. I lifted the hatch so she could grab whatever she needed. I let her in the trailer, saying, "I'll give you fifteen minutes," before leaving her alone.

In just over ten minutes, she'd gotten herself ready. She had pulled her blonde hair up into a high knot on her head which showcased her long neck and prominent cheekbones. This was the first time I'd seen her without any makeup on her face. Her natural beauty stunned me. Not doing me any favors, she'd slipped on a tight pair of denim shorts with a t-shirt that accentuated her chest. I couldn't help checking out her fine ass as she walked in front of me back to the vehicle. After tossing her bag in the back, she slid right into the passenger seat without argument. I hoped she cooled off some. I didn't like her acting unpredictable because it made what little resolve I had around her slip.

"You hungry?" I asked as we headed out of the industrial area onto the main road.

"No, although I'd do some pretty bad things for caffeine right now."

I glanced at her. "Addict." I shook my head.

She snorted. "It's healthier than drugs."

"I wouldn't know. I've never done them." That earned a look of shock that I found hilarious. "I sell the shit. The stupidest thing I could do is lower my inventory as well as my profit by using."

She nodded. "Smart."

"I'll stop somewhere before we get on the freeway." Other than telling me her order at a Starbucks, we didn't speak.

It wasn't until two hours later that she finally said something. When she did, it caught me off guard.

"I've never been this far away from home before." Her voice was quiet as if she were thinking out loud.

"Where are you from?" I asked in spite of myself. Getting to know her went against every professional aspect I tried to maintain. Still she intrigued me, so I couldn't help asking her questions.

"Winthrop. It's a small town northeast of Seattle on the other side of the mountains. There's nothing there other than fields and farms."

"Is that why you came to Seattle?" I merged into the right lane to take an exit for the next highway.

"Yeah, although I don't like it as much as I thought I would."

I grunted in response. Perhaps she'd leave town after we were done with this job. I was tied to Seattle, raised on the streets surrounded by people. If I were given the chance to disappear, I'd possibly take it, although that didn't seem like an option for me. Even after leaving the business my father may still need me occasionally. Plus, Simon and Mackaela were here.

She turned slightly in her seat to face me, searching my face. "Can I ask you something?"

"Sure."

"Why is it so important that you get this Ricky guy?"

"That's a loaded question," I replied before passing a semi-truck. "Long story short, he betrayed me by nearly killing my brother while attempting to kidnap my best friend."

"The quiet girl with the long brown hair." I raised a brow at her. She shrugged. "You were always watching her like a hawk at your parties. Cory said she was your main bitch. I don't think you slept with her though."

I bit back on my molars. *Main bitch.* I'd shoot him just for calling Mackaela that. I didn't want to talk about her to Claire or anyone else. She was the one person that really knew me, that brought the part of me I buried deep down to the surface. Speaking of her would lower my defenses.

"Why is that?" I asked, keeping my voice even.

"She didn't fawn all over you like the other girls did. Plus you always ended up with some drunk chick in your lap at the end of the night before disappearing." I winced. How observant of her. "Will one of your *girlfriends* be joining us at the place we're going?"

Scoffing, I shook my head. "You think so little of me." There were a lot of people that thought similarly. While it typically didn't bother me, it did coming from her. I didn't want Claire thinking I was some man whore who couldn't abstain. I got around because I feared commitment, however I wasn't about to tell her that.

"Does that really surprise you?"

I glanced at her, squinting. "For your information, I don't have *girlfriends.* So no, we won't have company where we're going. Mackaela's off limits. Don't bring her up again."

"So you can pry into my life but I can't ask you questions?" She snorted. "That's fair ... *partner.* I don't even know why I'm bothering. It's not like I care about your stupid life."

"We're not partners," I growled. "We're temporary colleagues at best. Once this is over you walk away. You can go wherever you want."

"I intend to," she snapped. "I'm going as far away from Seattle as possible. I never want to see yours or Cory's faces ever again!"

"You know what I think?" I bit out as I merged around another semi. "I think you used Cory to get whatever you wanted at the time. You got bored, wanted to move on but were too chicken shit to say anything before he gave you an excuse. That's why you lack any emotion that he left you."

She laughed without humor, pinning me with an intense look. "Yeah? Well *I* think you're too much of a coward to face the fact that you're not all that. You're threatened by this Ricky guy, by Cory because you're afraid."

"Nothing fucking scares me."

"Oh yeah?" she asked, leaning over the console. I inhaled deep, immediately regretting it. That scent of hers drove me crazy. "What if you fail, Mick? What if he doesn't react when he finds out that you kidnapped me? What are you going to do then?"

"He'll care. You said yourself that he hated me. He won't like that I have you."

She righted herself in her seat again, folding her arms across her chest. "*I* hate you."

"Good."

We didn't speak again after that which was just fucking fine with me. After another hour, I needed to stop to fuel up. I exited the highway, pulling into a simple gas station with a small convenience store.

"Wait in the car," I ordered. Claire rolled her eyes but obeyed. Once the tank was full, I parked near the front of the store.

"We're going to go in to use the bathroom. You're not going to speak to anyone. You'll keep your head down. When you're done, you come straight back here. Got it?"

"Fine." She started to open her door. I shot my arm across her to pull it closed. My face was inches from hers, my lips so close to her throat that I felt her swallow. Damn, I wanted to taste her skin to see if it was as sweet as her scent.

"I mean it, Claire. We're incognito here. Ghosts."

Her eyes closed as her lips parted, capturing my attention. I hadn't leaned back yet, still all up in her business like she was a magnet keeping me close.

"You'll be a good girl for me, won't you, darlin'?" Her throat rolled in another swallow. It took every ounce of strength I had to pull back from her. She nodded. "Let's go."

I let her walk in front of me while scanning the store as we entered. She headed straight for the back where the restrooms were. I followed, grabbing her hand before she pushed the door open. She blinked up at me.

"Straight to the car when you're done."

"Got it."

I released her, loosening a breath as I went into the men's room.

Ten minutes later, we were back on the road without incident. It was another thirty miles or so to the house. I was more than ready to get there. Being cooped up in a confined space with Claire was pure fucking torture. She didn't seem angry anymore, although she was distant, almost morose looking. I probably hurt her by saying what I did about Cory leaving her. While I felt like a real dick for that, it was better than showing sympathy. I wouldn't dare tell her she was better off without him, that I hoped she truly hated him and wished she would run far away from the both of us so that she'd be safe.

I couldn't tell her that every time she looked at me my heart beat faster. That all I could think about was kissing her lips. That what she said about me being afraid was partially true. That I was worried I'd be stuck in this damn business forever or die trying to get out.

Claire

The sooner I was out of this vehicle, the better. I wanted a hot shower, a moment of peace, and maybe a good cry. How dare Mick accuse me of being heartless, of using Cory. He didn't know what I'd been through, what I'd done to protect myself from getting caught up in someone I knew had the potential to destroy me. Cory wasn't innocent. He undoubtedly gave me good reason to check out of the relationship mentally. It started when he cared more about selling drugs than he did about spending time with me. It became more prominent when he threatened to kill me if I ever told anyone his secret. What was I supposed to do? Walk away only to be left watching my back the rest of my life?

The secret was the biggest reason I wanted to get away from Seattle. Because if Mick found out what I knew, what I'd sworn not to tell, he'd probably kill me, too. I should have never agreed to this deal. I should have left after that first night at *Rosie's* when Mick showed up. I could have skipped town and fallen off the radar. I could've gone back home like I'd lied to Bianca about. Yet I didn't do that because the money Mick offered was too enticing to pass up. It was life changing.

After another half hour or so Mick drove us up a long winding road surrounded by tall evergreen trees. The further we went, the fewer houses there were. Each home we did pass grew in size as we climbed the steep drive. He finally hung a right down a private drive, stopping in front of a large black iron gate with a keypad set up. After rolling down his window, he entered whatever code was needed. The gates swung open soundlessly before closing again once he'd pulled through. My mouth fell open at the sight of the house beyond.

It was an incredibly modern looking home like what you'd see in *Architecture's Digest* or something. The exterior was made up of wood and stucco with daylight pouring into the many windows, giving a perfect view of parts of the interior as well as the view beyond through the floor to ceiling windows in back. Mick eased the car around the front of the house toward a garage. The front walkway caught my attention with a large tree sitting in the middle of the concrete path that had been built around it, leading up to the front door.

I'd never seen a home like this before. I was struck speechless in awe of the beauty and simplicity of it. It felt like it belonged up here, nestled into trees on three sides yet open in back to overlook the Columbia River atop a massive cliff.

Mick stopped in front of the three car garage, cutting the engine. Running a hand through his hair, he turned to look at me, his jaw tight. He searched my face for a minute without saying anything. After a few moments, he exhaled soundly, pushing his door open. I did the same, meeting him at the back of the vehicle.

"Come on," he said, reaching for my hand then thinking better of it.

I followed him down the walkway to the glass front door that he opened without a key because of course, why would you need one when your property is secluded on top of a cliff? We stepped onto stone tiled floors that were an off-white color. To the left was what appeared to be a brand new kitchen with a large center island adorned with quartz countertops in a charcoal gray color. To the right was a narrow hallway tucked back from a set of stairs leading further down in the house. The large windows in front of me offered such a breathtaking view, I barely noticed the living room with a long gray leather sectional and modern looking armchair in the corner that sat in front of a glass gas fireplace.

"There's one bedroom on this floor, the others are downstairs. You'll sleep up here," Mick said quietly, heading down the hall.

I continued on the tour, following him into the large bedroom. It was nearly the size of my entire apartment in Seattle. A large bed was fixed against the wall facing more windows with that un-believable view.

"I usually stay in here, but you can have it this time. There's a bathroom connected." He opened a dark wood door. "You can shower or bathe, whatever you want. Everything is stocked."

I nodded. "Thanks."

"I'll go get your things."

I couldn't stop turning in circles as I took in the massive room. The bed was made up with white linens while the headboard appeared to be carved from wood and stained in dark colors. It was like the ritziest of hotels yet this was Mick's home. Well his father's technically. I'd never been anywhere so nice before.

I found myself inching toward the window to observe the mountain off in the distance along with the river below. A place like this tucked away from the world would be a dream come true. I knew right then that's what I wanted though on a smaller scale. Space, freedom, solitude. I needed to find something to do with my life that was honest. That didn't involve showing my body to men who weren't satisfied in their relationships or single with no intention of ever settling down.

Maybe I could open a dance studio somewhere to teach. I day-dreamed about a future I wasn't sure would ever be possible when the sound of my suitcases dropping to the floor pulled me from my thoughts. Mick stood at the foot of the bed where he'd deposited them with his hands at his sides studying me.

"My favorite thing about this place is the view. I don't have that back home."

"It's gorgeous," I said.

"Yeah. Listen, I think it's best we lie low for a couple of days. Let the news of your disappearance spread to the right people. Then we'll contact Cory, see if I can draw him out."

"Okay."

"I'm going to need you to sell the whole kidnapping thing. I don't ... I won't really harm you. You understand?"

Swallowing, I nodded.

"Despite what you might think of me or what I might say or do to you, I'm not a complete monster."

Ice filled my veins. "*Do* to me?"

His gaze shifted out the window as he squinted. "You can settle in, clean up if you want. You hungry?" He glanced at me again.

"Yeah."

"Cool, I'll whip something up for you." He left abruptly, closing the door behind him. I let out a heavy breath.

What was he going to do to me? A tight knot formed in my stomach as I placed my suitcases on the bed to go through them. Collecting a change of clothes, I made my way to the bathroom, stopping just inside the door.

The space was huge with white marble flooring and a matching long vanity that had two sinks. A stand up shower large enough for five people with a clear glass door was set up off to the right. Mick wasn't kidding about having the essentials. The shower was stocked with three different body washes, shampoo, conditioner, and even a razor and loofah. At the end of the long room was a marble half-wall with a small gas fireplace enclosed. On the other side of the wall was a deep garden tub with a picture window spanning the length of it.

This was overwhelming yet incredible. I both loved and hated that I was here, that this was mine to use for a little while. While I was itching to try the tub out at some point, for now I decided to use the shower.

I stripped down after ensuring the water was situated to the perfect temperature. Stepping in, I let the rain shower-head thoroughly soak me. The shampoo was a kind I'd never used although it smelled good, like green tea. Grabbing the loofah, I scanned the different body washes before halting at the one in the middle. I frowned at the small cylindrical container wondering how he'd known. It was the exact kind I used back home. A kind that was expensive along with only being sold at one store in town.

I tried not to read too much into how sophisticated his stalking skills might be as I lathered up. Once I was dressed in a pair of cotton shorts and a baggy t-shirt, I brushed out my long hair, leaving it down. As I wandered down the hall, I was smacked in the face with the glorious smell of bacon.

Mick was standing at the island, frying what looked like an omelet in a pan. A heaping plate of bacon sat across from him near the edge of the counter in front of two bar stools. Snagging a piece, I took a seat on one of them. The hot grease slid down my throat with the first bite causing me to moan involuntarily. Mick raised his head examining me carefully.

"You're a meat eater," he said with a small smile playing on his lips.

"Absolutely," I said around another mouthful of the salty goodness. "You cook?"

He lifted his shoulder in a slight shrug while focusing back on the omelet. "I dabble a little." He plated the omelet, sliding it toward me. "Ham and cheese." He grabbed a fork from a drawer, passing it to me.

"Thanks." My stomach growled as I wasted no time taking a bite of the fluffy eggs. "Where did this food come from?"

Mick slid onto the stool next to me, plucking up a piece of bacon. He finished the strip in two bites before grabbing another. "I had someone stock the kitchen yesterday. Taste okay?"

I nodded, not stopping long enough between bites to speak. He ate three more strips of bacon before wandering to the refrigerator. He grabbed two bottles of water, placing one in front of me before taking his seat again.

"You have a lot of people that work for you."

He nodded, checking his phone. "Not many I trust to know where we are. There's a housekeeper that comes a few times a month when no one is living here. I had her grab groceries."

I finished the last of the eggs, rolling my eyes. "How convenient." Of course, he had a housekeeper.

Ignoring my response, he said, "Sounds like Cory's already aware of your disappearance."

I took a drink of water before frowning at him. "How is that possible?"

"I was going to ask you the same thing." His tone was even yet there was a hardness to his stare. I hated that he still assumed I was somehow conspiring with Cory.

Irritation laced my voice when I replied to his rude accusation. "When would I have talked to him? I don't even have my cell phone ... " I panicked when I realized I had no way to communicate with the outside world here. The eggs settled uncomfortably in my stomach.

"It was intentionally left. I can't risk someone tracking us. I have burner phones for contacting Cory as well as the few people I trust."

Scowling, I said, "How nice for *you*. Meanwhile I'm just stuck here? You know in prison you at least get one phone call."

His jaw tightened. "This isn't a prison."

My brows rose. "Are you serious? You're keeping me locked away while you hold me for ransom. Might as well be jail."

"You're welcome to leave," he snapped. "Although you'll have to give me back your deposit and find your own way home."

"You're an asshole."

"Who do you need to talk to anyway? Bianca? You want to tell her I'm the one that took you? That it was all a plan you agreed to? I can't allow you to ruin this for me," he growled.

"Yeah, it's all about *you*, isn't it, Mick? Never mind the fact that I'm being held captive for some ridiculous vendetta."

"It's not ridiculous!" His voice boomed throughout the kitchen. I stood abruptly.

"Do not yell at me," I warned.

His nostrils flared, jaw muscle ticking as he met my glare. It was a stare down that lasted a solid minute. When he spoke again, his voice was lower though it still held a slight edge.

"Things are progressing quicker than I initially thought. Hopefully, it's only a matter of time before he caves. I'll contact him tonight if you'd like."

"How do you have his number?"

"He called me the other day. Right before he had a rookie cop cuff me and throw me in jail for a night."

Mick had mentioned spending a night in jail to get the information he needed. I found it hard to believe he'd willingly let a cop pull him over. I wasn't sure if he could read the confused expression on my face or if he'd simply felt the need to explain.

"Your boy is blackmailing me by threatening an informant will go to the FBI to turn me in. Not my father, not my brother, *me*. My record is clean. No one knows what I do for a living outside of the ones on my payroll. This happened a few days after we paid you a visit. *Someone* told him I talked to you at *Rosie's*."

I sat back on the stool taking another healthy gulp of water. There was only one person I told about Mick questioning me. Unless someone else was paying attention that neither of us were aware of. My heart crept in my throat.

"Bianca," I said in a hoarse whisper.

"That girl has a big mouth. She can't be trusted."

"She's my friend," I argued. "She wouldn't ... why would she contact Cory?"

Mick shook his head, blowing out a breath. "She had a thing with Delgado years ago. I'm sure she still stays in touch. Either she's the mole or someone else at that club is. Your boss Clint or maybe the bouncer."

Heat crept into my cheeks at the memory of that night. God, I hated the way I was affected by him. How knowing I was turning him on, turned me on. Mick cleared his throat loudly, stealing my attention.

"Um, yeah, maybe," I mumbled. "Clint's pretty quiet. He doesn't like trouble at the place."

His cell phone rang, startling me. Mick plucked it up before making his way to the living room near the couch.

"Yeah?" He kept his back to me as he spoke to whoever it was. I noticed that he'd removed his shoes and socks. The sight of him in his faded jeans with bare feet made him look so ... normal. It was as if he was in his comfort zone here. Interesting.

"So you've got a trail on him?" A pause. "Good." He scratched at the back of his neck. "Let me know when you have him." He ended the call before tucking the phone into his pocket as he turned back to face me. "If I'm making the call tonight, we've got to start planning."

Chapter 7

Mick

"What's the best way to successfully convince him?"

Claire and I were in the living room. The way she had her knees bent against her chest made the little shorts she was wearing damn near non-existent. It was difficult not to stare at those long legs while she talked about not being sure how to persuade Cory to walk away. I'd wanted to fly over the kitchen island when she'd let out that moan around a mouthful of bacon earlier. I imagined something else in her mouth in that moment.

Dragging a hand through my hair, I stared out the window. Jesus, I needed to get a hold of myself here. Every minute I was near this girl I found my resolve slipping. It had only been a few hours so far and I was already questioning if I'd made a mistake in bringing her here. If I weren't careful I'd end up blowing this whole thing up by doing something dumb like actually kissing her or eye fucking her long enough that she'd be creeped out and run away.

"He hates you enough that if he already knows you took me, he's ready to listen. You have an advantage there. Although whether I'm actually in danger or not probably matters, too.

He's the one that chose to leave me but that doesn't mean he wants me with anyone else."

"What do you mean?" I glanced at her briefly before staring out at the view again. Those violet eyes were fixed on me. Not helping.

"I don't know if it will anger him more if you've potentially harmed me or if you've ... "

I clenched my jaw. "Fucked you?" Her breath caught. I kept my attention out the window. I didn't want to see her face to find out whether she was picturing that or not.

"He knows I'd never do that willingly. Not with you."

I snorted. "Wow, that stings." My gaze swung to hers. "It doesn't matter because I've never taken anything from a woman that wasn't offered to me."

Her narrow throat rolled in a swallow. "If he thinks you—"

"Not. Happening," I growled. "I won't taint my name with those kinds of accusations. You don't joke about crying rape." That was a hard limit for me.

Ever since Mackaela was taken advantage of when we were teenagers, I vowed to never take a woman without her consent. If she had too much to drink that was a deal breaker. No meant no as far as I was concerned. Even making up a lie to hurt Cory or get him to back off with Ricky wouldn't be worth it.

"Okay, I understand." Her voice was quiet. "Then you're going to have to rough me up a bit."

I scowled at her. "I told you I'm not going to hurt you. It's a phone call, Claire, not a Zoom meeting."

She nodded slowly, stretching her legs out on the cushions beside her. Her painted toes wiggled slightly making my dick twitch at the movement. Feet never gave me a hard-on before, but hers? Yeah. Everything about her affected me. I shifted uncomfortably while dragging my hand through my hair again. I had forbidden fruit at my fingertips and the urge to take a bite was killing me.

"You can say you tied me up somewhere. I took drama in high school so I can scream if you want or beg him to help me."

I nodded, leaning forward to rest my elbows on my knees. "That might work. I don't want you saying much though. I'd prefer if I do the talking."

"Yeah, that's good. I'm just the bait anyway." Her lips turned down as she picked at a piece of lint on her shorts.

"Is there anything specific I can use to goad him? Blackmail him into backing off?"

"I told you before, I don't know any more than you. He likes money, he wants to see you burn."

So I could pay him out more money than I had or what, jump off a cliff? Not happening. I couldn't really understand his disdain for me, although I wasn't shocked by the news. I'd made a hell of a lot more enemies than friends throughout the years.

"Okay let's do this." I stood, digging the second burner phone from my pocket. Her head snapped up as a look of panic settled on her face.

"Now?"

"Yeah." I cocked a brow. "You ready?"

"Sure." She lowered her legs, planting her feet on the floor. I sat back down, dialing Cory's number. After the first ring, I put the phone on speaker before setting it between us on the couch.

It was time to see just how much Claire could handle. As much as I was hoping for a few days of rest before we were doing this, I was eager to get it over with. I needed to get to Delgado and the less time I spent with this woman the better.

Claire

Anxiety bubbled inside me as the phone rang once then twice. When I heard Cory's voice, bile rose in my throat. He sounded livid and I could just imagine the vein in his forehead popping, his face a dark shade of red.

"What the fuck, Silver?!" he snarled.

Mick's lips slowly tipped up in a mischievous grin that had my heart rate increasing for other reasons not related to fear. "Well if it isn't the worst employee ever. Wait, *second* worst."

"Where is she?"

"Who?"

"You know who! Where is my girl?"

His girl? That was a big fat nope. I bit down on the inside of my cheek to keep from saying something.

Mick looked at me, holding my attention. "Didn't seem much like your girl since you left her in *my* town." His eyes swept over me before meeting mine again. "Thanks for the early Christmas present. A perfect little doll to play with." Heat pooled low in my belly. He was looking at me like I was a plate of bacon.

A loud growl sounded on Cory's end. "I'll kill you if you touch her."

Mick chuckled darkly. "Tell you what, Wilson. Get out of my way with Delgado so sweet Claire can be set free. She really is sweet, too. Smells like cotton candy, and the way her ass felt in my lap the other night was like fucking heaven."

My mouth popped open. *What the hell?* I mouthed. Mick shrugged.

"You had no right to go to her work, to bring her into this."

"Oops, too late," he said indifferently.

"I'm not backing down! We've got a viable business starting up. Release her or Watson's going to the feds!"

Mick pursed his lips, nodding though Cory couldn't see him. "See, that's the thing though, man. You're leverage is gone. *Finite*. Completely null and void."

"What are you talking about?" Cory demanded. I watched as Mick stood, pacing the floor in front of the couch. He scratched at his chin before folding his hands behind his back. Although he was dressed casually, he still had this business-like air about him.

"Thanks to your tip I've had some men trailing Ken Watson. Imagine his surprise when my brother showed up at his door ready to finish what he'd started a year ago. That *'main bitch'* Ken threatened is *his* woman. He doesn't take kindly to dirt-bags who don't listen the first time."

It sounded like something shattered in the background as Cory growled again.

"You listen to me, Silver. You release Claire or I'm coming for you. I'll put you down myself. Delgado's got nothing on me. You understand? I'll bust a cap in you and make it look like you committed suicide. We're bringing your business to its knees whether you comply or not."

Mick halted suddenly, stopping in front of me. Before I could register what was happening he withdrew a gun from the back of his pants, one I hadn't realized was there. At the same time, he reached for the phone, holding it up to me. With a wink, he used the barrel of the gun to lift my chin placing the cool steel against my throat. I froze, eyes wide as I stared at him, too afraid to move.

"That's cute." He cocked the gun, the 'click' noise resonated throughout the entire living room. "However, I've got a bullet with this pretty little thing's name on it. It's pointing at that delicate throat of hers." He gave me a single nod before glancing at the phone.

Trembling in fear, I tried to speak but my voice was strangled. I cleared my throat, the movement causing the barrel to glide along my skin. "Cory, please," I breathed. "I don't want to die." Tears formed as I stared at Mick.

He said he'd never hurt me no matter what. Was this what he meant? Pointing a gun at me? What if his finger slipped making him accidentally shoot me? Anger mixed with the fear whirling inside me. I found myself saying the next words easily because the panic was genuine.

"He's going to kill me, Cory. He sent his men for me early this morning. I don't know where we are. I'm scared."

Mick lowered the gun. "Time's wasting."

"You wouldn't dare," Cory seethed.

"Darlin' why don't you stand up for me," Mick said. I blinked up at him, hesitating. "Now!" he ordered in a loud voice.

On shaky legs, I stood and shrieked when he wrapped an arm around my waist, spinning me until my back was to his front. He held me firmly against him.

"What are you doing? Claire!"

Mickey placed his lips at my ear, whispering slowly as I repeated what he said. "He's got a gun to my head. He's going to shoot me. Please, Cory, do the right thing. Just give up."

"Good girl," he murmured in my ear before speaking to Cory. "I'm giving you twenty-four hours to make a decision. Next move is up to you. Call me on this number. If I don't hear from you, I'll send you a little video of *your* girl becoming *mine*." He disconnected the call, tossing both the gun and the phone on the couch cushion behind me.

"Hey." He turned me around, placing a hand against my cheek, his thumb grazing my trembling lower lip. "I told you I wasn't going to hurt you." His eyes searched mine, worry etched into his features. "Hey, it's okay."

I shoved away from him, darting toward the hallway. "Stay away from me!" I screamed rushing for the bedroom.

I slammed the door, bolting it before collapsing into a heap on the floor. Tears streamed down my face faster than I could swipe away as my vision blurred. I let myself let go, releasing the anger along with the fear I'd felt moments before. I was held at gunpoint, my life threatened for Mick's stupid revenge. I wasn't rescued or bartered for by the man that I'd spent over a year with.

How had I fallen so far?

*

I ended up staying in the room the rest of the day into the night. I didn't want to be around Mick at all. I definitely didn't want to talk to him or hear his meaningless apologies. Once the tears ran dry I felt empty, worn out, and used. I let the tub fill up with scalding water before sinking beneath the surface, staring out at the purplish orange sky. It was peaceful in here, safe. I could pretend this was my home for a while where I could forget the outside world, where I could just be.

I stayed in the bath until the stars filled the night sky and the water went cold. The bed was incredibly comfortable, like a giant cloud. As I lay there in the dark, I wished that it would carry me far away from here to a new life in a new city.

My first attempt at starting fresh had gone completely wrong. Now I was stuck with a man I feared and loathed. The only silver lining was what I'd get in return for my willingness to be held captive. The thought of what that money could do for me kept me from breaking down again. I needed to stay strong, to finish what I'd started.

Before long, I fell asleep dreaming of a bright future with no violence, no drugs, and only happiness with abundant opportunities.

The following morning I made the difficult decision to leave my private sanctuary if at least to fill my stomach. I'd missed both lunch and dinner yesterday. Plus, after all that crying, I had a pounding headache. I needed coffee like I needed air at this point so if Mick got in my way I'd put a gun to *his* head.

I padded down the hall on bare feet, wrapping my fuzzy oversized cardigan around me. It was cooler here than Seattle and I was glad I decided on leggings instead of shorts to sleep in. I smelled fresh coffee brewing as I entered the kitchen. I stopped dead in my tracks.

Mick's back was to me, his bare back. Etched in multiple colors on the majority of his skin was a massive tattoo of an angel and a demon at war with each other. I couldn't stop staring at the incredible detail of both ethereal creatures battling. Good and evil, how fitting for him.

He reached into a cabinet for a mug, his muscles flexing with the movement. Jesus, it was like he'd been carved out of marble. He was wearing a pair of gray sweats that hung so low I could see the upper curve of his ass. I needed to get a freaking grip, to stop gawking before I got caught. Rolling my eyes at my moment of stupid weakness, I continued into the kitchen toward the coffee pot.

Mick gave me a brief glance though wisely said nothing. He let me pour my coffee first, grabbing a sugar free almond creamer from the refrigerator and sliding it across the counter to me. I stirred a little in before taking my mug to the living room. I frowned down at the sectional.

There was a blanket scrunched on it along with a pillow as if he'd slept there instead of a room downstairs. Sighing, I moved the blanket to the side as I curled up in the corner staring out at the morning sky. A few minutes later, Mick sat in the modern armchair kitty corner from me. We sipped our coffee in silence. When he finally spoke, I tried not to let the softness in his voice change my attitude toward him.

"The gun wasn't loaded. I'd emptied the clip beforehand."

I took another drink of coffee while glaring out at the pale blue sky.

"I'm sorry." He cleared his throat. "Really. I overreacted and lost my cool."

I finally met his hazel eyes that looked tired with dark shadows beneath. "Lost your cool? For all I knew I was a goner. To make it worse, he didn't even fight that hard for me. You could decorate this pretty house with my brain matter, still he wouldn't care." I could feel tears forming again so I willed them away. "I just want this over with. What's next?"

His jaw flexed. "It all depends on when or if he calls. I thought he'd cave easier, that he'd give Delgado up."

"I don't think he gives a shit about that guy. You're looking at this all wrong, Mick."

He squinted at me. "What do you mean?"

Scoffing, I said, "Did you ever think that maybe Cory Wilson has just as much invested in this new business venture, if not more, than your Delgado guy?"

"What do you know that you're not telling me?"

"Nothing." I glanced back out the window. "It just sounded like he would do whatever it takes to stop you. Maybe I'm not as valuable as you thought."

"Are you always this pessimistic?"

"Have you ever lost? I know you want revenge for whatever that guy did to your family, but couldn't you just let it go? I'm sure there's other bad guys out there you can torture."

He took a drink of his coffee, shaking his head. "It's my final task. The one loose end that needs tied up before I can quit for good. You think I enjoy this?" His voice rose as I looked at him again, noticing how white his knuckles were around the mug in his hands. "You think I don't want a *real* future that doesn't involve watching my fucking back every single day and toting a gun for protection?"

Hearing him basically say he wanted to leave the business surprised me. "What would you do instead?" Despite my hostility toward him for what he pulled yesterday, I was curious.

"I'm part owner of a shop in Seattle with my brother. It was his dream which I helped finance for him. I want to help him out more, maybe settle down eventually. Maybe open another business or something. I've got money, plenty to keep me afloat into my golden years if I invest it properly." He shrugged.

Say what you will about Mickey Silver but I never once doubted his tenacity. Hearing him speak of a future and investing had me wondering if I really knew anything about him outside of the exterior. Was he actually capable of being a responsible, tax-paying citizen?

"Sounds like you've thought a lot about it," I said.

He huffed out a laugh. "Yeah, I have. Ever since Simon was shot." He cringed at the memory. "I could have lost him, my own brother, my blood. I could have lost my best friend, too. It took that among other things to realize that life is short. That slinging illegal narcotics while also selling sex isn't nearly as satisfying as it seemed when I was seventeen years old trying to follow in my father's footsteps."

"Wow," I breathed, earning a glare from him. "Mickey Silver might have a heart after all."

He finished off his coffee before standing to his feet. "It's buried pretty deep but it's there. You staying?" I arched a brow.

"Do I have a choice?"

He licked his lips, the hint of a smirk forming. "No. Though I thought you might try to make a break for it so I slept on the couch last night. That way I'd be able to hear if you tried to leave."

I inhaled a deep breath before letting it out slowly. "I want this over, fast. Since I don't have a choice and because I need the money I guess I'm staying."

He nodded. "You need to know that what happened yesterday was all an act. I'm a man of my word despite my moral compass being hopelessly all over the place most of the time. I won't let anything happen to you."

"The gun really wasn't loaded?" I asked.

"Hell no it wasn't loaded. You think I'd hold a loaded gun to any part of your body? Did you notice how I didn't point it at your face? That was intentional, Claire. I'd never threaten you or lay a finger on you with the intent to inflict pain." His voice was full of conviction. Once again, I was unsettled by the sincerity of his words.

"Okay," I replied. "I'm not going to tell you I trust you. However, I ... believe you. For now."

He grinned, winking at me. "That a girl."

Chapter 8

Mick

"Where is he now?"

"He's at the warehouse with Tyler and James. He won't talk ... yet."

I ran a hand through my hair, rolling my neck to crack it. "He'll speak up if he knows what's good for him. Does his wife know of his affairs?"

"Not yet, though we're ready to taint his reputation should we need to," Simon replied.

"You're too much of a natural at this, bro. How's Mackaela doing? Is she still pissed?" She hadn't been happy about the whole kidnapping Claire thing before. Then when I enlisted Simon to help with Ken Watson, our number one rat, she threatened to hunt me down and kick my ass. I didn't doubt she'd do it, too.

"She's cooled down a bit. Other than the initial beat down, I've got the guys covering the rest. Dom's handling the interrogation. How's the girl doing? Dom said she's fearless."

"Yeah, a bit. She's got an attitude as well as a mouth that lacks restraint, but she's compliant for the most part."

He laughed. "Sounds like she's perfect for you. Any word from Cory yet?"

"He texted me a counter offer. Said if I let Claire go, he'll try to turn over Delgado, although he's not stopping the business plans they have. He also mentioned not knowing where Delgado is so that's not at all reassuring."

"That guy is slick. How does he keep disappearing?"

"No idea. I'll get him though, I have to. Get someone on Bianca Rogers to see if she can't lead us to him. I have a fairly good suspicion she's been in contact with him somehow."

"Will do. I'll hit you up later, bro."

"Sounds good."

After hanging up with Simon I sent a text to Cory.

Me: Denied. For every day you continue to operate against me, the girl gets a new bruise.

I slid my phone in my pocket as I headed upstairs. I'd shared too much with Claire earlier by telling her I wanted a future. Something about the girl had me ready to spill my guts which made me uneasy. I was doing my best to steer clear of her, to give her space. As little interaction as possible was best for both of us. Although that didn't stop my dirty mind from wandering.

I was likely demented for holding her against me yesterday during that phone call. It wasn't really necessary without an audience. The darkest parts of me reveled in the way she felt against my chest and how my fingers fit her waist like her body was made for me. I wanted to touch her again, to feel those perfect pouty lips on various parts of my body. I'd never been this sprung on a woman before. I started to wonder if it was only because I couldn't have her. Knowing she was untouchable definitely made me want her more.

Claire was watching some documentary on the TV in the living room that might have been about the ocean or whales or something. I wasn't paying attention to the screen. She was wearing the same thing she'd woke up in except she'd removed her sweater. In a thin pair of leggings, I could see the perfect curve of her ass while she lay on her side, head propped up with a fist. Her hair fell in loose waves over her shoulder, curving around the swell of her chest.

I was being a total fucking perv by checking her out as I stood there at the top of the stairs without her noticing. If she were mine, I'd curl up behind her and wrap her in my arms.

Not mine. She'd never belong to me.

Thank the good lord that my phone vibrated in my pocket to distract me.

Cory: You so much as lay a finger on her I'll cut them off!

Me: What if she wants me to? She sure enjoyed touching me at Rosie's.

Cory: I want a video proving she's safe.

Me: I want you to give me Delgado.

Claire glanced up at me, her brows knitting together. "Is it him?" she asked, moving to sit up. Well damn, there went my view. Fucking Wilson.

"Yeah, he refused to back down and told me not to touch you." I leaned a hip against the back of the couch. "Said he'd cut my fingers off."

"Did you tell him you touched me?"

Shrugging, I said, "I told him you enjoyed stroking my cock at *Rosie's.*"

Her mouth popped open, cheeks turning a dark shade of crimson. I chuckled, finding her embarrassment endearing. For a stripper she was kind of being a prude.

"I'm messing with him. I didn't say that exactly. He wants a video of you to prove your safe."

"Should I hold up a newspaper with the date?" She scanned the living room. "How are you going to sell holding me captive in a place like this?"

A slow grin formed. "Haven't I told you about my dungeon?"

Claire

I stood at the edge of the yard watching the cars pass over the bridge from Oregon to Washington. It was the first time I'd been outside since we arrived nearly a week ago. The entire property was gated so Mick wasn't worried about me running. Not that I had the desire to anyway. He'd hunt me down if Cory didn't get to me first. Truth be told, I wasn't sure who would be worse to deal with in this totally outrageous lock-down situation. At least Mick always had coffee ready in the morning when I woke up.

Cory didn't even drink coffee which was some sort of devil magic. What did you drink in the morning to perk you up for the day if not coffee or an energy drink of some sort? Water or orange juice? No thanks.

I was starring in my first live video this evening because Cory needed proof that I was unharmed, that I was still alive. Mick decided to make him sweat for five days in order to up the ante and get him to cave. So far it hadn't worked and I wasn't sure how to feel about that. I'd be free if he'd just agree to stop whatever business he had going on Silver turf. Seemed like a simple solution to most though if you knew Cory, he had his reasons.

The secret he was keeping probably had a lot to do with his desire to take over Mick's territory. He'd always wanted to cut him deep. Even if I wasn't afraid of being killed for spilling the secret, it wasn't necessary to tell Mick. Not now anyway. It'd likely only piss him off further or create a bigger mess. Besides, if Cory wanted him to know he'd tell him himself. He hadn't done that yet or even hinted at it to my knowledge. The less I was implicated, the better. If that meant holding my tongue, so be it.

Mick and Cory were actually a lot alike because getting Cory to walk away from his own personal vendetta would be just as difficult as Mick letting go of Delgado. They were at a stalemate with me caught in the middle. That was unless tonight changed everything. Mick had a plan to nudge Cory in the right direction which also involved roughing me up on camera. Actually, it was partly my plan because after six days in his father's beautiful home, I was starting to grow restless.

Quarantine was cool when you chose it, however having it forced upon you beyond control was a special kind of torture. Even the most introverted person would go stir crazy. I'd begun to fear that this might take a while. If I had to spend one more week alone with Mickey Silver, I might just jump off the cliff the house overlooked. He'd been pretty busy on the phone while holing up downstairs which helped. Although there were still times I couldn't avoid him.

Every morning he was in the kitchen wearing nothing other than those gray sweats. His muscular form along with the vibrant tattoos called to me like he was some sort of male siren pulling me under. I'd learned that he got up early to work out. When I found out there was a gym downstairs I'd taken it upon myself to get a run in on the treadmill before bed every night. Ever since he'd talked about his future, I couldn't help seeing him differently. Instead of harboring hate for him or finding him arrogant and selfish; I found him diplomatic and disciplined.

Last night was the first time he'd joined me in the gym to work out. He was lifting weights in front of the floor to ceiling mirror which also happened to be in my line of sight. There was a moment I'd caught him staring at me through the mirror with an intensity compared to a starved man at an all you can eat buffet.

I'd thrown my hair up in a top knot, wearing a pair of sneakers with shorts and a sports bra. In hindsight, I probably should have worn an actual shirt, but he'd never interrupted my workouts before. I looked like a train wreck anyway after forty-five minutes on the treadmill, sweating in places I shouldn't be. The exercise helped manage my anxiety so I didn't really care. I'd been ze-roed in on the way his back muscles flexed with every lift he did. When I happened to look up, I'd seen his reflection examining me.

I should have been repulsed by his interest but I wasn't. When our gazes collided, he'd shamelessly smirked at me. My stomach coiled at the look on his face. I found myself remembering how he'd felt beneath my palm when I'd danced for him, when I'd had his undivided attention. It was enough to cut my workout short. I ended up bolting upstairs to take a cold shower before putting myself to bed.

I needed to get out of here as soon as possible. With a heavy sigh, I turned back toward the house, making my way across the long walkway to the front door. I headed downstairs to what I now knew not only had the gym but two bedrooms, an office, and a living space with a ton of bookshelves. I was headed for the door at the end of the main living area that led to the three car garage.

Mick's dungeon. He'd gone as far as painting one of the con-crete walls black before laying down a white sheet on the floor so there would be nothing distinguishable in the video. See, dis-ciplined and careful. I began to wonder just how often he'd been in similar situations.

A card table was set up opposite the black wall with a laptop on it as well as a webcam setup. So much for not having a Zoom meeting. Although this particular video was a one way feed for security reasons. Mick would be streaming the video using en-crypted technology I couldn't comprehend directly to Cory while on the phone with him. That way we could hear Cory and vice versa. I was to stand against the wall where he could see me to ensure I was alive and well.

Mick was tinkering with the equipment and stopped when I'd wandered in, closing the door to the house behind me.

"Take your hair down," he said as he re-positioned the camera on the laptop until it was exactly right. I yanked the ponytail out of my hair, sliding the tie onto my wrist. He scanned the length of me from my head to my bare feet. "Dirt. Nice touch."

I shrugged. "Figured I wouldn't be getting three square meals or regular showers."

"Smart. Although you're gonna have to lose the shirt darlin'." Crossing my arms, I pinned him with a glare as he sauntered over to me. "It's clean and fits you well," he explained. Grabbing the hem of his shirt, he yanked it off over his head holding it out to me. "Wear this instead."

I glanced between him and the t-shirt with a frown. "I'm not wearing a paint splattered t-shirt that you got all down and dirty in."

One of his brows rose. He lifted the shirt to his nose, sniffing it. "Smells okay to me. Come on, lose the top."

Pursing my lips, I stared him down. It made more sense for me to wear something unclean, but I hated the fact that it was *his*. Rolling my eyes, I snatched the t-shirt away from him before heading for the door.

"Where are you going?"

"Duh, to change," I said.

"I've seen 'em before, sweetheart, no need to be shy."

"You were a paying customer then. Unless you've got another stack of cash for me, no deal." I heard him laugh as I disappeared back in the house.

I quickly removed the shirt I'd been wearing before pulling Mick's over my head. Falling to just above my knees, it was warm, soft, and smelled like him. My stomach fluttered as I inhaled the neckline. The fact I could have that kind of reaction over his scent alone from an inanimate object annoyed me. I needed to compose myself better. I shouldn't be getting caught up in anything other than the ultimate goal here. The only endgame that mattered was getting paid after making it out alive.

When I went back in the garage, the lights were dimmed. Mick was leaning against the wall with his arms folded over his chest.

He tracked me with those hazel eyes that captivated me when I didn't want them to.

"Here's how this is going to go." He placed a hand on my shoulder and the contact felt like an electric current surging through me. "I'm going to tie your hands in front of you. I won't gag you because I don't want to tarnish those pretty lips. However, you won't speak until I command it. Understand?"

I swallowed as my pulse beat wildly in my throat. "Yes."

"If I touch you, flinch. If I grab you, act like it hurts."

"Be utterly repulsed by you, got it."

His gaze sharpened as he released me. "You're a little monster." He went to a plastic crate, grabbing a short nylon rope out of it.

"Do this often?" I asked. His brows rose.

"Yeah. Though I've never had such a beautiful and willing participant before." He shot me a wink. I wasn't sure if I should cringe or melt into a puddle at his feet. "Put your wrists together."

I held my hands out to him, wrists resting side by side as I interlocked my fingers. Mick's long fingers moved deftly as he bound me with the rope. He'd definitely had practice in securing knots. Guiding me by my shoulders, he positioned me against the cool concrete wall. I shuddered involuntarily. He stepped back with his brows creased as he gave me a once over.

"Can I confess something?" he asked, dragging his teeth along his lower lip. I shot him a questioning look.

"I guess?"

His hazel eyes pinned mine in the dim light, sparkling back at me.

"You look good in my t-shirt."

Heat crept up my cheeks. "You look good with no shirt." It tumbled out of me before I could stop it. My brain to mouth filter completely obliterated by his thick voice and hungry stare.

His nostrils flared. "So do you."

The impact Mick had on me was growing stronger which frightened me. I was supposed to hate him because I always had in the past. He was my boss, a selfish man with no heart. Even so, he was sexy as hell and absolutely delicious standing before me in low hanging jeans with vibrant tattoos spanning his upper body. I was his prisoner, literally. Yet instead of being afraid, some perverse thrill ran through me at the thought.

Suddenly he was directly in front of me, his chest brushing mine as he dipped his chin. I could almost taste him as cinnamon mixed with scotch invaded my senses, making my toes curl. He lifted his left hand, his index finger slowly sliding along my cheek.

"You're a wicked temptress, sweet Claire. I'm finding it increasingly difficult to resist my urges around you."

My breath caught, my gaze colliding with his.

I opened my mouth to say something but the words wouldn't form. He angled his head, resting his cheek against mine as his lips brushed the shell of my ear. He let out a low growl, creating an ache between my legs.

"I want to run my tongue over every inch of your body. I want my hands all over you and I want to hear you scream my name as I bury myself inside you, leaving you begging for more."

Oh for the love of all that was holy!

I whimpered as my head fell back against the wall behind me. I was on fire from his words, from his proximity. My nipples hardened as his chest pressed into mine. I shivered though I wasn't cold. Would he make a move? If he did would I stop him? My body was fired up and ready to go, my mind totally lost. Why did he have to say that kind of stuff?

"Damn," Mick groaned, stepping away from me abruptly. He ran both hands through his hair while taking in a deep faltering breath.

I lifted my bound hands to my chest, feeling my heart pounding ruthlessly. Grounding myself, I turned my head to rest it against the cool concrete as I released the breath I'd been holding. Clarity slowly began sinking in, though the ache between my legs had yet to cease.

A shrill beeping noise sounded from the card table startling me. Mick blew out another breath, grabbing his phone. Glancing up at me, he said, "It's time. Remember what we talked about? Stick to the plan."

I nodded. "Be repulsed. Don't speak yet. Act scared."

"Good girl."

I slumped my shoulders slightly, making my face blank as he clicked the camera on.

I could see myself on the computer screen that faced me from the table. My violet eyes looked larger than normal, my cheeks a faint pink. I took a few cleansing breaths. I could do this. I *had* to do this. I just wanted it to be over. Pretending to hate Mickey Silver was easy right? I'd always hated him.

Up until recently.

Mick

It was going to be challenging selling the whole kidnapper act when all I could think about was the way Claire looked in my t-shirt. How her nipples poked through the cotton, taunting me as she stood there with wrists bound and legs bare. I was rock hard, trying like hell to hide that fact by filling my mind with every disturbing image I could think of. It's sad that I had a lot of source material for that.

She undid me. Made me feel like I'd die without her or something. Although it had only been a few days alone with her, I already found myself drawn like a moth to a flame. I couldn't explain why I'd constantly sensed that when it came to her. It started the first time I saw her at one of my parties. I'd ended up fantasizing about her when I took some other chick, Becky or Becca or something, to bed that night. It didn't matter because I could never have Claire the way I wanted her. I could never sample what she had to offer because the moment I did, I'd be snared completely. It was just so difficult not to react when she looked at me with those brilliant eyes or those luscious lips as she moaned when I told her what I wanted to do to her.

I had to table whatever this was right now though because it was time for business.

The plan was simple, show her off to Cory who would be able to view her on a live video screen and hear her via my burner phone. The selfish part of me put her in my shirt to mark my non-existent territory. The genius part wanted to play up the fact that she was being held captive, not treated well.

I answered the phone, hitting the speakerphone button. I held it as I stood in front of Claire to block his view of her initially. I could hear her taking deep breaths, preparing herself for the roll of a lifetime. This had to go well. I needed him to back off, to give me Delgado or help me find the bastard.

"I don't want to see *you*." He growled. "Show me her!" Lifting my head, I smirked at the camera.

"You'll see her when I say you can. Any word on Delgado?"

"No. I told you I couldn't give a shit. Release Claire, then you can have him if you can find him. I've got men of my own."

Quirking a brow, I said, "Is that so?"

"Yeah, they're loyal like damn dogs."

"If you think you can make it in this industry, Wilson, you won't. I promise you'll fail. Give up now. Quit while you can or you'll be spending the rest of your life behind bars or dead."

He snorted. "Not likely. I told you I've got connections, too. We're operating in Oregon not Washington. Different cops here, none on your payroll."

"So you think."

He growled which made me smile at the camera again. Goading him was oh so fun but I had little time for this elementary school showdown. "I'm not releasing her until you fuck off. Now that I know you won't back down in trying to take over my territory, I have new conditions."

"Such as?"

"You're a traitor. You betrayed me, and those that forget their place are often shot first before I ask questions. You're a special breed though, Wilson. You see, I can't find you and you haven't slipped up like I was hoping you would. Just like Delgado. I'll give you credit for not being as dumb as I thought you were. However, I guarantee you're desperate. I'll give you half a million dollars to leave the country. Never show your face again. Go live happily ever after. All you have to do is hand me Delgado."

It was more money than he'd ever seen in his life. If he refused, he'd be far worse off. I hated to admit the fact that I was the one who was desperate. All I wanted was to get Delgado. I really didn't care about Cory's bullshit at this point honestly. I figured someone else could deal with it later. Everything slipped further from my control the longer I was in this, the longer Claire was here. I didn't like not being in charge.

"Let me see her," Cory said.

Releasing a frustrated sigh, I glanced back over my shoulder at Claire. She stood with her head down, hands clasped together. Such a patient woman to allow me to use her for my ultimate goal. How Cory Wilson ever kept her as long as he did was beyond me.

"Fine, I need your answer still." I stepped to the side, showing her on the screen.

She glanced up at the camera, her eyes brimming with tears, her cheeks now void of that incredible blush I'd given her just minutes ago.

"Oh my god, babe, you're alive."

Babe?

That word was like a punch to my gut. Fuck him calling her pet names when he abandoned her. Claire smiled slowly, lifting her hands to her face to wipe the tears away. She nodded.

"Are you hurt? Did he touch you?" Cory's voice was suddenly laced with concern. What a joke. Claire shook her head as she lowered her hands. "Say something."

She glanced over at me, remaining quiet. I stepped back into the sight of the camera at her side. "She's alive. You got what you wanted." I reached out to cup her cheek. She flinched slightly, looking everywhere except at me. "You will not speak to him or I will punish you. Do you understand?"

A soft gasp escaped as she nodded.

"What the hell, Silver!? You have her trained like some sort of animal. Claire! Look back at the camera, talk to me."

"I broke her down little by little. It didn't take long," I mused, staring into her violet eyes as she lifted them to mine. "She's tough as steel though. Really put up a good fight. However, I can be *very* persuasive." I held her chin with my thumb and index finger, tilting her head toward the camera. "Isn't that right, darlin'?"

"Get your hands off her!" Cory yelled. "I'm going to kill you! Claire, I'm going to get you out of there. Hold on a while longer, okay?"

I bit back on my molars, glaring down at the phone. "You'll never see her again! Not unless you take the deal. What's your response?"

He didn't speak right away, and the hesitation angered me further. How could he even have to think about this? The woman he wanted could be free if he'd only take the bait. Why would he risk her life? How did that make her feel to know he couldn't so easily give up his hatred of me in order to save *her*? It was as if he was biding his time, waiting for something.

Realization hit me then like a ton of bricks. I shoved her out of the way of the camera so she was no longer in sight. "Where is he?"

"I told you, I don't know where—"

"He's looking for me, isn't he? Looking for her." I grabbed the rope at her wrists, tugging her to my side. "Tell me where he is or I'm going to hurt her," I growled.

It made sense that he'd send Ricky out to track me down. That he'd lie about not knowing his whereabouts. He thought he could get to me before I knew it was coming. Cory thought he was a big boss man now, ordering Delgado around like a puppet on a string. His arrogance was repulsive as well as utterly ridiculous considering he wasn't worth more than the dirt on Claire's legs.

I held the rope, forcing her arms up over her head with my free hand before planting them against the concrete wall. She whimpered. My gaze slid to hers for half a second to see if I'd actually brought her pain. She gave a slight shake of her head. The fact we could read each other so easily was incredibly advantageous right now.

"Jesus, okay, okay!"

"Where is he?" I asked again.

"He headed down the coast after he got word from someone that you might have taken Claire to Oregon."

"Where did you get that information?" I bit out, squeezing the phone in my palm. "Choose your response carefully. I'll know if you're lying."

"Bianca Rogers. She knew you were sniffing around before Claire disappeared. She didn't say who gave her the tip but she's right, isn't she?" Cory asked.

Releasing Claire, I stalked toward the camera, blocking her from his view again. A low growl erupted from the phone. I ignored it. Let him be angry, I didn't care. I set the phone down on the card table in front of the laptop before making my way back to her at the wall.

I slid a palm up the front of her shirt from chest to throat before wrapping my fingers around her neck. Glancing back at the screen, I saw what he could. Me standing in front of Claire, blocking half her body with my fingers poised to cut off her oxygen.

I felt her swallow beneath my palm. "Don't be afraid," I whispered so only she could hear.

"Let her go!" I heard him scream.

"I'm going to apply a little bit of pressure." I stayed quiet so he wouldn't hear me. "You ready? Blink once for yes, twice for no." When she gave me the go ahead, I turned back to the camera, speaking louder.

"I'm giving you one last chance to end this! Tell me you'll take the money. That you'll leave and give up Delgado or the princess here gets to take a nap." I squeezed her neck, making her gasp.

"Don't hurt her! Stop, Silver!"

"That's not a yes!" I snarled.

"Give him what he wants! Cory, please just let this go!" Claire shrieked.

Releasing my hold on her, I lifted my hand as if I were rearing to smack her in the face. She cowered away.

"I told you not to speak!"

She bared her teeth, shoving against my chest with her shoulder which actually made me stumble back. "Let me go! Cory, please save me." She rushed up to the camera, crying out. "Tell him whatever he wants. Take the money, you need it! End this," she begged.

"Babe, it's not that simple. We have to do this right," he said.

I grabbed her arms from behind, hauling her into me. I tangled my fingers in her hair as I tugged her head back. She moaned. The sound went straight to my cock, jarring me for a minute. Her gaze lifted to mine when my free hand slid to her waist before curving over her hip as I guided her flush against me.

"I'm going to have a lot of fun putting you in your place, *princess*. Seems like your boyfriend doesn't want you that bad."

"Stop touching her!" Cory ordered. My hand inched up her flat stomach over the t-shirt, stopping just under her glorious chest.

"Please." Claire's voice was breathy, unsteady. "Please," she said again. When I looked at her, her lashes were fluttering closed.

Cory continued hollering about me releasing her but I ignored him. Was she begging for me to touch her? My fingers glided up to the lower swell of her breast as her eyes flew open. Her sweet ass pressed against my rock hard dick taking everything in me to keep my composure. Releasing her hair, I lowered my lips to her ear.

"You're fucking perfect," I whispered before shoving her forward. I looked into the camera again. "I want an answer, now!"

"Do what he wants," Claire said with a shaky voice. "Please, Cory, end this."

"Come with me," Cory replied quickly. "Say you'll come with me if I take his money. We'll leave the country, get away."

Like hell! He wasn't taking her.

Claire stumbled. "What?"

Cory's deep chuckle resonated from the other end of the phone as venom filled my veins. This motherfucker didn't give a shit about her. He was playing some game I hadn't anticipated. "We're gonna find you before you find us, Silver. Keep the bitch, she means nothing to me. I'm going to bring you to your knees." The line went dead abruptly.

"No!" Bolting to the laptop, I slammed it closed before grabbing the phone. "Fuck, fuck, fuck!" I yelled as I dialed Dom's number.

"Hey, Mick, what—"

"Grab Bianca Rogers. Now!" I hung up the phone, tossing it back on the table. When I turned to Claire she was standing as still as a statue, staring at me with fresh tears.

"What happened?" she whispered.

"I underestimated him." I approached her slowly, worried she'd scream at me like the other day. When she didn't move or speak, I untied her wrists, letting the rope fall to the floor. "I've got a backup plan that might draw Delgado out while also scaring Cory enough into taking the deal."

"What are you going to do?"

"Nothing I haven't done before." I shook my head. "It doesn't matter right now. How are you feeling? Did I hurt you?"

She shifted her focus to her hands that were still clasped in front of her. "No. He ... doesn't want me. I'm sorry. I ruined this."

"Hey," I lifted her chin with my index finger, forcing her to look at me, "you didn't ruin anything. I knew there was a chance this wouldn't work. That's why I have other cards to play, okay? You were perfect, you did everything you were supposed to."

"What happens now?"

"I show them I'm serious. I force my hand which will hopefully get them to back down while also drawing out Delgado. I know he's coming for us now so that's a good thing." I could still do this.

"What are you going to do to Bianca?" she asked with trepidation.

My brows rose. "You really want to know?"

Chapter 9

Claire

I definitely didn't want to know what Mick had planned for Bianca, yet somehow I felt like I already did. I was smart enough to understand that she'd given up important information and that snitches got stitches. Or worse, ended up in a body bag. I told Mick I was tired instead, retreating to my room to take a shower. You'd think I'd be angry at Cory for saying he didn't care what happened to me. I should be heartbroken or distraught. I was just ... numb.

After my shower, I changed back into Mick's t-shirt because I liked the way it smelled. I wasn't sure what kind of message that sent. Honestly, I didn't care anymore. I was too exhausted from what had transpired over the last week. I wasn't sure what would happen now that my being here was no longer beneficial to Mick's revenge. The thought of running away held less appeal now than it had days earlier. Would he pay me off, sending me on my way as early as tomorrow?

I tugged on my cotton shorts, leaving my hair down. It was late and while my body was tired, my mind couldn't seem to shut down. After an hour of failing to fall asleep, I headed to the kitchen for some water. I stopped at the edge of the hall when I heard Mick's hushed voice.

"She's not safe. I have to keep her here until this is over." Was he talking about me? "He claims he doesn't care about her but keeping her still gives me some leverage. Once I take care of Delgado and his woman, he might wise up."

I lifted my hand to my mouth to conceal the gasp that escaped. So I wasn't off base with my thinking. He was going to kill Bianca for ratting him out.

"Yeah, she's fine. No doubt shaken up. She didn't punch me or scream at me this time." *Yet.* I thought. "No I haven't touched her. Jesus, Mackaela, why does everybody always assume that?" So he was talking to his friend, the girl I'd seen around last year who was with his brother. Mick chuckled. "Yeah, well, as much as I'd love to do something about it I can't. I need her to trust me. I'm not going to sabotage that." He paused for a few moments, listening.

My heart pounded against my rib cage. What did he want to do, *me*? Instead of revulsion, the idea made my stomach flutter nervously as butterflies sprang to life. I thought about the way it felt when he'd pulled me against him earlier while negotiating with Cory. His fingers were so close to my breasts at the time. I'd gotten lost in the warmth that spread through me, the ache that formed between my legs.

"Thanks. I don't know how much longer we'll be here, hopefully only a few more days." He heaved a sigh. "Yeah, you too."

I peered around the corner of the hallway wall to see him sitting on the couch with his elbows on his knees and fingers in his hair. "Shit," he muttered, shaking his head.

I took a breath before stepping out from behind the wall, making my way toward the kitchen. I grabbed a bottle of water from the refrigerator, deciding it best to just go right back to bed. I didn't want to impose on whatever thinking Mick was doing. He obviously had more on his plate than I did at the moment.

"Where you going?" he called as I walked by him. Stopping, I turned around. His lips tilted up on one side as his eyes roamed over my body. A flood of warmth rushed over me, prickling my scalp at the sight of his predatory stare.

"Couldn't sleep,." I said while fumbling with the cap of the water bottle.

He stood then and I bit down on my bottom lip, stifling a groan. He was basically naked which I hadn't noticed until now. He was shirtless like before, yet instead of a pair of jeans, all he wore were a pair of bright blue boxer briefs. My mouth went dry, scanning the ripple of muscles in his abdomen to the lower parts of him. Yeah, that underwear left extraordinarily little to the imagination. Although I wouldn't call what it showcased 'little' at all.

My skin hummed with electricity as I swallowed the lump in my throat. I looked back to his face. His hazel eyes were sparkling in the soft buttery glow of the lamp on the end table as he stared back at me. I should have retreated when he sauntered toward me but I couldn't. I didn't dare so much as breathe when he stopped in front of me.

"You really shouldn't look at me like that," he murmured as he coiled a strand of my hair around his finger.

"Like what?" My voice came out breathy.

"Like you want me." The back of his fingers brushed the top of my left breast, making me shiver. "Like you're hoping to act out all the naughty things I said earlier."

"What if I am?" Even if it was wrong in every single way, even if it didn't mean anything, I totally wanted Mick. Hearing him admit he felt the same just minutes ago had me curious as to how far he'd go.

Maybe it was due to the sting of rejection from Cory or the need to disappear for a while, to forget what was happening. Maybe it was the way my heart tripped over itself when he'd manhandled me earlier in the garage. His breath faltered as he blinked at me, dropping his hand.

"Sweet Claire, don't tempt a man with no morals."

Licking my lips, I risked a step closer to him until the tips of my toes touched his. I tilted my head back to meet his gaze. "You assume *I* have morals?" I did to some extent; however, I was a modern American woman. Giving in to what my body desperately wanted didn't make me a bad person nor did it him.

He stared down at me, eyes darkening. We were locked onto each other, standing still while waiting for the other to make the next move. A thrill ran through every nerve in my body as it trembled in anticipation. The bottle of water I'd been holding crashed to the floor as my arms wound around his neck. His hands connected with my hips, pulling me into him. The second our lips met my brain clicked off. I acted only on instinct after that.

He didn't kiss me gently. He didn't wait to see if I was ready for him. His tongue brushed mine in the most tantalizing way before his teeth grazed along my bottom lip, making me cry out. I gave as much as I was getting, clinging to him in fear that if I let go he'd disappear, which I didn't want right now. I wanted him to ground me, to give me something to hold onto. To help me forget for a while about my empty life, about his selfish desire for revenge. I think he needed this, too.

Mick's hands slid over the curve of my hip, gripping roughly as he lifted me up against him. I wrapped my legs around his waist, tugging the ends of his hair as he pivoted, slamming my back against the wall in the living room near the kitchen.

He kissed a path to my neck when I tilted my head back to allow him access to the sensitive skin at my throat. I tightened my legs around him. Feeling his hard length against my center ignited something in me that thrummed violently. I moaned when he palmed my breast, stroking my nipple with his thumb through the fabric of my shirt, his shirt. He made quick work of removing it, pinning me against the wall with his hips as he tugged it up over my head.

His mouth was all over me after that. I slid my hand down his chiseled abdomen to the bulge in his underwear, slipping inside the cotton to stroke him. His skin was soft as velvet yet also hard as stone. He sucked in air through his teeth, lifting his head to look at me. Gliding my thumb over the gathering wetness at the tip, I reveled in the way his eyes fluttered closed and the noise he made in the back of his throat.

"God that feels ... *fuck,*" he stammered as I continued sliding my palm over his shaft. He gripped my ass cheeks, carrying me into the kitchen before planting me on the island countertop. Holding my hips, he tugged me to the edge before stepping out of reach. He turned to a drawer, tugging it open. Pulling out a foil packet, he faced me again. Condoms in the kitchen? That was a first.

"Ask me," he demanded in a breathless voice.

I blinked at him in confusion. I thought based on my actions, I'd already asked. He crossed his arms over his chest, shaking his head.

"I need to hear you say it."

I wet my lips, dragging my teeth along my lower lip. "I want you," I said in a voice I didn't recognize.

He darted toward me again, yanking my shorts down my legs after removing his boxer briefs like he'd practiced the move a hundred times. He probably had, but I didn't care about his past or his future right now. This moment was all that mattered. It was our escape. His knuckles brushed over the bundle of nerves between my legs, making me moan.

He glanced down, watching himself as he trailed a finger along my slick center until it sunk inside of me. I cried out as he slid it in and out repeatedly.

"You're so wet for me." He groaned, glancing up at me. "I'm gonna try really hard to go slow but I've been dreaming of this pussy for days now."

My breath caught in my throat. Well, that was kind of hot. Removing his finger, he fisted his cock, stroking it as he situated the condom. Stepping forward, he pressed the head against my entrance. He eased in gently, allowing my body to adjust to him while observing where we connected. I watched as well, biting down on my bottom lip as he filled me.

I inched closer to the edge of the counter which forced him deeper. He held my hips as I gripped his shoulders, lifting up slightly to move against him. A shudder of pure pleasure rolled through me, my head falling back as my breath quickened. I continued the rhythm, already so close to tipping over the edge.

Mick growled, placing one hand on my lower back while the other rested on the side of my neck. He guided me until my back was against the cool countertop. He palmed my breasts, leaning over me as he nibbled my skin, driving me wild. I locked my ankles together behind him, urging him closer. He grunted in approval as he thrust into me faster. I felt the pressure building between my legs, my muscles coiling tight like a spring ready to snap. His lips hovered at the shell of my ear, the low growl he released sent me spiraling as the intense orgasm rocked through me.

His hips slowed before he stopped moving completely. I felt him pulsing inside of me as my body vibrated with a new desperate need taking over. My eyes flew open as I gaped at him.

He lifted me so that I was sitting up. "You're going to come twice for me, darlin'." With a wicked smile, he began moving to work me up all over again.

It didn't take long. This time when the pressure released with a vicious force, I screamed his name. His body tightened as he clutched my hip tight, pounding into me. Seconds later, he found his own release, collapsing against me as we caught our breaths. After a few minutes, he gathered me in his arms, carrying me to the living room. He sat down on the sectional, positioning me on top of him with my legs on either side of his.

He cupped my cheek as his lips brushed against mine. "Don't move, okay? Not yet," he said before kissing me.

I nodded against him, letting him continue exploring my mouth until my lips felt swollen and numb. My body was free of tension, my mind completely and blissfully blank. For the first time in a long time I felt comfortable.

Mick

There was a warm body tucked against me and a perfect ass nestled between my hips. Long, smooth legs tangled with mine. My arms were wrapped around her, my finger gliding along the soft skin above her rib cage. I inhaled deep, the scent of cotton candy surrounding me. I opened my eyes to find her still asleep with swollen lips parted as she breathed softly. My beautiful dirty secret.

I should have felt regret, should have realized that we made a mistake. One that I'd be paying for the rest of my life. I didn't care about that right now when I could hold her in a way that I'd never done before with any of the women from my past.

Last night had been as mind blowing as I'd expected. Not that I was expecting to do what we'd done, not really. Although, I had made sure condoms were in the house. It was more wishful thinking on my part, but I was so fucking glad I had them in that moment. I'd put them in the kitchen as a way to help resist the temptation because who the fuck needs condoms in a kitchen? Apparently, I'd need condoms in every damn room of the house if I didn't get a hold of myself.

It would be even more difficult to resist her now when she responded to me so perfectly. The sight of her coming undone because of me was a high greater than any junkie could ever experience. Kissing her, listening to the little whimpers she made when my lips were on hers, shook me to the depths of my tainted soul. I shouldn't have kissed her, shouldn't have tangled my fingers in her hair or caressed her cheek. I shouldn't have fallen asleep with her on this couch.

It made what we did that much more painful because eventually I'd have to let her go. I already knew I didn't want to do that because it wouldn't be easy. Sadly though, like everything in my fucked up life, I didn't have a choice. Every decision, every single move I made, was based on the possibility of ulterior motives. Whether conscious or not, I didn't react without thinking about the repercussions. Only this time I'd been purely selfish, been well aware that the decision I made was going to be the death of me, yet I'd done it anyway.

Claire stirred slightly as I sat up to slide my leg out from between hers. I needed to get away from her before I mauled her again. Damn, I wanted another taste of those lips, to sink into that beautiful body once more. The morning wood I was sporting was truly painful. Raking a hand through my hair, I shot up off the couch, high tailing my ass downstairs. I needed a shower, needed to get rid of her scent on my skin.

After cleaning myself, I turned the faucet on cold in order to attempt ridding the visions from the night before. Before I knew it, I was jerking off to the memory of what being inside her felt like. Pure fucking paradise was as close as I could get to explaining it. That was probably the nearest to heaven I'd ever be. Once I was done, I dressed quickly and grabbed my phone.

Dom had better have Bianca Rogers in his grasp or I was going to burn the entire state of Oregon to the ground. I was desperate to send a message, to catch Delgado now more than ever. He answered his phone quickly, giving me good news which helped ease some of the tension.

"Got her. We're headed South," he said.

"Thank fuck!" I scrubbed a hand over my face as a small amount of relief ran through me. "Did she put up a fight?"

"Didn't have time to. Kyle bagged her as she left work. It was late so no one was around."

"Perfect, that kid needs a raise." He'd been steadily pulling his weight. He was always willing to help when called. I'd have to let

Hawks know that he was a good recruit so he'd be taken care of after I walked. Speaking of … "Where's Hawks?"

"Heading down to Cali to meet with your father, I guess. Jack called him for a meeting with the cartel."

I pinched the bridge of my nose with my thumb and forefinger. Jesus Christ, when it rained it poured. "So *I* have to be the executioner."

Dom sighed as a silence stretched between us. I knew he understood what was going through my mind. He was my best friend, had been for a long time. I didn't just want out of the business, I wanted away from the violence. Save for putting a bullet between Delgado's eyes, I no longer dabbled in the whole death for dishonor punishment. I'd told him to be available yet here he was letting me down.

"Is there another way?" he asked with no spark of hope in his voice.

"Not if I want to get my point across. Wilson made the mistake of dismissing Claire. It seems pretty obvious Bianca's loyalty lies in Delgado. I want him rattled when he comes for me."

"I stand behind you, Mick. I always have, you know that. I wish it didn't have to be this way."

"You and me both," I said. "Take her to the safe house off Hamilton. I want *your* eyes on her. I'll be there tonight."

"What about the girl, Claire?"

"She'll be safe here." Before he could question me or ask about her further, I disconnected the call.

Putting a woman before my job wasn't typical behavior for me. I certainly never gave a shit about people knowing what I did before because it gave me all that cool street cred. However, Claire didn't care about street cred and she sure as hell didn't need to be there when I shot her friend. Even if their friendship was far less meaningful than she originally thought. She didn't know the truth like I did. Once she found out the real reason Bianca took her in she'd be heartbroken. Causing her pain wasn't on my to do list. Ever.

After shooting a text to Hawks informing him of what was going down, I reluctantly headed back upstairs. Claire was no longer lying naked on the couch which I was grateful for. I was pent up with so much frustration that I couldn't think straight. The chances of me throwing myself at her would have been incredibly high if that were the case. Although dressed or not didn't really make a difference when it came to her.

I found her sitting at the dining table with one leg tucked beneath her as she stared out the window. It was an incredible view so I didn't blame her for fixating on it as much as she could. There had been times in the past that I would escape here to get away. I'd sit out on the deck just being still. It was peaceful, which wasn't something I had a lot of most of the time.

The view that I had right now nearly surpassed what she was looking at though. Her long blonde hair was damp from a shower. She was wearing a tank top and leggings. Even in lounge-wear, she was the prettiest damn thing I'd ever seen. A perfectly manicured nail slid along the rim of her coffee mug. It stilled when I walked by her toward the kitchen.

I kept my back to her as I poured myself some coffee.

"Morning," she mumbled.

I grunted a response before taking a sip of the hot liquid, relishing the burn as it slid down my throat. I deserved far worse pain than this. Setting my mug down, I gripped the edges of the counter, staring at the different flecks in the stone. Might as well get it all out there now.

"I have to leave. You're to stay here until I come back." I kept my voice even, though it still came out harsher than I anticipated.

"Where are you going?" she asked. I knew she was nothing other than genuinely curious, although she had to suspect something because she wasn't stupid. "Wait, don't tell me. I don't want to know."

Rolling my neck, I glared at the gray cabinets in front of me. "Best that way, darlin'. I'll be back tonight, tomorrow morning at the latest."

I heard her chair scrape across the floor, the hair on the back of my neck standing on end as she approached. The fact that I could feel her presence made my heart beat unsteadily. I wished I hadn't screwed everything up by giving in to my selfish desire last night.

"Mick," she started. Her voice was soft as if not to startle me. I continued gripping the countertop until my knuckles turned white. Inhaling a deep breath through my nose, I turned to her.

"I broke a rule last night. One to myself that I'd been holding onto for years. I did it for you because my longing got the best of me." She stared at me with a questioning look. "I don't kiss women, don't give them more than the thing between my legs. I fuck them from behind without caring if they come before me."

Her lips parted in a gasp. I smirked at her.

"With you I wanted to feel every single part. I wanted to see you come undone beneath me. I craved it so bad that I didn't care if I got off or not, but of course, I did. You're amazing, being inside of you is … addictive." Unable to help myself, I stretched my hand out, placing it against her cheek. "I kissed you because I've had the urge to drink from those lips, to sink my teeth into them since the first moment I saw you."

Her breath hitched. We were locked in an intense staring contest that neither of us wanted to break. I felt her fingers curve around the wrist of the hand that held her face, causing my body to spring to life. That fire I couldn't deny licked up my skin, coursing straight to my dick. Before I could stop myself, my lips were devouring hers.

I pushed her into the refrigerator, rattling the contents inside as I clutched her perfect hips that were made for me to grab hold of. Anger at myself for not being able to manage how much I wanted her tasted like ash on the back of my tongue, yet I swallowed it down. I was a pro at deflection and she was the perfect distraction.

She moaned in my mouth, sliding her tongue against mine. A low rumble vibrated in my chest as I pressed against her body to show her just how much she affected me. Her answering whimper along with the eager hand tightening around me almost unraveled me. Jesus, she was insatiable. She was perfect, she was *mine*.

I pulled back just enough that I could speak. "Tell me you want me."

"I want you," she rasped before her plump lips came crashing back to mine to enforce her response.

Damn it all to hell, I couldn't resist her. It didn't take long to remove her clothes. Lifting her in my arms, she wrapped her legs around my waist. I quickly undid the zipper and button on my jeans to free myself. After grabbing protection, I eased her onto me slowly, all the while watching her face as I filled her and kept her pinned against the refrigerator. Her eyes fluttered closed for a moment before opening to lock on mine.

"Don't close your eyes," I ordered, placing a hand on her hip to steady her while putting the other against her neck, gently squeezing. I slid my thumb along the soft skin of her throat.

She nodded, rocking her hips while using her hands on my shoulders as leverage. I gave her full control, enjoying the way she rode me with her tits bouncing against my chest. When I felt her tighten around me I focused back on her face, taking in the way her violet eyes glazed over, her lips trembling as she came. I was a goner after that, following almost immediately. I held her up as she collapsed against me, her forehead falling to my shoulder. My heart was hammering in my chest like I'd just finished running a marathon.

When I finally lowered her to her feet, certain she wouldn't fall over, a coldness seeped into my veins as irritation took root. She got dressed mechanically, pulling her hair to one side. I zeroed in on the round red mark on her throat. Fuck. I'd marked her at some point. It was a good thing she wasn't coming with me tonight. Though the prospect of leaving her now made my stomach hurt. God, I was a masochist with her.

"When are you leaving?" she asked, making her way to the mug she'd left on the table.

"Soon."

She grabbed her mug, carrying it back to the coffee pot to refill it. We were both silent for a while before she turned to look at me. "How many people have you killed?"

"More than I've wanted to." I couldn't lie to her.

"Do you ... like it?"

What? That was a scary question. The fact that she felt she needed to ask stunned me, although I guess I couldn't blame her, considering who I was. I'm sure she'd heard about me from those around her.

"No, I don't like it. I mean anyone I've taken out deserved it, but it's not like I was itching to pull the trigger." It was the truth. I did what I had to do either to save my own ass or someone else's. I wasn't sorry for what I'd done but it's not like I got off on it or anything. "Claire, whatever I have to do I'll do because it's part of the job. I need to put this Delgado shit to bed. What they're doing is treason. It goes against every rule. They know that. I can't stop until this is over."

I didn't expect her to comprehend my motives. As bad as it sounded, I'd never be able to rest until this was finished. It was ingrained in me since an early age to follow through. I could leave my father or Hawks to deal with it, but the guilt would surely eat at me. It would kill me to dip out when the going got tough. That kind of death was worse than being shot in the head by a rival business or some random idiot.

She squared her shoulders as she held the mug between her hands. "I want to go with you."

"Hell no!" I growled. "Are you fucking crazy?"

She frowned. "You expect me to stay in this house, *your* house, while you skip town to kill my friend? At least let me be there to say goodbye. What if this Ricky guy comes for me when you're gone? What if Cory does?"

I shook my head. "He's after me, not you. You're safer here."

"Be that as it may, I don't want to stay here. Bianca was my friend." I rolled my eyes and she snapped. Setting her mug down she stalked up to me before shoving her finger in my face. "I am not backing down on this! She may have betrayed you and your business but without her I don't know where I'd be."

"Probably better off," I muttered.

"Yeah," she scoffed. "Yeah, I would be. I certainly wouldn't be dealing with this shit you dragged me in to."

My hands balled to fists at my sides, the resentment intensifying inside me. "I'm not to blame for your current situation. That's your loser boyfriend's fault," I said through clenched teeth.

Her brow rose. "Yeah? I don't think he's losing sleep over the fact that I'm here. In fact, why don't you call him up, tell him that I had sex with you. See if it changes his mind. It won't. He doesn't care!"

Her voice wavered slightly, making my chest tighten. It hurt her that he so easily dismissed her. Whether she cared about him or not the rejection was evident. That soft side of mine she'd successfully tapped into along with the urge to defend her had me reeling. I knew she was safe here. Although next to me she'd be just as safe because I'd never let anything happen to her. Hell, she could ask me for the moon and I'd find a way to build a ladder tall enough. I was a wreck in her presence, becoming someone I didn't recognize. What the fuck was wrong with me?

Releasing a breath, I said, "Your safety is important to me. Not just because I'm responsible for you right now but because I care about you." Shaking my head, I added, "Don't think that means I'm in love with you or some twisted shit like that. I don't love. My heart bleeds for few, however I do care." This was getting way too deep. I'd admitted to far more than I wanted. She had a way of getting under my skin that left me far more vulnerable than I intended.

Damn Claire Evans bringing out some sort of knight in shining armor persona in me that I didn't even want. What fresh hell was this?

She watched me as I worked out in my mind how to walk away, how I could leave her here alone. My intentions were good, gallant in fact. I was protecting her. However, like I'd said before, I'd never been known for my honor. I was inherently selfish.

"If you come with me, you stay with me. No wandering off, no talking out of turn, no fucking my head up. Got it?" I couldn't believe I was caving.

Her violet eyes sparkled as a small smile graced those tantalizing lips. "I swear I'll behave. Thank you."

I lifted a finger. "Except ... " Her face fell. I knew what I was about to say would hurt her. She'd probably think I was a dick. I mean really though, I was Mickey fucking Silver, what did she expect? "You can't say goodbye to her and you can't be in the room when it happens."

"Why?"

"Saying goodbye to her won't help either of you. You're going to be exposed to a different side of me tonight. A side that is likely to scar you for life on top of making you wish you'd never let me in. I'm not going to further that nightmare by allowing you to bear witness to my greatest sin."

Chapter 10

Claire

I couldn't make heads or tails of what transpired between Mick and I the last twenty-four hours. All I knew was that I liked the way he touched me. I craved the pure carnal bliss he'd elicited. I'd never experienced so much passion from a man before. I found myself irrational and explicitly smitten. Days ago I loathed him, couldn't bear the sight of him let alone the idea of being so close. Perhaps it wasn't hatred that I'd felt toward him all this time. Maybe it was mere frustration. Because he drove me crazy in ways that were equally good and bad. He had a way of rendering me weak in the knees, forcing me free of any coherent thought.

The only thing I knew for certain was that staying here in this house while he went to end Bianca's life would be wrong. I needed to be there, to see exactly who Mickey Silver was. If only to rid the positive thoughts that seemed to now outweigh the negative when it came to him. Surely seeing him in all his bossy glory would kill the desire that rattled my brain since I tasted his lips. Especially if he ended up murdering Bianca. There was no possible way I'd entertain anymore thoughts of him if that happened.

What startled me the most was that he seemed to be as equally enamored. He said he cared about me which confused me further. I didn't know what would happen after tonight or a month from now. All I could do was hold on tight while hoping to survive the ride.

He told me to pack an overnight bag in the event we needed to stay somewhere. After I'd packed, I found Mick waiting for me at the front door. He seemed tense, his face a mask of unspoken irritation.

We were headed north to a safe house that was supposedly often used during unsafe times. It was completely off the grid and he'd made sure to stress the fact it was incredibly remote several times. I was certain it was his way of trying to talk me out of going.

He should know by now I didn't scare easily. I'd rather be surrounded by people or at least him, than alone in that too large house with it's expensive furniture. Besides, he couldn't say for certain that Delgado wouldn't be able to get in. If I were left alone I'd be a sitting duck.

We were in a different vehicle than the one we'd arrived in. It was a non-de-script sedan that was parked in the bay of the garage, not normally used for nefarious purposes.

Most of the trip was spent in either silence or with him speaking on the phone to whomever was helping orchestrate the events that'd be taking place. We turned off the main road to travel up a steep winding gravel one. My stomach twisted into knots. The late afternoon sun was high but it didn't help the ever-present darkness that seemed to trickle in hours ago. My friend was going to die at the hands of a man seeking revenge. A man I'd been with intimately, twice.

"Before we get there I have to ask … " Mick's voice was low, breaking through my thoughts. I turned to look at him. "Have you ever shot a gun before?" He glanced at me briefly before focusing back on the road.

If you could even call it a road. He wasn't kidding, this was like *Deliverance* style remote. I prayed to God I didn't hear a banjo playing.

"Once. Although I wasn't aiming at anything in particular." I chewed on my bottom lip. "I hesitated when I aimed that gun at your guy, so I can't say I'd want to shoot someone,." I added quietly.

He nodded. "Yeah, well don't be too upset about that. I think James is grateful you spared his life."

I frowned. "Why do you ask?"

He licked his lips before glancing at me again for a moment. "Knowing Delgado is somewhere out there means we have to be extra careful. He has to know by now we have his woman. Others may be looking for her so if things go sideways you're going to need to be ready. I'll have Dom with you. However, you've got to protect yourself if push comes to shove. Understand?"

I blew out a breath as the knot in my stomach grew. "You're giving me a gun?"

He snorted. "Against my better judgment, I'm considering it. If this goes south."

My eyes narrowed. "What do you mean 'against your better judgement?'"

"You're my hostage, remember? How do I know you won't put a bullet in my back?"

I couldn't help the slow smile that formed. He thought I'd shoot him? It felt kind of good to know he didn't trust me. "Mickey Silver, are you afraid of me?"

His head whipped in my direction, nostrils flaring. "I've said before nothing scares me."

I shrugged. "I don't know, it sounds like you're worried."

The car came to a halt. I glanced out the windshield to see a cabin sitting about twenty feet in front of us tucked into the tree line. Mick put the car in park before killing the engine. He pinned me with a glare, his jaw muscle clenching.

"I have another confession," he growled, leaning toward me. "*You* frighten the fuck out of me." He reached for my face with both hands, clasping my cheeks as he drew my face to his. His lips hovered over mine, forcing my heart to speed up. "I'm a very bad man, sweet Claire."

I opened my mouth to say something, but the words died on my tongue when he pressed his lips to mine in a searing kiss that left my body aching with need. When he pulled back, he opened his door, giving me a quick once over.

His brows scrunched together with a look of remorse as he promptly got out, slamming the car door before rounding the front toward me. After opening my door, he gripped my upper arm, tugging me out of the seat.

"Start walking, don't ask questions," he said in a low voice, nudging me forward. I did as he said, letting him guide me toward the cabin. He'd told me earlier I'd see a side of him that I wouldn't like. I guess that started now.

As we trudged up the long staircase to the front door of the cabin, it opened. Dom stood at the threshold. His dark eyes fell to mine before sliding to Mick.

"What is she doing here?" he asked, giving me another brief look.

"Can't trust her alone. She threatened to leave. She's also already broken her restraints once," Mick said easily.

Dom's head fell back in a laugh that thundered. "Damn, man, I told you she was going to give you a hard time." We brushed past him into the cabin. Mick deposited me on a tattered floral couch that looked like something my grandmother used to have in her living room.

"She's a hellion, drives me crazy, and I didn't want to risk her running." Mick ran a hand through his hair. "Any news?"

"No one seems to know she's gone still. It's not uncommon for her to disappear for a few days."

That was true. Bianca was pretty detached when it came to most people. There were times I had no idea where she was or when she'd come back. She'd never been gone for more than a day or two though. I wondered now if it had to do with this Ricky guy. I'd never met him that I knew of, although lately he was all I heard about. If she was dating him or whatever I had no idea. It had me wondering if I ever really knew her at all. I'd put so much trust in her because she helped me out when I first came to Seattle. She gave me a roof over my head, a job, and I'd felt so grateful. Was it all an act? Did she ever really care about me?

Mick nodded. "Good, that gives us time. Where is she?"

"Kyle's bringing her in any minute."

"Thanks, Dom. I know it's a lot to ask but I'm going to need you to hang out. This one," he hitched his thumb at me, "can't be in the room when I decorate the wall with the bitch's brain matter."

A wave of nausea rolled through me as tears sprang to my eyes. That was awfully colorful of him. No one paid me any attention, either ignoring my surprise or oblivious to it. Nerves began to build steadily inside me.

Dom nodded. "Yeah, no problem. Sadie's with Mackaela anyway. They're wedding planning."

A slow grin appeared on Mick's face. He looked genuinely happy which caught me off guard. Especially since he was on the freaking cusp of potentially murdering someone. What a strange world I was living in right now.

There was a commotion outside forcing the grin on his face to a scowl. "Time to get to work," he said.

"Let me go, you stupid motherfucker!" Bianca shrieked as who I assumed was Kyle yanked her through the front door.

I tried to keep my expression blank even though inside I was filled with a heavy sense of dread. Her usually perfect hair was disheveled, tattered around her face and tangled in the back. Whatever lipstick she'd been wearing was smudged, her mascara had run to the middle of her cheeks. She was wearing a pair of loose lounge pants with a t-shirt that fell off one shoulder. They'd definitely taken her when she least expected it. It was rare for her to not have on a designer outfit.

Mick knelt in front of me, his hazel eyes dark and unyielding.

"If you breathe a word to her your fate will match hers. Understand?" Swallowing the lump that formed at his venomous words, I nodded disjointedly. He squinted at me. "Don't move." I nodded again. He stood then, blocking Bianca's view of me as he faced her.

Her hands were bound behind her so when Kyle tossed her into a beat up armchair, she swung her leg out, kicking him in the shin. He looked young, like he'd barely graduated high school, with dark hair and sinewy biceps. His tan face darkened as he lowered it close to hers.

"I wouldn't do that if I were you," he warned. Bianca rolled her eyes.

"You're a child! I'm not afraid of you."

Kyle glared at her before stepping back, heading for what appeared to be a small kitchen. I heard drawers opening and closing.

"He's right," Mick said. His voice was eerily calm, deadly. "If you attack my men, you face the consequences." Her gaze sharpened as she looked at him.

"He's going to kill you for taking me!" she seethed.

Mick chuckled, clucking his tongue. "Ah, yet he's not here, is he? I heard you've been running that filthy mouth of yours. Couldn't find a dick for the night to keep it occupied so you had to gossip about your roommate's disappearance instead?"

"I don't know what you're talking about!"

"No? Well that's not what Cory Wilson said. In fact, he admitted that Delgado was after me, that *you're* the one who told them it was me that took Claire." He stepped to the right, putting me in view of her. Bianca blinked at me as her brows inched up her forehead.

"Claire! Oh my god, you're here." She gasped.

I bit down on the inside of my cheek trying not to show any emotion. I wanted to cry, to tell her I'd trusted her, that I'd cared about her. I wanted to ask her if she ever really cared about me but stayed silent.

"Don't look at her, look at me!" Mick ordered in a loud voice that had me recoiling. "You're a snitch, a waste of life taking innocent girls to turn them into whores. You're the little mule, aren't you?"

Bianca bared her teeth. "Clint's gotta get girls somehow. No one has a flock like you," she seethed, staring at him in disgust.

It felt like I'd been punched in the chest. *What the hell?!* Rage boiled within me as tears threatened to spill. She'd been using me.

Mick turned toward me, crossing his arms over his chest.

"You hear that, darlin'? They wanted you to turn tricks for them. She was grooming you, trying to make you a sex slave." There was a bite to his tone. I knew he was holding back unbridled fury. "I should kill her for that alone," he added before turning his attention back to Bianca.

"Fuck. You." She reared her head back, spitting at his feet. "She's bumpkin white trash, the perfect specimen. Would have made us a lot more money. She was the favorite at *Rosie's* because of it."

Mick stomped toward her, grabbing her hair to tilt her head at a sharp angle. Bianca whimpered. "Disrespect her again and I'll slit your throat." Releasing her roughly, he stepped back just as Kyle entered the living room with a long rope and duct tape.

"Want me to tie her to the chair, boss?" he asked in a tone as easy as if he worked at a Wetzel's Pretzels or something.

"Secure her good, start with the feet," Mick said. "Your life is on the line here," he said to Bianca. "Tell me where Delgado is."

She attempted to kick at Kyle again, so Dom knelt in front of her, capturing her legs. They had her bound from her ankles to her thighs in no time. Under different circumstances, I might have been impressed at how fast they worked. Or not. This was something I never wanted to see or be a part of again. The regret of wanting to come was heavy.

"He's coming for you. He'll make it count!" she shouted. "You won't get shit from me." Kyle ripped off a piece of duct tape from the roll before smashing it against her mouth.

Mick shrugged. "That's a shame. Kyle, go get the plastic."

He wandered down a narrow hall, disappearing again.

Dom pulled Bianca's cell phone from his back pocket. I recognized it because of its glittery pink cover. He handed it over to Mick who dialed a number before pressing the speakerphone button. A shrill ringing filled the small room until a man answered. His voice was deep and menacing.

"I'm going to stab you in the heart, Silver."

"Too bad I don't have one. We've got your girl here, Delgado. I'm about ten minutes or less away from burning her body in a barrel. Care to meet up?"

"You're bluffing," Ricky growled.

"I wish I were. Trust me, her presence is not at all welcome." He stalked toward Bianca, once again standing over her. Her eyes filled with tears as she stared at the phone. "You want to talk to him honey?" She nodded vehemently.

Mick grabbed a corner of the duct tape over her mouth, yanking hard. The sound of it ripping from her flesh made me physically cringe. Good lord, he was brutal.

"Ricky, he's got me tied up at some cabin! You need to get here. Now!" she cried. Mick replaced the duct tape before she could say anything else.

He held the phone up to his mouth, glowering at the screen. "I've got two girls in my possession that belonged to both you and Wilson. Your FBI informant Watson is out since my associate so kindly broke his legs after scaring the piss out of him. Although I'm sure you're partner filled you in on that. You know what that means? Check fucking mate, bitch."

"You are out of your mind, Silver. I have no clue what you're talking about, though it's about time someone new takes over. When are you gonna realize you're nothing?"

Kyle came back into the room with a large roll of what I assumed was some sort of painter's drop plastic. He began rolling it out around Bianca methodically. My stomach lurched. Holy shit this was really happening. He worked so meticulously, like it was just another ordinary day, and that made me incredibly uncomfortable. Sweat formed on my brow as my heart pounded in my ears.

"When are you going to realize that I run this motherfucking coast?" Mick asked, his voice dark.

He pulled a gun out from the waistband of his jeans. My breath caught in my throat. He straightened his arm, aiming the gun at Bianca's chest. The sound of the gun cocking reverberated around the small room, deafening and ominous.

"If you kill her you're going to start a war you won't be prepared for. I'll make sure to burn everything you love to the ground!" Ricky threatened.

Mick snarled. "You comply or I add another piece of jewelry to her face. You have zero leverage now, asshole. Meet me so I can do to you what you tried to do to my brother."

"Tell you what," Ricky said, "I'll let you in on a little secret. Let's see if you really want to continue defending that father of yours. My immunity in exchange for important information."

"What are you talking about?" Mick demanded, lifting the gun to Bianca's face.

"If you let her go, I'll tell you."

"Mmm, nope. Not the way it works here, dumbass. I call the shots." Mick turned abruptly, his eyes landing on mine. "Head shot or straight through the heart, darlin'? You choose." I gaped at him in horror. He was a madman right now, completely unhinged. His gaze slid to Dom. "Take her outside."

Without hesitation, Dom grabbed my arm, hauling me up from the couch. He wasn't overly aggressive about it but he wasn't gentle, either. Shoving me toward the door, I stumbled to it, yanking on the handle.

"Thirty seconds until this bitch becomes a ghost."

"Jesus, Silver, don't do it!" Ricky begged.

"Twenty." Mick's voice was faint as I was led out of the cabin. Dom closed the door behind us, tugging me down the stairs.

The moment my toe touched the bottom step a gunshot blasted. I collapsed onto the ground, my stomach tilting as my chest heaved. He'd actually done it. He'd shot Bianca. He was a murderer, a criminal, an unbelievably bad man. I should have known., I *did* know. Although actually witnessing the behavior was a different kind of proof. Hearing the gunfire sent a wave of terror through me. It wasn't until Dom put me on my feet again that I realized I was crying. My body shook brutally as sobs rocked through me.

He didn't say anything to me, just kept a hold on my arm as he stared up at the evening sky while the sun sank behind orange clouds.

My friend, my roommate, the person responsible for me being *here* was gone. She'd used me, groomed me as Mick had said. Clint, my boss, was a bad man, too. I was so very stupid for falling into the trap the moment I set foot in Seattle. I'd been in danger since day one without ever realizing it. In a totally twisted way, Mick rescued me from her, from everything I'd gotten wrapped up in without even knowing.

That didn't make me feel better because he was as bad as they were. No, he was *worse*. Because he murdered Bianca in cold blood. Used her as a weapon against another person that he wanted to screw over. All for something that ended up working out okay in the end. Simon was still alive, Bianca wasn't. He was no better than the rest of them.

Everything hit me all at once and I couldn't stop the emotions that engulfed me as I stood there sniveling like a child. I heard the faint sound of a door open and close before footsteps thudded down the stairs. As Dom released me, I was hit with the scent of cinnamon and the distinct musk of Mick. His hands landed on my shoulders. I think he was looking at me but my vision blurred with the tears that I wasn't sure would ever end.

"Help Kyle," he said to Dom. I heard him sprint up the stairs, slamming the door behind him. Suddenly, I was pulled into Mick's body as his arms circled my back, crushing me to his chest. "Shh, I know. I'm sorry," he murmured as he placed a hand at the back of my head to stroke my hair.

I wasn't sure how long we stood there with him consoling and suffocating me at the same time. I wanted to move yet I couldn't. The warmth of his embrace, the familiar scent of him was comforting me as much as it was killing me. That made me cry even harder. I felt like some sort of Stockholm syndrome victim. Mick was my captor *and* protector. Everything was falling apart and I couldn't even run. I couldn't fight the hold he had on me because I was frozen in disbelief and misery.

As the tears subsided, my wailing turned to sporadic hic-cups. He hesitated for a moment as I pulled back, sighing when he released me. The sky was dark now with tiny stars pep-pered throughout the expanse. I focused on them, taking in gulps of air to regulate my breathing. Mick stood beside me silently. There was nothing he could say to make this better. I was grateful he seemed to understand that.

The door to the cabin opened again as Dom called down to Mick. "Place is clean. Josh is on his way to help with disposal."

"Thanks," Mick hollered. The door closed again as he turned to face me. "Claire ... "

Shaking my head, I bit down on my bottom lip. "Don't." My voice was hoarse so I cleared my throat to try again. "Don't say you're sorry. Don't lie to me and tell me everything's okay." I folded my arms over my stomach, staring straight ahead at the car now.

"Is there anything I can say?" I caught the hint of concern in his voice.

Inhaling a deep breath, I turned my head to look at him. His hazel eyes were full of apologies and fractured promises. "Tell me it was worth it. That whatever happened in there will make things better than they were before. Tell me that you found what you were looking for."

His throat bobbed in a swallow as he searched my face. "I can't say that."

A humorless laugh escaped. "At least you're honest." I glanced back toward the car feeling empty. I wanted to leave this place behind, although something told me nightmares would haunt me for years to come. "What happens now?" I asked after a few minutes of silence.

"Cory has a secret that somehow involves my father. Del-gado offered to share it with me if I agreed to let go of my per-sonal vendetta against him."

My heart skidded to a stop. I tried to keep my face blank, to not give anything away. "What are you going to do?"

He blew out a breath. "Not sure. He made it sound like it's something I definitely want to know. Although I can't let him get away with almost murdering my brother."

I thought that killing Bianca would be enough yet kept the thought to myself. "Do you have any idea what it is?" I asked, keeping my voice even.

"No. The way he made it sound, I wouldn't worry about anything else once I knew what Cory was hiding." He moved to stand in front of me. "You wouldn't happen to know what it is?"

The response was automatic, ingrained in me since the night I'd discovered it. Cory had threatened to end me if I breathed a word. "No."

Mick nodded, holding his hand out to me. I raised a brow at him as he gave me a halfhearted smile. "Come on. Let's get out of here."

Chapter 11

Mick

I'd made the executive decision to stay at a hotel for the night.

The images of what I'd done kept replaying in my head like a never ending nightmare. I deserved them. A pang of regret settled in the second I pulled the trigger. The feeling had only grown since. I couldn't dwell on that though. Claire witnessed a side of me that I wasn't proud of. The fear I'd read in her tear laced gaze gutted me. I'd warned her, but that didn't change the fact I was probably now a monster to her. I needed to let her go, to find a way to get her as far away from this place as possible without word getting out to the wrong people. There was no doubt I'd endangered her life further with this stunt.

Bianca had to die. There was no other way around it. As much as that fact bothered even a soulless bastard like me, it was the truth. The only way to gain any sort of leverage from Ricky was to hit him where it hurt. Not only that, Bianca was baiting women. Leading them into a life of pain they didn't deserve.

This entire situation was becoming a lot more involved where Cory Wilson was concerned which I hadn't expected. The thought crossed my mind that I'd done enough, that now may be a good time to cut ties with the business, though it was fleeting. Ricky mentioned something that didn't really hit me until we'd left. The more I dwelled on what he'd said, the more I worried that I'd never get out.

He claimed he didn't know where Cory was, that since last year he hadn't been to Oregon. He was supposedly hiding out across the border in Canada. He also mentioned that while he scored drugs off him to sell for money to evade me, he wasn't working *with* him. I was under the assumption he'd been talking out of his ass to save Bianca. Now I wasn't so sure.

Not being able to grasp what was actually going on really pissed me off. There was only a small extent of leverage I had at the moment. It made Wilson and Delgado far more dangerous than I'd originally planned. It made me doubt everyone, including my own business associates.

I pulled into the busy parking lot of a large hotel chain, opting for a place with more people. I thought it might help Claire feel safer than some seedy motel. She was asleep in the passenger seat and had been since before we even hit the main road. I felt like an asshole for waking her, but I was too on edge to leave her out here while I checked us in. I hadn't shed first blood. Ricky had done that when he shot Simon last year, but I knew he meant what he said when I'd be unleashing a war. The trouble was I didn't know exactly who that was with anymore.

Killing the engine, I grabbed my phone from the center console. Dom had been texting me since I'd left the safe house. Typically, his communications after these events were fairly minimal. Not tonight. He'd reminded me I did the right thing. Eye for an eye and all that. He'd told me he backed me completely as usual which was his way of making me feel better. Then he pissed me off by acknowledging my weakness.

Dom: Don't think I didn't notice the hickey on her neck
Me: Rope burn?
Dom: Be careful Mick

Me: Noted

I slid the phone into my pocket as I exited the car. Claire didn't even flinch at the sound of my door closing. I opened the passenger side, gazing down at her. The dark circles under her lashes made my chest hurt. I rubbed the skin above my heart as I inhaled a deep breath. I let it out slowly as I placed my hand against her cheek, gliding my thumb over her bottom lip. God she was beautiful, so innocent in all of this. If this were a fairy tale, she'd be Red Riding Hood and I'd be the big bad wolf. She let out a soft moan, eyes blinking open slowly. Her brow furrowed as she stared up at me.

"Where are we?" she mumbled while gazing out at the parking lot.

"We're staying at a hotel. It's safe."

She yawned before stepping out of the car. As soon as her door closed, I reached for her hand. She pulled away and crossed her arms over her chest. Clenching my jaw, I quelled the urge to snap at her. We were sitting ducks like this. She was clearly still bitter about what happened back at the cabin, which it's not like I could fault her but fuck, she could at least stick close to me for safety. Damn insufferable, independent woman.

The sliding doors opened for us before we approached the front desk. A woman with bright blue eyes and brown hair greeted us cheerily.

"Can I help you?" She glanced from me to Claire.

"We've got a reservation under Hartwell," I said while pulling my wallet from my back pocket. I slid the credit card under the false name toward her along with the fake ID. I'd reserved a room this morning in the event I needed to stay behind.

She took it before clacking on the keyboard in front of her. Handing them back, she printed out a copy of the receipt which I signed. "Here's your room key. Number 206."

"Thanks." I grabbed the key card, tilting my chin at Claire to follow. She remained quiet until we exited the elevator on the third floor.

"Hartwell?" she asked as I scanned the room numbers.

"You ever see Breaking Bad?" She shook her head. "You really should. It's a great show. Hartwell's the middle name of the main character. He makes methamphetamine. I thought it'd be funny, you know, me being in the line of work I'm in."

"Cute." She rolled her eyes, tightening her arms across her chest.

Okaaaay, so she was still pissed, which meant my chances of getting an earful once we were in the room was topping out at one hundred percent. Either that, or she'd kill me with unrelenting silence. I squeezed the back of my neck as I stopped in front of room 206.

Once the door was unlocked, I swept my arm out to allow her to enter before me. When the door shut with a loud click behind us, she decided to whip around fast as lightning to get all up in my face. So we were going with the earful.

"I don't want to be here with you. I don't want to be a part of this any longer. I've thought long and hard about it. You know what?"

"What?" I ground out. She was standing so close I could smell her sweet scent which put my body at war with my mind. I despised that she thought she could talk to me like this but damn, it was also a total turn on.

Her face was a mask of pure fury with those violet eyes burning up at me. "I did my part. You owe me the rest of my money. I'm. Done."

It felt like I'd been roundhouse kicked in the chest as my lungs restricted, forcing the air out of me. *No!* Anger mixed with an emotion I couldn't place at the moment. Maybe panic? It tunneled deep inside of me as every muscle in my body locked up tight. While I knew letting her go was best, I hadn't realized she'd kill me so soon. This tempting viper of a woman, who stood before me with all the confidence in the world, had a stony gaze that cut me down where I stood. To think, this entire time I thought *I* was dangerous.

She didn't waiver, didn't show one single ounce of fear as she stood toe to toe with me making ridiculous demands. I clenched my jaw, glaring down at those violet orbs that haunted me. Maybe it was the fear of losing her that made me say what I did next, or maybe I was an idiot. It was likely both yet it didn't stop me.

"No."

Her mouth popped open. "Excuse me?" Her hands landed on her hips. "You're not the boss of me."

My brows rose. "I absolutely am your boss! You work for me or did you forget that? You don't get to quit. The answer is no."

Scoffing, she lifted her hands before letting them fall noisily against her thighs. "You've got to be kidding me." She turned away from me then, stomping toward the one queen-sized bed in the room. Scowling at the white comforter, her head shook. "Why?"

Lord give me patience. This woman was not unintelligent though she sure wasn't thinking right now. I stepped toward the small desk in the room, leaning against it with my arms crossed.

"I just killed a woman because she meant you harm. I shot her at point blank range in the head for sick and twisted revenge against a man lesser than me. One of two men conspiring against me who want me out of their hair as well as dead now if they didn't before. You're seriously standing there demanding I let you go? You think you can just walk out of here now as if nothing ever happened? As if they don't suspect taking you into their possession or worse, killing *you,* will turn me into the Incredible fucking Hulk and destroy myself along with anyone in my path to get you back?"

Her shoulders tightened.

She was an accomplice now whether she liked it or not. Plus, she meant too much to me to let her go so easily. I knew it was wrong, but I wanted at least a few more days with her. I needed time to prepare so that she could disappear cleanly.

"You said before they didn't want me, that they want only you. You told me I was safe at the house," she argued.

"Yeah, except you didn't stay, did you? Now you're a witness to a crime I committed. An accessory. Like it or not, you're in this, Claire. That was your decision not mine." Her face fell as she let what I said sink in. "I'm sorry, you have to stay right now." I was more than sorry. I should have never dragged her down like this in the first place.

Her gaze sharpened. "I'll go to the police. Tell them all about you and Cory and that Delgado guy. I'll turn you *all* in."

Okay, now she was throwing a hissy-fit that I was so not down for. Something snapped within me as hurt and fury clawed its way up my throat. Darting forward, I grabbed her by the biceps, pinning her against the nearby wall.

"You think I won't go to great lengths to maintain my innocence? That I won't take you down with me if you open your fucking mouth to the cops?" There was a fear in her eyes that I hadn't seen before. My murderous glare reflected back at me through them. I dropped my hands as if her skin burned my palms. Raking a hand through my hair, I took several steps back. "I'm sorry."

She didn't speak and the room grew quiet with only the sound of her occasional sniffling. I'd made her cry. Again. I was digging an even deeper hole with no way to climb out. This wasn't what I wanted for her. It wasn't how it was supposed to be.

Sitting down at the foot of the bed, I lowered my head. "I know you're scared, that you don't comprehend any of this like I do. I get that it seems easier to walk away. I assure you, it isn't. Not only is it dangerous right now, I ... I don't want you to leave." I risked a glance at her. The sorrow in her gaze pierced straight to my heart. "Confession number three," I began, clearing my throat, "I think I'm starting to fall for you."

My words hung between us as I squeezed my eyes shut, burying my head in my hands. It's not like I loved her. I didn't. But there was something about Claire Evans, there always had been. She needed to know that. If only to slow her down or at least keep her from running out of here the minute I turned my back.

I was intrigued by her, challenged by her. There was this pulse that radiated between us that I couldn't get rid of. Even when we were fighting, I wanted her. I cared about her more than myself. I'd lay down and die for her if I had to. If it took sacrificing myself to take away all the violence, all of the wrongs she'd been handed, I'd do it without a second thought.

How was that for my morality?

Claire

I couldn't have heard him correctly. There was no way that Mickey Silver just told me he was falling for me. Not after everything he'd done or said up until this moment. It couldn't be true. He had to be messing with me, trying to find a way to tug at my heart to make me stay. Right?

Although, there was this morning, when he'd admitted he'd never been with a woman the way he had with me. He'd told me that he cared. He'd also been brutally honest when I questioned him after he'd shot Bianca. I understood that it was partially his fault, but deep down he wasn't a sociopath. He had a conscience and knew I'd be affected by his actions because he'd warned me. Yes, he'd killed someone and yes, he was a drug lord who went about things in a violent and criminal manner. However, he'd never been that way toward me. He'd never threatened my life and meant it. He'd never physically harmed me.

Even minutes ago when he'd grabbed me, it was gentle. The rapid movement startled me, not the grip. His words, while harsh, didn't matter as much as the look in his eyes. There was a level of fear in them, and a pain that shown through when he glared down at me after I threatened to tell the police.

Mick was scared. I got the notion that it was a different kind of fear he'd never showed to anyone before. He was vulnerable around me, he opened himself up to me with these random confessions. This latest one made my heart swell and break simultaneously.

I wasn't sure what to say. I couldn't tell him I was falling for him, too, because I didn't trust what I'd been feeling. We'd known of each other for a year, yet up until a few weeks ago we'd never spoken. There was this odd connection between us that had us at each other's throats one minute and stealing delicate moments the next. I found myself drawn to him, forgiving him slowly even after what I'd witnessed tonight. It was why I said what I did. Everything was too heavy. The crushing weight of what transpired had me more determined than ever to leave quickly. Staying with him now when it likely couldn't get much worse would mean something. It would solidify my feelings that I was too afraid to admit. That I simply wanted to be around him because I liked him a whole hell of a lot more than I ever planned.

My legs were moving before I'd made up my mind. Suddenly, I was standing in front of him. When he raised his head, those hazel eyes held mine. They were softer than before, full of guilt and apprehension. I wasn't sure what to say but that didn't mean I couldn't express the whirlwind of emotions he stirred within me. I lifted my hand, sliding it against his cheek. His breath caught as I bent forward until our lips were aligned.

"Claire," he began to protest, and I shook my head.

"No more talking," I said before kissing him.

Every time we spoke to each other, we ended up in some sort of argument. Our bodies were different, they seemed to come together without hesitation. This way of communication was an easier way to resolve things. I wanted to forget the last few hours. Knowing what little I did about him had me thinking he wanted that, too.

Mick kissed me back while reaching for my hips to tug me forward until I was straddling his lap. I removed his shirt hastily, allowing him to do the same to me. I ran my fingernails over his broad shoulders, down his muscular tattooed arms, to his equally decorated hands before guiding them to my skin. His lips trailed a fiery path to my chest. I rocked against him when he bit down on the tightened peak before soothing it with his tongue, then doing the same to the other one.

Sometimes it felt like he knew my body better than I did. I loved the way he brought me pleasure that I'd never experienced before. But I wanted to do something for him, to show him that even though I was disappointed and terrified how things were turning out, I was falling for him, too.

I pushed away from him gently, standing to remove the jeans I'd been wearing along with my panties. Mick stood as well, going for the button on his own jeans. I grabbed his hand to stop him. Flicking my gaze up to his, my lips tilted up on one side.

"I want to undress you," I said, my voice sounding steadier than I felt. There was a measure of control I had over him this way which was something he didn't give up easily. If he could do this for me, it would prove that what he'd said was true.

With a clipped nod, he let his hands fall to his sides. I undid the button, then the zipper, before kneeling in front of him as I lowered his jeans along with the underwear to his feet. He toed off his shoes so I could remove his clothes the rest of the way, including taking his socks off for him. His breath faltered when I straightened, lightly grabbing his rock hard length.

Glancing up at him through my lashes, I saw the hard set of his jaw, his eyes darkening as he stared down at me hungrily. I licked my lips slowly and he let out a groan that sent a wave of gratification through me. Liquid heat flowed between my legs.

"Can I taste you?" I asked in a sultry whisper.

His chest rumbled. "Fuck yes. *Please.*"

Smiling to myself, I eased him into my mouth slowly. My tongue trailed along his length as I explored how far I could take him. I'd made it midway before he hit the back of my throat. A moan erupted from his lips as his hand tangled in my hair. I continued my exploration of him, gaining momentum while quickening the pace. Mick panted above me, his fingers flexing in my hair as the other hand balled into a fist at his side.

"Damn, I don't think ... " Before he could finish his sentence, he exploded. Hot liquid rushed down my throat, spilling past my lips. He pulled out, releasing a shuddering breath as I ran the back of my hand across my mouth.

He immediately dropped to his knees in front of me, tilting my chin up with his index finger to study my face. There was an emotion there I couldn't quite place. Gratitude maybe? I started to speak and he shut me up with a deep kiss that made my toes curl, further igniting me. He pressed me back onto the floor as his lips traveled down my neck to my chest and beyond. There wasn't an inch of my body he hadn't tasted as he worked all the way down to my toes. Coming back up, he placed his hands on my knees, spreading them apart.

His gaze zeroed in between my thighs and I gasped at the predatory gleam in his eye. With a wink, he lowered his lips to the inside of my right thigh before licking a path up to my center, hovering there. His breath was hot against me and I felt like I was going to combust when he peered up at me through his lashes.

"Confession number four," he began in a gruff whisper. "You're my first." He gave me a devilish smirk before going in for the kill.

If he hadn't just admitted to that, I'd think he was a liar. I kind of still did because the way he worked my body with his tongue set me on fire. I clutched at his hair, bucking my hips against his mouth as he lapped at me while flicking his tongue. It was like a cord was tightening within me, my spine tingled as he brought me closer to release. When the cord snapped, I squeezed my eyes shut, writhing and shouting his name.

As I came back to reality, Mick swept me up in his arms before tossing back the covers of the bed and lying me down. He crawled in, folding his arms around me as I rested my head against his chest, savoring the comfort of him while my breathing evened out. He stroked my hair absently, his heart beating steadily against my ear.

"I don't know what to do." His voice was distant like he'd been thinking out loud. I pulled back to look at him. "I don't have control of the situation anymore. It makes me feel reckless. I'm not sure what the next move should be."

"Do you think they'll catch up to us?" I knew how Cory operated because I'd witnessed his OCD tendencies and methodical behavior. He was smart, albeit an asshole with a temper, but cunning when he needed to be. For all we knew they were hot on our heels.

Mick's throat rolled in a swallow as his fingers tangled in the ends of my hair. "Ricky doesn't know about the house even though he worked for me. He's Dom's cousin."

"The guy who helped you kill Bianca?"

He nodded. "Yeah, he's been a good friend of mine for years. I can trust Dom, which is why I let Ricky in the business in the first place. However, he hadn't proved his worth. I pissed him off by calling him out on it. He wanted more money or something so he went after me. He got to Mackaela first."

He'd said before she was off limits, yet he brought her up so easily now. Maybe he really was falling for me, trusting me with more of the things he held dear in his life.

"He went after her to hurt you," I guessed.

"Not exactly." He scratched at the stubble along his jaw. "She got in the way, so he decided he'd take her hostage, or at least try to. That's when Simon showed up and got shot." His eyes closed as pain etched into his features. When he opened them again they were full of a thousand emotions. His voice was thick as he continued. "I saw him on the ground, blood pouring out of his body as Mackaela knelt beside him trying like hell to stop the bleeding. He begged me to help him. Told me he didn't want to die."

"Ricky got away," I said.

Mick snorted. "Yeah, the coward took off after he fired the round. He left Mack behind. Things would probably be a lot different if he'd taken her. He'd be dead by now because I would have stopped at nothing to save her. I haven't been able to track him after all this time. After seeing my brother that way, almost losing him when I'd only just had him in my life, filled me with the need to make Delgado pay. It's all I've been focused on since."

I propped my head up with my hand, looking at him. "You care a lot about her." You'd think it would be difficult to hear about another woman, someone he allowed to know his heart and so obviously loved, but it wasn't. In fact, seeing a different side to him, this softer side was altogether unique and fascinating.

"I love her," he said with conviction. "I met her when I was fifteen years old. She's lived a rough life, and the idiot I was dragged her down with me when I thought I was helping her. If it weren't for my brother coming along to give her something to believe in, who knows how she'd be now. She's better than ever, so I'm glad he could help her when I couldn't."

"Why isn't he in the business like you are?"

"We have different mothers. He's a few months older than me which is really weird when you think about it. My father fucked around a lot apparently. I was raised by my dad while Simon was raised by his mother. I was alienated from him by my father."

My brow crumpled. Jack Silver was a piece of shit. That's what Cory always said, which on that one fact I actually agreed. With my free hand, I trailed a finger over Mick's chest in slow circles. "Why would he do that?" Maybe he already knew Cory's secret.

He shrugged. "It turned out to all be a misunderstanding, I guess. He thought Simon was living it up with a rich step-dad, that he didn't need him or me. Turns out that wasn't the case at all. Last year after he served time, Simon sought me out."

"How did your dad react to that? I imagine Simon was angry at him for not being involved in his life and for keeping you out of it."

Mick let out a heavy sigh, rolling over me until he was situated between my legs. "I don't want to talk about my family. We'll stay here tonight and head back to the house tomorrow." His lips hovered above mine, his breath warming my face.

My heart hammered in my chest as I felt him harden against me. He let out a low groan that gave me goosebumps.

"Can we forget about everything for tonight? All I want to do is get lost in you."

My body loved the sound of that but my mind was spinning. There were things I knew involving Jack Silver. Namely what Cory was hiding. It made me feel like a traitor for not telling Mick the truth.

What did it say about me as a person that I'd intentionally fail to mention something important because it didn't outweigh my own need to escape reality? He'd opened up to me, yet I couldn't bring myself to share this important piece of information. When he found out, would he blame me? If I didn't tell him before Cory, would my knowing already cause Mick to lose what little trust he had in me?

I tried to tamp down the anxiety steadily building. He must have caught on to it because he lifted his head, pinning me with a concerned look.

"What's wrong?"

Shaking my head, I wrapped my arm around his neck, drawing his lips down to mine. "I want to get lost, too."

Chapter 12

Claire

Things had shifted between me and Mick. I wasn't sure if it was the events that took place at the cabin, the newfound intimacy, or both that had me feeling some type of way. All I knew was that I felt different about him. Cory's secret went from the back of my mind to front and center. It nagged at me, causing a fear that was different from before. I wasn't so much afraid that Cory would kill me because how could he reach me now? It was more the dread of what the truth would do to Mick. He'd likely be angry and while I didn't want to be on his bad side, it was the potential damage I'd trigger that gave me pause. The thought of being the bearer of bad news after what he'd confessed to me had my heart at war with my mind.

After checking out of the hotel Mick stopped at a drive-thru for coffee and breakfast. I wasn't really hungry but forced myself to eat most of a muffin. He was being unnaturally quiet which didn't sit well with me. I'm sure he had just as much on his mind as I did, if not more, but I was kind of hoping he'd pull me out of my negative thoughts.

Part of the anxiety his silence caused was from him checking the rear view mirror constantly as well as tensing when vehicles passed us on the highway. There was this air of worry surrounding him that I wasn't used to seeing. Mick was always confident about everything. Witnessing this cautious side of him forced my own feelings of uncertainty to bubble to the surface.

Once we arrived back at the house, he mumbled something about making calls before heading downstairs so I retreated to my room to shower. I wondered if he was going to ask around about the secret Cory was keeping. He'd have to give up his revenge on Ricky Delgado for it which was a decision he wouldn't make lightly. One of the things I'd learned about him in our short time together was that he rarely quit. The guilt continued eating away at me as I cleaned myself up, taking a lot longer than necessary.

The night I found out about Cory's secret, we were drinking at one of his friend's houses. They were passing around a joint while I was sitting in a chair staring at the TV screen. An old episode of *SpongeBob SquarePants* was on. At the time, I felt that was more entertaining to watch than being involved in the drug related conversations around me.

"Silver's going to get what's coming to him one of these days. I know a guy that's looking to take over an area in south Oregon and eventually steal Washington," Cory had said before taking a large hit from the blunt between his fingers.

"No shit?" his friend Billy Bobby or something asked. "You gonna quit on him?"

Cory shrugged, passing the joint to Billy Bobby. "Maybe. Mickey Silver needs to be knocked down from his pedestal. He's a prick like his dad. Fucking murdering bastard." He growled.

Billy Bobby snorted. "Murder?"

"Yeah, Jack Silver killed my mom." He'd sounded so nonchalant about the admission. I'd wondered if it was due to the effects of the joint.

I'd whipped my head in his direction, gaping at him. Billy Bobby sat up straight. "What the hell?"

Cory glared at the television, his jaw tightening. "Apparently my mom got pregnant by the bastard so she tried to abort the baby. She chickened out, I guess, so when the kid was born she told Jack to handle it. He kept the kid and ghosted her. A few years later when I was four, he came back. Called her a bitch before shooting her right in front of me."

My hand flew to my mouth as I gasped. Cory's gaze snapped to mine, his eyes narrowing to slits. "He thought she was running her mouth about him. Telling people he had her kid. He capped her for being a big mouth. At least that's what my dad said." He reached for me, gripping the back of my neck. "You tell anyone about this, I'll kill you. Understand?"

I nodded as he shoved me back in the chair.

"Turns out she wasn't saying anything at all. He only did her in because she said she wanted the kid back. Wanted to make amends so she could spend time with him." He shrugged. "Got killed for loving her other son."

"Dude." Billy Bobby stared at him stunned. "You're saying ...
"

Cory chuckled darkly. "Mickey Silver's my half-brother. I'm going to make him and his dad pay for what happened to my mom."

Mick

"There's some secret Wilson has. I need to know what he's keeping."

"Does your girl know what it might be?" Dom asked.

"She's not *my* girl," I growled. He snorted.

"Whatever you say, man. I saw that mark on her neck. You seriously telling me you didn't tap that when you've had her locked away this entire time?"

"Watch it," I warned in a threatening voice. "Why do you care?"

Dom chuckled. "Gee, man, I don't know. Maybe because you've had a thing for her since the first time you saw her. Mack called it last year. We knew you of all people would end up falling for someone you could never have." I scowled.

"This is off topic. Back to the task at hand," I said. "Have you heard any rumors on Wilson?"

"Nope. Whatever he's keeping is locked up tight. He doesn't have many close friends, you know that. The only people who might know what he's hiding is the girl or Billy Franklin. Bill's in county doing time for a B&E gone bad."

I muttered a curse. That wouldn't help me. Delgado claimed I'd call off my plans if I knew whatever Cory had to say. I didn't like being left to react when I heard it directly from him. Being caught by surprise usually ended up with me overreacting. Case in point, what happened to Bianca and deciding to ransom Claire. I'd already asked her about what he was hiding and she'd said she didn't know. It was possible she was lying to me to protect Cory.

That thought made my stomach hurt. After bitching out by telling her how I felt about her, I'd be a mess if she betrayed me. I hated how right my friends were when it came to her. I had noticed her last year, watched her everywhere she went when she was around. I'd always been hopelessly distracted when it came to her.

That didn't matter right now. What mattered was coming up with a plan.

"See if you can't get more information," I told Dom. "Do you have a visual on Delgado yet?"

"Not exactly. I just got word from someone that he was found dead this morning."

My spine stiffened. "What the fuck?"

Dom blew out a breath. "He was capped, Mick. Someone took him out and we don't know why. The strangest part is that he was in fact in Canada, which means—"

"He was telling the truth," I mumbled as the memory of what I'd done to Bianca came back. A violent wave of nausea rolled through me. Pinching the bridge of my nose, I inhaled deep, releasing the breath in a rush of air. "I need to call Hawks. See if he can grab Wilson if he's available." There was a chance Wilson called for a hit on Delgado. Although he couldn't have known about him informing me of whatever secret he had.

After hanging up with Dom, I called Hawks who answered immediately which caught me off guard. For being totally unavailable the last week, he sure was present now. I didn't know what to make of that.

"Hey, Silver."

"Done with the cartel business?" I asked, plopping into one of the arm chairs in the office downstairs.

"Yeah, Jack's with me. We're heading up the coast."

"I need you to do something for me. Cory Wilson's in Portland somewhere or so I hear. Track him down, but don't let him know you're there yet."

"You still on that? Don't you have his woman?"

My nostrils flared as a kernel of anger sprouted in my gut. She wasn't *his,* either. "Yeah, although apparently he no longer cares. Delgado claimed Wilson's got some secret I want to know."

Hawk's snorted. "What is this, high school? Why are you even wasting your time, Mick? I heard Delgado isn't an issue anymore. Now you can walk away like you want to."

Well that was awfully ballsy of him. "Are you telling me how to do my job?" I bit out. "Last I checked it's *Silver* Enterprises. I call the shots here. I do what *I* want."

He heaved a sigh. "Yeah, I know. I'm just saying, leave Wilson to me. He ain't getting the turf. Are you letting the girl go?"

"Not yet. I killed Bianca Rogers and now Ricky's dead, too. I'm not going to throw her out with the chance of someone harming her."

"Why would you care if that stripper gets offed? She's just a pawn," he snapped.

Okay, that wasn't just ballsy of him, it was downright sense-less. Who the fuck did he think he was suddenly? I bit back on my molars, quelling the urge to lay into him. "She's innocent," I said. "We don't need any more bloodshed."

"As long as she doesn't run her mouth once you release her. I'll take care of Wilson."

"Is that a threat?" I growled, unable to contain the rage that festered with his statement.

Hawks snorted. "Calm down, Silver. I'm sure she knows better than to talk."

I didn't know how to respond to that so I let it go for now. If he so much as joked about shutting her up again, I'd deck him in the face and kick him in the balls before shooting him. "Keep me updated on Wilson. I can't really make a move right now when I don't know what this secret is. If you figure it out, contact me im-mediately."

"Yep," was the only response I got before he disconnected the call.

It didn't sit right with me that he promised to take care of Wil-son. Knowing he was with my father right now had me wondering if they had their own intentions that I wasn't privy to. I was dip-ping out on my own but I didn't want to be phased out by some arrogant prick like Hawks. Especially when I wasn't entirely sure anymore where his loyalties lie.

Why was I allowing Delgado to make me question everything? Maybe that was his plan, throw me off to confuse the hell out of me. But then, who killed him? Everything was quickly falling apart after all my careful planning.

Ricky was dead, Wilson was likely somewhere in Portland, and we were smack dab in the middle of them with fuck all going on. I needed to clear my head, needed to get away for a minute. I wouldn't leave Claire alone though. Hopefully, she was up for a little adventure. One that for once had nothing to do with the business.

*

Claire was still in her room with the door closed by the time I'd showered and made my way upstairs. I approached her door cautiously, rapping my knuckles a few times. When she opened the door, my heart stopped. Like literally ceased to beat when her violet eyes collided with mine.

I'd slept with her last night in a way I'd never done before other than with Mackaela, although that was different. Sharing a bed with Mack was like sharing a bed with a sister. Holding Claire through the night, skin to skin, then waking up with her head on my chest, was as sweet as claiming her body.

She looked amazing in a hot pink t-shirt that fell off one shoulder showcasing her trim waist. It was paired with denim shorts that hugged her thighs perfectly. God damn, I was sprung on her. My body immediately wanted to explore all the skin I could see. It took everything in me to focus back on her face while resisting the temptation.

"Busy?" I examined the loose waves of her hair cascading over her chest.

"No." Her brow creased. "What could, I possibly be doing? There's nothing here for me."

My lips tilted up on one side as I leaned against the door frame, crossing my arms. I was itching to touch her, but I knew if that happened, I wouldn't be able to stop.

"Good point. You want to do something?"

Her gaze slid from mine as she bit down on her bottom lip. I stifled a groan. Could she be any sexier? She wasn't even trying yet I was standing here salivating like a wolf stalking its prey. I didn't miss the way her cheeks flushed as she looked me up and down. Yeah, she wanted me, too. That made my chest swell with an emotion I wasn't ready to entertain. She wasn't mine and she never could be. Even if I was falling for her, I knew it was wrong.

"What do you have in mind?"

I cocked a brow. "Do you trust me?"

She scoffed. "Are you serious?" I gave her a wide grin. I was glad she didn't say yes. I'd be questioning her sanity.

"Grab some shoes. We roll out in ten minutes." I headed back downstairs to grab my wallet and keys.

There was a pretty cool little spot a few miles away that was secluded enough I wouldn't have to watch our backs, yet open enough to ease the stifled feeling. That was one of the things I'd been struggling with when I thought about leaving the business. What exactly was I going to do with myself? Be all domesticated or some crazy shit like that? I snorted to myself at the thought. Mickey Silver wrapped up in a woman with a mortgage or possibly even a family? Hell would have to freeze over before that ever happened.

I stumbled up the stairs as an image flashed in my mind of Claire standing in a white dress, her hair done up all fancy with a dreamy smile on her cherry colored lips. I screwed my eyes shut for a moment.

What the actual fuck was that? Nope. No way was that happening. I didn't love her. I couldn't. I'd only destroy her life while also obliterating mine in the process because I'd ruin her and I would never forgive myself. She deserved someone who was stable in life. Someone who could go anywhere without feeling paranoid. I'd never be able to give her anything normal with all the trappings of some Disney movie. That's what she fucking deserved.

She was waiting for me in the living room with a pair of running sneakers on her feet. I made my way for the door with her following behind me.

She was surprisingly quiet as I pulled out of the gates, hanging a right. Maybe she was having doubts after last night or maybe being out like this scared her.

"We're safe," I said, fumbling with the stereo as I turned off the main drive, heading down a back road.

She turned to look at me. "How do you know that?"

Licking my lips, I said, "I talked to one of my guys. Delgado is dead and Hawks is headed for Cory in Oregon."

Her sharp intake of breath made me glance at her. "What is he going to do with Cory?" she asked.

"I'm actually not sure," I replied honestly. "I don't like that I'm being left out of it."

She nodded. "Did you find out what his secret is?"

I stopped messing with the stereo, leaving it on a slow rock song. "No. You sure you don't know what it is?"

"No." Her voice was quiet.

"Let's not talk about business right now. We're taking the day off." Cranking the stereo, I rolled down my window to let the warm breeze flow through the cab.

Every once in a while I'd glance over to see Claire's hair flapping wildly in the wind as she sang the lyrics to a few of the songs that played. I could be happy with her if I didn't feel like she'd be settling. I wouldn't mind being around her every day like we'd been the last week. That was new for me. While the thought of commitment didn't necessarily scare me when it came to her, the worry of how much I'd hold her back did.

The rest of our drive was quiet other than the music. As I pulled into the empty parking lot near Trailhead Pass, I felt a small amount of weight lift from my shoulders. It had been a while since I'd come here. I missed the seclusion and serenity the area allowed. I pivoted in my seat to look at Claire as she studied the trees surrounding us.

"Where are we?"

"I don't like sitting around. I'm not used to it so it makes me anxious. When I've got the time, I like to disappear for a while. This is my favorite place to do that."

"I didn't really take you for the outdoorsy type." Her lips twitched. I glared at her playfully.

"Prepare to be amazed. Come on." I met her at the front of the vehicle. After locking it up, I stuck my keys in my front pocket before reaching for her hand. To my surprise, she actually let me take it.

We wandered toward a sparse line of trees as I led her toward an old trail that very few knew about. I inhaled the scent of pine and rich soil, feeling more of the heaviness dissipate. Despite what she thought, I loved being outside. I used to go camping with friends when I was a teenager but then once I got more into the business, I didn't have the time. I missed the feeling of the cool breeze against my skin, the sounds of birds and insects as I wandered aimlessly. Sometimes I'd camp on my own, simply sitting in peace with a small fire and good scotch.

We continued on the trail in silence for a while until the sound of rushing water filled the canopy of pine trees. I released a breath, or maybe it was a sigh of relief as we broke through the clearing.

It was just like I remembered even though it'd been a few years since I'd last been here. Bridal Falls ran down a cliff that sat about twenty feet above us. It fell fast into a small pond that was maybe ten feet wide. Claire released my hand before stepping over a large boulder to get closer to the shallow creek beyond the pond. It traveled underground toward the river.

I watched her explore with a smile ghosting my lips. My chest swelled as she crouched down, dipping her hand in the water. She seemed to be in her element, too. That sparked a sense of pride and happiness in the hollowest parts of my chest.

"Seeing as you're from a small landlocked town, I'm guessing this is new to you," I said as I made my way over to her.

She glanced up at me still swirling her hand in the water. "We have the Methow river that runs near town. It's good for floating and fishing. There's far less trees or greenery though." I nodded, crouching beside her. "It's hotter there, too. I like it here."

"I used to camp in the area sometimes with my friends. There's a campground a few miles away." I glanced up at the top of the waterfall, squinting against the sun.

Standing, I skirted the side of the pond heading toward a secret place I'd discovered one of the last times I was here. Gently moving a few branches to the side, I disappeared behind it, taking in the dark granite that naturally formed a shallow cave. The stagnant air made it warmer behind the flowing water. I stepped forward, bracing my hand on the rock as I closed my eyes.

Why did Hawks suddenly seem so eager to hunt down Cory Wilson? Why was he so challenging on the phone earlier? It didn't make sense for my father to phase me out, yet I couldn't help thinking about that possibility now. I'd told him I wanted to make things right for Simon with Delgado and he'd all but literally kissed my ass about it. He said I made him proud, that he appreciated my follow through. Maybe he'd been lying.

At the time, it felt good because impressing my dad was what I strived for. It's all I'd ever cared about. Though I'd gotten Mackaela out of the business and didn't let Simon get roped in too far in the first place, leaving it behind myself made me feel guilty. Like I'd be letting my father down. Seeing how much better both of their lives were was the kick in the ass I needed. There was no doubt in my mind that it was time to move on regardless of Jack Silver thought.

Although telling him I wanted to quit had troubled me to the point that I'd spent an entire month trying to figure out the best way to broach the subject with him. Once I'd finally given him the news he'd been cool about it, told me to just make sure I tied up loose ends. I was relieved and also surprised at how well he'd taken my resignation.

Hawks wanted to know why I wasn't walking away yet. To be honest, I'd been asking myself the same question since last night. I'd killed Bianca which was as close to the law of retaliation you could get. Plus, Ricky Delgado was dead now, so the entire premise of my original vendetta had been resolved.

Ricky's confidence in my reaction to learning Wilson's secret still gnawed at me. For all I knew he was just trying to mess with my head. However, Dom had proof the guy was across the border. He hadn't lied. Something told me that of all things to be dishonest about, where he was would have been it, not this secret.

Claire's sneakers squeaked on the rocky floor as she joined me behind the waterfall. I lifted my head, glancing at her over my shoulder. "Would I be less of a man for walking away now?" The words tumbled out at the sight of her honest eyes. I clenched my fist against the granite, frustrated that I was so easily vulnerable around her.

She stopped a few feet from me, twisting her long hair to one side. "Sometimes revenge feels necessary in theory but it's better served by walking away."

I snorted, turning around fully. "Okay, Confucius, that's not the response I was looking for. You sound like Mackaela."

She lifted her shoulder in a slight shrug. "She's a smart woman then. You want to know if I'd think less of you? I wouldn't. This Delgado guy is dead now. I know you don't want Cory taking over your turf, I get it. If someone were trying to steal from me, I'd probably want to mess them up, too. However, that doesn't make it right. You already took one life—"

"Don't!" I barked, my shoulders tightening. "Please don't talk about what happened to Bianca."

She stared at me with contempt. "You killed her out of anger. She paid for a crime she didn't commit just like Simon almost had."

Frustration flooded my veins and my body shook as I stalked toward her, not stopping until she had to tilt her head back to look at me. "She was still a mule, Claire. Do you know how many women disappeared under her care? How many missing posters are hung up around the entire city for girls that won't ever come back?"

Shaking her head, she opened her mouth to argue. I cut her off. "No! Some of those girls were as young as sixteen. I wish I'd known sooner, done something about it then."

"How can you justify taking a life?" she protested. "A *woman's* life at that. You could have turned her into the police."

Yeah that's what I was struggling with. I'd never hurt a woman in the past. I *should* have turned her into the cops. I shouldn't have been the one to end her, even if Bianca Rogers was no saint. She was trying to groom women, including my sweet Claire who didn't deserve any of what lay ahead. Who knows what would have happened if I hadn't intervened when I did. However, I wasn't thinking straight at the time. I'd had tunnel vision since finding out I might finally get Delgado. Everything was a mess now but it all boiled down to one simple fact: I couldn't take any of it back. Dwelling on it would only weaken me further. I was already struggling to stay afloat with whatever I was feeling for this clever woman standing in front of me.

"A *woman* who wasn't looking out for other women. What is it with you and the cops? I couldn't turn her in because it would be my word against hers. At the very least, I'd be labeled a nark. Come on, Claire, you're smarter than that."

"What about you?" she asked, her voice rising over the rushing water. "What happens if you're the one that dies at the end of all this?"

"Then I die. Then I go out knowing I tried. That I avenged my brother, my blood." It's not like I was in a hurry to face death. I'd simply do whatever it took to make sure Simon and Mackaela were safe. That they wouldn't have to watch their backs in fear of someone hiding in the shadows.

"Okay." She squared her shoulders, thrusting her hands on her hips. "Then what about me?"

Confusion swept over me as I raised a brow. "What about you?"

Her features smoothed slightly, the anger turning to something else. Fear mingled with apprehension in her gaze. "If something happens to you then what will I do? Where will I go?"

Well now I felt like the biggest piece of shit to walk the planet. Closing my eyes, I pinched the bridge of my nose. When I opened them again her head was bowed, her arms circling her waist. I placed my index finger under her chin, tilting her head up to look at me.

"You can go wherever you want. Wherever you were planning on going when all this is over. You'll do whatever it is you wanted to do before. You don't need me for that."

"I don't want you dead. I ... don't want to say goodbye to you."

She blinked up at me like a wounded puppy I'd just kicked across a football field. I'd never hated myself more than I did right then. She cared. She actually gave a shit about me, and even though she didn't admit to it last night, her actions said everything. I needed to send her off before I broke her heart or caused so much damage it was irreparable.

"Claire ... " I wasn't sure what to say. I didn't want to hurt her but there was no way I'd be able to tie myself down. Not until this business was handled, maybe not even after that. I wanted to be free to live my life, but I couldn't be responsible for someone else's heart when I barely had one of my own.

"You can't tell me you don't feel a connection between us. That you want me to walk away from you after confessing to falling for me."

I ran a hand through my hair, releasing a heavy sigh. "I told you that because I can't seem to shut up around you. Yes, it's true, that doesn't mean anything. It can't."

"Bullshit," she snapped. The anger was back with a vengeance yet there was an underlying sadness in her glare as well.

"Listen, I like you. I mean I *really* like you," I said. "Still, whatever we have now can never go any farther than this. I'm no good for you. Do you understand?"

A flash of agony filled her eyes as she closed them, taking a step back from me. When she opened them again they were laced with unshed tears. "You're an asshole."

I huffed out a laugh. "Yeah, I am. I've admitted that already. Clearly, you have zero issue frequently reminding me. It's not news, cupcake, however I'm not going to sugar coat the truth. I'm not going to stand here making empty promises to you when neither of us know what's going to happen tomorrow. I could die. You could die. The whole world could get bombed."

A growl of fury rumbled from her chest. I wasn't sure if I should be worried or totally turned on. Honestly, I was a little of both.

"That's a cop-out, Mick. You're just a coward. You don't want to face the fact that eventually you'll let someone in. That you'll have to risk the pain that might come once your defenses are down. You know, for a badass, gun toting, drug boss you sure are soft."

My mouth fell open as a wave of shock and irritation consumed me. Who the hell did she think she was talking to?

Clenching my jaw, I glowered down at her. "I am *not* soft. I'm Mickey fucking Silver so you better watch your mouth when you talk to me or I'm going to—"

"Cut my tongue out?" she spat. "Yeah, I know. What about *those* empty promises? You won't do a single thing and do you know why?" I didn't say anything. I couldn't. God this woman had balls as big as mine. "You. Need. Me."

I stared at her in disbelief. Need her? I didn't need anyone. Was she clinically insane? "Newsflash, you're of no use to me anymore. I'm only letting you stay with me to keep you safe," I ground out, my chest bumping hers. She didn't budge which had me wavering between kissing her or abandoning her here to teach her a lesson.

"Liar!" she shouted, not backing down. She stood on her tip-toes nearly matching my height. "You also want someone to talk to. Someone to confide in. You won't admit it because you're afraid to appear fragile, but you need me."

"What I *need* is for you to stop talking. I *want* you." I lifted my hand, grasping the side of her neck and lowering my lips just above hers. "I want you really bad, Claire. Always. I don't need you. You're not giving air to my lungs or pumping blood to my heart. You're not nourishment for me in any way. I can live without you." I brushed my lips against hers once, twice. "You don't need me, either. Hell, you probably don't even want me yet here you are because you're a nice girl. Even with that foul mouth and tough exterior, I know deep down you're a saint compared to me and every other miserable waste of life you've befriended."

I remained still with my mouth so close to hers I could taste her sweetness, but I wasn't going to move. She could admit defeat and choose to walk away with her tail between her legs, or she could step up to the plate and prove to me how much I supposedly needed her. I'd welcome her putting me in my place, so when her trembling fingers slid over my stomach then up to my chest, I smirked. She was about to teach me a lesson and I was so fucking here for it.

Chapter 13

Claire

This ridiculous man had taken me as a hostage, used me for personal gain, and completely stripped me bare. I was an absolute wreck in his presence. Nothing made sense anymore. One minute we were at each other's throats then the next I was pressed against the warm stone as he devoured my mouth like a man who'd just relinquished priesthood. It was maddening and intoxicating and every single time resistance was futile. Especially when he ran his tongue along my neck while fisting the hair at the back of my head.

I rolled my hips against him, moaning as my head fell back. My legs wrapped around his waist as my hands roamed over his chest and shoulders. His hand slid along my thigh, fingers dipping into the hem of my shorts. He lifted his head with a growl that turned me on further.

"These shorts are tight. You're gonna have to lose them."

I was so not about to toss my shorts somewhere inside this cave. Shimmying down his body, I undid the button and zipper before sliding my shorts and panties down to my knees. I grabbed a handful of his rock hard cock, squeezing lightly when he pressed against my hand.

"Damn," he groaned.

Releasing him, I turned abruptly to plant my hands on the stone in front of me. I glanced back at him over my shoulder, raising a brow. "Better?"

"That'll work," he muttered before reaching out to grab my hip, pulling me into him.

He'd already made quick work of freeing himself. When I felt him slide along my center from behind, I bit down on my lip. He entered me slowly, his fingers flexing against my hips, keeping me in place. Seconds later, he was thrusting into me from behind. The small cave filled with our vigorous grunts and moans as we moved together, punishing the other while seeking release. One of his hands slid in front of me to lightly grip my throat as he lowered his lips to my ear.

"I lied," he groaned when I lifted up on my toes. "I need you. I need this body. I want to fuck it and hold it and worship it for the rest of my life."

I glanced back at him with a smirk. "Careful, Silver, I might hold you to that." He started moving faster, gripping me tight as I lost what little control I had. My body tightened as the orgasm rocked through me. I convulsed in his arms as he shuddered behind me, finding his own release and pulling out quickly.

Neither of us moved for a few minutes as our breathing regulated. I readjusted my clothing, tugging my shorts up to fasten them again. When I turned around Mick was staring at me with a peculiar expression. Suddenly, he grabbed my face with both hands before kissing me. I was breathless and dizzy when he pulled back to rest his forehead against mine.

"I want out. I swear to God, I do," he murmured. "But I can't walk away quite yet."

"Okay." I could see the war waging in his mind through those hazel eyes. He was wrong about needing me earlier but he was right, too.

Mickey Silver didn't rely on others to get the job done. He was a one man show that made shit happen. There was something admirable about his tenacity and endurance. I found myself appreciating him in a different way. Beneath the façade he had a good soul, a bleeding heart. What had he said the other day? That his heart bled for few, yet he cared. He was guarded, cautious, and he had every right to be. I felt even worse for harboring this secret of Cory's. Still, I was afraid of what would happen once he knew the truth.

Selfishly I didn't want to ruin this moment because he was baring himself to me in a way I never expected. I wanted to soak up as much as I could. I kept the doubts locked up tight, ignoring them when he reached for my hand again.

I held on to him, allowing him to lead us out from behind the waterfall. I didn't let go until we made our way further up the trail deeper into the woods. There was a fallen tree that he sat down on before running a hand through his hair. I was beginning to learn that was a nervous habit of his.

I took a seat beside him, plucking at the long grass surrounding us. It was so peaceful out here in the middle of nowhere. The trees acted as a blanket, keeping us out of sight as if we were in our own little world. It wasn't a single planed valley like back home. I found I preferred this environment with the smell of rich earth and wildflowers.

We were both silent for a while, taking in the scenery. There was a peace with him that I'd never felt. When Mick finally spoke, his voice was soft.

"I've been in the business so long that sometimes I worry if I can survive with a normal lifestyle. Since I was young I looked up to my father, I did whatever I could to prove I'd be an asset working for him. He'd have me run little odd jobs after I turned sixteen, then when I was eighteen, he offered me half of the business. Said I had clout and wouldn't let him down."

I tried to imagine Mick as a teenager. I wondered if he'd ever really had a chance to be a kid. When I was sixteen, I was dancing with friends in high school. I didn't know what I wanted to be or where I'd go in life. I didn't care at all, yet here he was preparing to take on an empire. I felt sorry for him.

"That's what you wanted?" I asked. He kicked at a buried rock with his left foot.

"I thought it was. At the time, I was eager to start working. Plus there were other motivations as well." He tilted his head toward the sky. "Mackaela was in a real bad situation with her mom. I got my own apartment at seventeen, so I had her move in with me. I felt like I needed to protect her, to keep her safe. I guess in a way I felt responsible for her. After she was ... " He released a breath shaking his head. "I owed her because I wasn't there when I should have been." He glanced at me again.

"Working for my dad was incredibly lucrative. By the time I was nineteen I'd bought a house and was running my own office downtown. At that point, I was just in it, you know? I couldn't really walk away nor did I want to. I had money, cars, women, a nice place to rest my head."

"That's quite an accomplishment at that age," I said. Honestly, I couldn't blame him. If I'd been handed power and money at that age I may have done the same.

"Yeah, except I never felt fulfilled or happy. Once Simon came around, after I found out what he'd been through, I began to feel guilty about my life compared to his. We bonded quickly and seeing things from his perspective changed me. Mackaela's mom died during that time, as well. He was there for her when I should have been. She was hurting, going through her own issues while I was too busy making sure our supply was flawless and steadily distributed. My focus was misplaced which kills me to this day. I chose the business every time over her."

Unsure of what to say, I placed my hand on his knee. He stared down at it like it was the most peculiar creature he'd ever seen. I didn't move. "It's okay to feel guilt. Though I'm betting she still loves you and forgives you."

He nodded. "I still hate myself for it." I frowned. "If Simon hadn't been there for her I don't know what would've happened."

"She's better now though, right? They're together."

A smile ghosted his lips as he nodded. "He's perfect for her. Loves her unconditionally and thinks they were meant to be together." I smiled, too.

"That's sweet."

He shrugged. "If you believe in that stuff."

"You've never wanted someone enough to be their only one? Never felt a connection you couldn't ignore?" Personally, I hadn't really felt that way, either, though I'd dated a few guys in the past. I was always monogamous even when I knew Cory had messed around on me. Relationships were a lot of work.

"It's funny, Mackaela asked me something similar once. At the time, I told her it never happened for me, that it probably never would. Now ... " He trailed off.

My heart leapt to my throat. "Now?"

His hazel eyes locked on mine as he grabbed the hand that was on his knee to interlace our fingers. "You radiate this warmth like you're thawing me out. There's something about you that makes me more open. I don't mind it as much as I thought I would. I can't really explain it."

Wow! I was shocked he'd admitted that to me. Especially after our fight earlier. There was a tightness in my chest near my heart.

"I don't believe in soul mates or destiny. However, I think you can be drawn to someone and click," he added.

"You think we click?" My voice came out in a hushed whisper as my heart thudded against my ribs.

His grin was wide, eyes sparkling. "Definitely. You're cool as hell and you don't take shit. I dig it. Plus, you're damn pretty so that's a bonus."

I couldn't help but laugh at his enthusiasm. "Thanks, you're not so bad, either. I mean, while I still kind of hate you, I'm finding you to be a lot more tolerable than I originally thought."

He bit down on his bottom lip, frowning slightly. "I'll take it. I'm sorry that I dragged you into this mess with me." Something told me he didn't apologize often so hearing that meant more to me than admitting he thought we clicked.

"What are you going to do once this is over?" Part of me was worried about his answer, but I was also curious. Especially when he mentioned not being sure if he could live without the business.

He absently trailed his index finger over my palm with our hands still laced together. "I'm honestly not sure. Me and Simon have the shop. My heart isn't in it like his is though. I might like to travel or something. Vacations haven't really been a priority with everything I've had going on. What about you, what's your plan?"

"Now that I'll have the money, I'd like to go to another town or even a different state. I know I don't want to go back to Winthrop. Maybe I'd go somewhere less populated than Seattle. I like this, the trees and nature."

"What about work? Was *Rosie's* the career path you wanted?"

I immediately began shaking my head. "No. I never really enjoyed that even though I do love dancing. Maybe I could have my own studio someday."

His lips kicked up. "Yeah, that'd be cool."

We ended up talking until the sun began to fall behind the trees and a cool breeze picked up. Mick grabbed my hand as we headed back to the car. It was nice to just hang out with him, talking about nothing and everything. I felt like I knew him better. It was incredible how quickly someone could move from a stranger to a friend, or whatever we were to each other now. You'd think it was weird because we'd only spent just over a week together, but I couldn't deny the connection I felt to Mick. It's like he said, we just clicked.

The clarity was welcome after everything that had happened the last week and a half. Although the closer we got to the house, I felt a darkness creeping in that filled me with the anxiety I'd brushed aside. Cory's secret was weighing heavily as if a ton of bricks were on my chest.

Once it was revealed, everything would change. The fear of losing Mick was something I wasn't ready to experience yet, if ever. As if it were written in the stars, the sky lit up with a bright streak of lightning before thunder crashed around us when he pulled into the driveway.

A storm was brewing and while I wasn't sure what side I'd end up on, I knew without a single doubt that it was time to face the truth. I had to tell him before he found out from Cory or one of his business associates. Maybe coming from me it wouldn't be as cruel. Or maybe he'd take back everything he'd said this afternoon.

The risk was worth it though because I cared about him. Putting his feelings before mine would be the most selfless thing I'd ever done. Even if it hurt like a bitch, likely obliterating whatever new feelings we'd developed, it was my turn to share a confession.

Mick

After our getaway to Trailhead Pass, I found myself growing more attached to Claire. I both loved and hated the way my heart raced when she entered the room or sat next to me on the couch. I kept touching her in ways I shouldn't, like stroking her cheek or playing with her hair. A few days ago, I'd crawled into her bed just to hold her until we both fell asleep. I was a completely different person with her than I had been in the past. There was something about her that brought on a level of comfort I'd never experienced. It was as if we belonged together or something. Maybe all the romantic shit Simon spouted about Mackaela was starting to rub off on me, or maybe I was simply losing my mind.

We had this weird almost domesticated routine over the next week due to the stalemate between me and the bastard who was trying to steal the business. I hadn't heard a word from Hawks other than he was in Portland, trailing Cory Wilson.

I didn't care aside from learning whatever he was hiding from me. Once I had the information, I'd walk away. I'd made up my mind for good yesterday as I lay on the couch cuddled up with Claire while we watched some movie I wasn't paying attention to.

She'd said she wasn't ready to say goodbye to me. While I knew the time would come to let her go, I just couldn't bring myself to do it quite yet. There wasn't really a reason to stay here anymore, but I was afraid that going back to Seattle would ruin this temporary bliss. I also worried her life might still be in danger because I still couldn't shake the feeling I was being misled intentionally. If there was another traitor in the business, one that knew I had her, would they use her against me?

There had to be a reason Hawks was interested in Cory Wilson. The only thing I could come up with was that it had to do with whatever secret he'd been keeping. I killed Bianca, and Ricky Delgado was dead, so I no longer worried about him. However, Wilson and Hawks? Yeah, I needed to figure that out.

I tipped the beer I'd been drinking to my lips, taking a healthy swig. Claire sank onto the sectional next to me before curling into my side. She seemed to do that a lot lately which I didn't mind at all. She'd also been uncharacteristically quiet since we'd gotten back from our outdoor adventure. I tried not to dwell on it. Whatever we were developing was delicate so I wouldn't be surprised if she were just as afraid as I was about her impending departure.

I tried bringing it up a few times but the conversation never lasted long. We'd either end up fucking or fighting or both. She said she didn't want to think about it. Honestly, neither did I. There would come a time we'd be forced apart though so I wanted to ensure her safety and have a structured plan in place.

"My mom's freaking out over the thought of me moving somewhere else besides Seattle," she said, picking at lint on her leggings.

I'd let her use the burner phone to contact her folks since we'd been in hiding the last two weeks. The last thing I wanted was word to get back to them that she'd been taken. I didn't want her family involved at all because that would likely put them in danger, too.

"What did you tell her?" I set my beer on the coffee table before folding an arm over her shoulder.

"That I quit the club and moved out of Bianca's. She knew I wasn't planning on doing that for long anyhow. When I said I'd like to go to another city instead of back home, she freaked out. She doesn't understand why I can't just be happy in Winthrop."

I slid my fingertips over her bare shoulder. "Why weren't you happy there?"

She released a breath, meeting my stare. "I always felt out of place back home. Like there was something else meant for me other than working at my mom's salon or marrying some small town guy. I like adventure, trying new things. It was ... suffocating."

I could definitely relate to that. Although my town was much larger, I knew practically everyone thanks to my line of work so it felt smaller. There was no place I could go without running into someone that knew me. I longed to go to a place where I could be a ghost.

"You still don't know where you'll go?"

She shook her head. "Not yet. I was thinking maybe Colorado or something. They have small towns I'm sure."

I quirked a brow. "Why there?"

She shrugged, tucking her hair behind her ear. "I don't know. I've just always wanted to go there. Thought it might be a cool place."

"I could see you owning a dance studio there, skiing on the weekends or curling up in front of a fireplace to read." The mental image popped in my head as a warmth spread through my chest. She'd be content. I wanted that for her more than anything.

"Yeah." She gave a tight smile. There was something else on her mind that she wasn't saying. I didn't want to press her because what good would it do? If it had to do with her future, I couldn't be a part of it anyway.

My hand drifted lower to her rib cage before trailing to her hip. I lifted the hem, sliding my thumb over her waist. She shivered beside me. I loved the way she responded to me. I angled my body toward her as I lifted my other hand to cup her cheek.

"I want that for you, to be happy, to move on from all this," I murmured, lowering my lips to the corner of her mouth. "You deserve it." I kissed her because I felt like it. Because lately she was the only thing that grounded me. When she wrapped her arms around my neck, I took the kiss deeper.

Before long, I had her lying back on the cushions as I settled between her legs. We were still dressed and I didn't care. I'd take her any way I could whether it led to sex or not. That was another first for me. Everything about her was so perfect. I reveled in the way she moaned as I rocked against her while my hands roamed over her body through the thin tank top she wore.

It had been a few days since I'd been able to feel her like this so I was taking advantage of the moment. She sat up to remove her shirt and I did the same. Guiding her back again, I dipped my hand into the waistband of her leggings, inching toward her center. She stiffened, grabbing my wrist. My eyes flew to her face as I frowned. She was blinking up at the ceiling with her lips turned down.

"Hey," I said, moving over her to meet her gaze. "What's wrong?"

She exhaled a shaky breath before shifting her focus to the back of the couch. "Nothing it's just ... there's something you should know."

The fire burning through me died the moment those words were uttered. "What are you not telling me?" I could see the apprehension in her eyes, the way they pooled with tears. A definite tell that whatever she had to say was critical.

Her lips parted as if she were going to speak. I held my breath, waiting for whatever it was. Her breath faltered when she inhaled, a single tear rolled down her cheek. I shook my head, squeezing my eyes shut.

"Rip the Band-Aid off. Jesus." I dragged a hand through my hair as I lifted myself off her. She sat up, folding her hands in her lap.

"Mick, it's not my secret to share."

My brows lifted. "What?" Realization hit me like a fucking semi-truck. She'd been lying to me. Disappointment mingled with the unease that had already sunk in. "You know the secret?" She didn't say anything. Instead, she reached for her shirt to pull it back on. "Answer me!" I demanded as my patience thinned with each passing second.

"It's Cory's." Her voice was so quiet, I nearly didn't hear her. "There's something about him you don't know. It's basically his entire driving force."

My forehead crumpled in confusion. "You're just *now* telling me this." Anger reared its ugly head as I curled my hands into fists.

I'd asked her not once, but several times if she knew what he was hiding, yet she denied it. If this was his driving force, I should have known about it weeks ago. If Delgado hadn't said anything, would she have even thought to bring it up? Why did I suddenly feel like I'd not only been stabbed in the back but also through the heart?

"I'm sorry. Like I said, it isn't my secret to share. Besides, I don't think he ever meant for me to know; except I do. Once he realized that, he threatened my life. I don't want to keep this from you anymore. I also don't want to get killed for it."

The urge to protect her life with everything I had was strong and unwavering, even if I was mad. Yanking her to me, I cradled her head in my hands, resting my forehead against hers. "No one will *ever* hurt you. You understand? I won't let anything happen to you."

She nodded, taking in a breath. "How much do you know of your mother?" My hands slid from her face, my heart ceasing to beat for a moment before picking up erratically.

My mother had died when I was two years old. I didn't remember anything about her other than I obviously had a mother. She wasn't around anymore because she was dead. At least that's what my father told me. I never thought much about it because I had him. He took good care of me. He gave me everything I ever needed or wanted and raised me to be the man I was today. I never spoke of my mother to anyone.

"Mick?"

Blinking at her, I said, "She died when I was two. I don't know anything else about her."

Her gaze fell to her hands as a solemn expression formed. "Cory knows about her. He's ... her son."

The air in my lungs came out in a rush as the earth tilted. *No.* That couldn't be true. I wanted to tell her she was wrong, that whatever he told her was a lie. I didn't know which thread to pull from first. There were so many questions forming in my mind. So many memories flowing through from childhood that I tried to decipher if he'd ever been mentioned. Surely, I would have known about another half-brother. Simon had no knowledge of this, he couldn't because if he'd known he would have told me.

I was too young when my mother died to know how it happened. Jack Silver never said a word about her in all these years. Why would he when she was dead and gone? He wouldn't lie to me about that. I trusted him. If she were alive, I'd know, wouldn't I?

"Say something," Claire urged, placing a hand on my forearm. I pulled away from her, shooting up from the couch.

"Where did you hear this?" I demanded.

"Cory got stoned one night at a friend's house and I was there. He claimed he had leverage on you, that you deserved to be knocked from your pedestal. There was someone he mentioned who was trying to take over your business or something."

What the actual fuck?! How had she kept this from me the entire time? "When was this?" I gritted out.

"Last year," she said quietly.

Last year was when Delgado was trying to steal Ken Watson's business from me. He'd brought up ... fucking Hawks! Cory started dealing for me shortly after that. Were they working together? Was Hawks phasing me out while trying to turn my father against me?

My thoughts were bouncing around like a damn ping-pong ball. I couldn't focus on any one thing with all this new information. I ran my hands through my hair, pulling at the ends. Pinning Claire with a fierce look, I said, "What else did he say?"

"He said your mom was Helena Jennings. That she was his mother, too, and she was murdered in front of him. He was four when it happened."

My knees nearly buckled. "How old is he?" I murmured in a tight voice.

"He's twenty-six. How old are you?"

"Twenty-four." That meant that she had him before my father and her ever met.

"There's something else." She glanced up at me with a somber expression. I could see the hesitation there, the concern staring back at me in a way that had me trembling.

"Tell me!" I growled. "Now."

"Jack Silver's the one who killed her. He shot her in front of Cory."

My mouth opened as a strangled noise broke from my throat. What the ever-loving fuck was happening right now?

My father was a reasonable man. A man who wouldn't murder the woman he loved and adored. The woman who carried me for nine months and loved *me*. However, she was living with her other son after I was born. A kid who was older than me which meant I was some product of an affair. An unexpected bastard that she wouldn't want if she was already established with someone else.

How could she have another family, another son that she'd wanted to raise without me? My heart ripped open as a grief I'd never experienced and a loneliness I'd been trying to tamp down smothered me. My throat tightened as my eyes filled with tears that I tried to blink away. Son of a bitch, I was crying and I couldn't make it stop. My entire life was a lie. My father betrayed me. How could I ever look at him again without plotting his demise?

I wanted to kill him, to confront him while making him hurt as much as I did in this moment. It hurt really fucking bad, too. Worse than any gunshot or stab wound. It was an internal pain that would never heal.

So this was what heartbreak felt like. I abhorred it, cursed it, and tensed as I shoved the heels of my hands against my eyes, silently willing them to stop leaking.

"Mick, I'm sorry."

"Stop apologizing!" I barked as I lowered my hands. "You're lying, *he's* lying. You don't know what you're talking about."

"Don't take your anger out on me!" she yelled, springing up to stalk toward me. "That's not fair."

I let out a harsh laugh. "Fair? You really want to talk about what's fair right now?! You're telling me my father killed my mother. *Cory's* mother." I advanced on her, grabbing her by the shoulders while looking her square in the eyes. "That she didn't want me. That she chose *him* and Jack murdered her for it, right?"

"You don't know that she didn't want you."

Choking on a sob, I released her. Is that what they wanted? To allow her to use me instead of the other way around? Had she been in on it, too? "Did he put you up to this?" I needed to know exactly where her loyalties were.

Her violet eyes burned back at me. "Are you listening to yourself right now?!" she scoffed. "I slept with you! You think so little of me that I'd say I cared about you to *use* you?!"

My shoulder lifted in a slight shrug. A low growl sounded from her throat and in that moment I knew I'd messed up royally. Without another word, Claire darted to the bedroom, slamming the door so hard the windows rattled.

This was why I didn't get attached, why I didn't allow others in. Especially beautiful women who had the potential to gut me like a fish. I couldn't deal with her right now. My entire life was crumbling down around me. I needed to get to the bottom of this.

It's not like I could just call up Cory to ask him. If he really had threatened to kill Claire for what she knew, I'd be putting her life in danger. I didn't want that, even if she did betray my trust.

Grabbing the burner phone from my pocket, I dialed Simon's number, pacing in front of the window. I scrubbed my face with my right hand, brushing the tears away.

"Hey, Mick, what's up?"

"I need information, as well as Lorenzo's number." He was silent for a few beats. I growled into the phone. "*Now*, please."

"Bro, what are you doing? Who are you putting a hit out on?"

"Jack Silver. Get me his number. I also need you to call Sadie. I need information on the death of Helena Jennings. She's got to have access to hospital records or something."

"What happened, Mick? Why do you want to kill our father?" His voice was quiet as if he were trying to be covert. He was probably near Mackaela and didn't want her knowing about this. She'd never cared for my father which now made sense. Apparently, she was a far better judge of character than I was.

"Because he's a lying piece of shit," I seethed. "Get me the info, Simon!" I ended the call before grabbing the beer bottle off the coffee table to down what was left.

Once it was empty, I threw it against the dining room wall. It shattered into tiny pieces, leaving a dent, but I didn't feel any better. I wouldn't until Jack was six feet under. Even then, I didn't think I'd fully recover.

Hawks was invested in Cory, said he'd find him, promised to take care of him. Now I knew exactly why. Those pricks were working together which meant everything he spouted on about last year regarding working with me was a front. He'd been trying to steal my business this entire time. I'd been played and I was furious.

Everything shifted for me in that moment as a new kind of vengeance formed. I was no longer walking away from the business. I was burning the motherfucker to the ground.

Chapter 14

Claire

Screw Mickey Silver for thinking I'd used him. For accusing me of working with Cory. I'd happily give the money back to prove I wasn't lying, and if that didn't work, I'd march right down to Portland to confront Cory myself. This ridiculous cat and mouse game he'd been playing didn't matter to me anymore. It never did. I should have told him the truth when he'd originally asked. Maybe I should have told him before we ever ended up in this arrangement.

I was mad at him even though I knew this was my fault. At least part of it was because I didn't say anything. I was too much of a coward. I deserved the pain of my betrayal in his gaze minutes ago. I let him down. The guilt had been eating at me like a parasite, yet I'd still kept my mouth shut. I should have known better, should have used my brain instead of allowing my selfish fear of losing whatever it was we had win.

I stood in front of the bathroom mirror with my hands curled around the edge of the countertop. I squinted at my reflection, noting my fuller lips and the red mark along the side of my throat where Mick had lapped at my skin. The thought of him touching me now sent a sharp stabbing pain through my chest.

How could I have been so careless? I didn't like how much it unsettled me that I'd been the one responsible for hurting him. Despite my initial reservations, I was drawn to everything about him. The thought of losing him now brought on tears as my chest constricted, making it difficult to breathe.

I splashed some cold water on my face in an effort to conceal the tears that kept threatening to escape. Once I was composed, I left the bedroom cautiously and poked my head out to scan the hallway. Squaring my shoulders, I ambled across the tile floor toward the living room. Mick was sitting on the sectional still clad in only his jeans. He held a fresh beer in one hand while the other held his cell phone. He dialed a number before placing it to his ear.

"Hey, it's me," he said. "I need a favor. Jack is somewhere in Oregon I believe. I want to know how much it will cost me to end him."

I gaped at him, stunned that he'd go to such lengths. Before I could stop myself, I was sprinting toward him, shouting, "No! Mick, you don't want to do that!" I lunged for the phone but he easily sidestepped me after standing and moving toward the dining area.

There was a dent in the wall near the table along with what looked like broken glass on the floor. I frowned at the sight. He was pissed, I understood that. He had every right to be. However, he was crossing a line he may eventually regret.

"That's right." He snorted. "Fifty grand? I hate to know how much I'd go for." He chuckled darkly. "Nice. Okay, I'll get back to you soon, thanks, Lorenzo." He ended the call, placing the phone on the dining table.

His shoulders rose as if he inhaled a deep breath. When he turned around his gaze was dark, narrowed at me. His jaw muscle flexed.

"You can't kill your father," I said.

"I can do whatever the hell I want. He not only murdered my mother, he lied to me my entire life."

I risked a step closer to him. "Mick, I didn't tell you what I knew for *this*."

"Well *this* is what's happening, Claire. Do you have any idea how messed up I am from being raised by Jack Silver? How much I prayed for a woman in my life to teach me the things I had to find out by trial and error? I hated my own brother for years because of my jealousy over him having a mom when I didn't. That envy was planted by the bastard that raised me."

"I get it," I said, reaching out to him. He shrugged away so I dropped my hand. "Whatever you're thinking of doing is permanent though. What if you change your mind? Shouldn't you at least talk to him first?"

He stared at me with eyes as cold as ice. "Are you defending him?" His voice was laced with venom, making me flinch.

"No! I just don't want you hurting more than you already are." He might be devastated once his father was truly gone.

He took a tug from his beer before placing the bottle on the table alongside his phone. "You don't know a thing about my feelings. In fact, I don't understand why you even care."

"I care because I know you want out," I said slowly. "You could go to jail for this. Jack Silver is powerful, you of all people know that. What if this is what they want? To see you take down your own family. You're going to give into *them*?" I thought maybe deflection would be the best way to go about this. He'd be playing into the wrong hands by ending his father.

Mick blinked at me, the silence between us dragged on until it was unbearable. I couldn't figure out what he was feeling because his face was a stone mask, not giving anything away. When he finally spoke, a wave of nausea rolled through me and I nearly collapsed to the floor.

"We leave in one hour so pack your stuff. It's time for you to go."

I didn't even get a chance to rebuttal. He walked away quickly, down the stairs without a single glance back.

I stood there blinking at the wall. How could he dismiss me now? After everything I'd witnessed the last few weeks, after what we shared with each other, he'd so easily send me away? I had a target on my back just as much as him at this point.

Where was I going to go? Bianca was dead, and even if I could, I didn't want to step foot in that apartment ever again. Seattle was full of bad memories, of a life I never wanted yet somehow fell into. Mickey Silver didn't want me anymore and instead of being blissfully happy to take the money and run, I felt like my world was caving in around me.

Anger and hurt mixed together to create a dangerous cock-tail of desperation. I wasn't sure if it was the need for him or the need to make things right. Why did I let myself get wrapped up in him? It didn't matter because this was my life now. I had to atone for my sins and lying to Mickey Silver, breaking his heart, was my cross to bear.

I made my way back to the bedroom to begin packing. He wanted me gone? Fine, I'd leave. I'd hold my head high, re-fusing to break in front of him. He'd confided in me, told me about Mackaela and his brother. I knew a vulnerable side to him that very few others did. He was reacting out of frustra-tion. I knew there was nothing I could do or say to change his mind. What had he always said? He was Mickey fucking Silver and he did what he wanted. Well, I was Claire fucking Evans so I'd be damned if I were going to let him see me fall to pieces.

I packed mechanically, tamping down the ever-present de-sire to storm down the stairs and fight with him. I almost caved, then thought better of it when I remembered the way he'd looked after I told him the truth about his mother. He'd cried. He'd looked utterly devastated and I'd caused enough pain by doing that to him.

As I set my suitcases by the front door, I heard Mick's voice trailing from downstairs. I stood there listening.

"You've got visual on him?" he asked. "Perfect. I have a lot of questions that need answered." I wasn't sure if he was referring to his father, Cory, or Fred Flintstone at this point. Mick had a lot of disputes going on. It seemed like every day was a new one.

"I'll be there tonight. I have to get rid of the girl first." My spine stiffened. "I'll call you when I'm close. Don't make a move until I say so, yeah?" He was silent for a few beats. "Yep, later."

His sudden footsteps on the stairs panicked me. I darted to the kitchen, opening the refrigerator door so he wouldn't know I was eavesdropping. I grabbed a bottle of water, trying to ignore the way my body hummed as he stepped beside me. I hated how I responded to him on some twisted subconscious level even when we were at odds.

"I'm taking you to the airport. I've already wired the remaining payment to your bank account." I straightened, blinking up at him. "Go wherever you want from there, except Seattle. It isn't sa—"

"Safe?" I rolled my eyes. "You're genuinely worried about my safety yet you're throwing me out." I twisted away from him, setting the bottle of water on the island countertop.

"I'm not *throwing* you out. I don't need you anymore as leverage because plans have changed. Again. You need to be as far away from me as possible." His voice was smooth as if we were simply discussing plans for the weekend instead of saying goodbye.

I hated that none of this affected him like it did me. Although he'd been living this way his whole life. He was probably used to it.

"Fine." It was useless to argue.

I'd just end up saying something I'd regret, like how the thought of being away from him made my heart ache. Or how not knowing what he had planned terrified me because I wasn't sure if this would be the last time I'd ever see him again.

His lips turned down and he extended his hand as if to reach for me, pausing midway. Inhaling a deep breath, he instead ran the hand through his hair. "You ready?"

"Sure," I mumbled, scooping up the bottle of water before brushing by him to the door.

I'm not sure what I expected. It's not like we were more than temporary lovers or maybe friends at this point. Yet there was this sour feeling in the pit of my stomach that wouldn't go away.

As he loaded my bag in the car, I climbed in the passenger seat and unease swirled within me like a violent tornado. I felt like I was standing at the edge of the cliff on the backside of the house. Something wasn't right about all of this. I couldn't shake the feeling that we were headed for a battle neither of us were prepared to fight.

Mick

Kyle was staking the warehouse in Portland while Hawks supposedly held Cory. I'd managed to get in touch with Hawks who claimed he already had Wilson chained to a pipe until Jack Silver gave the go ahead. Both of them were traitorous pricks.

Even though I felt like everyone around me betrayed me right now, Kyle was different. He'd been completely loyal the past few months he'd been around, proving his devotion time and again these last few weeks alone.

I had to get Claire as far away as possible before I planned to haul ass down to Portland to get the real story from Wilson. Lorenzo would hopefully have my father soon. Outside I was calm despite the fact that internally my blood spun violently in my veins, whirling inside me like a hurricane that was ready to destroy everything in its path.

I didn't want to send her away, especially not like this, but I had no choice. Things might go extremely bad down in Oregon. Even if it meant the end of me, she needed to be secure. I took my responsibility for her seriously. I had since she signed those papers in my office weeks ago. Risking her life by dragging her along on an interrogation or possible gunfight would be the dumbest thing I'd ever do. Next to taking on my own father of course.

He'd pay for his betrayal, that I was now completely certain of. Before calling Lorenzo, I put the few trusted people I still had on notice. I also enlisted Sadie, Dom's woman, to run research. I felt like an idiot for not discovering the truth sooner. Dom pulled newspapers from twenty-two years ago that talked of my mother's murder with a suspect at large. Within a few weeks, the trail ran cold because of course it did. Jack would do whatever he could to keep his name out of it. Sadie was able to retrieve medical records of her being brought to the hospital before she was officially pronounced dead. She hadn't been killed immediately which meant that someone, possibly Cory, called for help.

I remembered asking about my mother years ago when I was maybe ten or eleven. My father said she died and that was that. He literally gave me no further information at the time. Right now, I was kicking myself for not thinking to press him further. Maybe it was because I trusted him so much. I'd emulated and admired that man my whole life. I'd wanted nothing more than to be like him. Now I was cursing my last name, wishing I'd done everything differently. I was going to fix this even if it might be the last thing I'd do.

I glanced over at Claire in the darkness as we headed some twenty miles to the airport. She had a foot up on the leather passenger seat with her elbow resting on her knee as she stared out the window. I should tell her the truth, tell her that it was killing me to let her go. That wouldn't change the fact it was happening though. I felt like shit for not even apologizing for my actions earlier. I hadn't meant to hurt her or accuse her of setting me up. I was still angry at her for withholding what she knew. However, a part of me understood why she'd done it. It was as if she knew me better than myself at times so she likely anticipated this reaction.

That knowledge made it even harder to let her go. Maybe I'd buy her a plane ticket to Denver or some quiet ass town where she could blend in like she talked about. Or maybe I'd tell her to go back home to her family. She wouldn't like it, but Winthrop was probably the safest place in the world for her right now.

I wasn't sure what to say to make any of this situation better so I remained silent. I turned the stereo up instead, letting a rock song drown out the dense quiet that ate away at me. My phone vibrated in the center console and I glanced at the screen.

Kyle: Hawks is not in the warehouse.

What the hell? Hitting the call button, the music stopped abruptly and Claire frowned at the dash as Kyle's phone rang twice before he picked up.

"Dude I think you're being set up." Kyle's voice filled the cab.

"What are you talking about?" I growled. "You said he was in there."

"*Someone* is in there. I can see Wilson, but the guy with him isn't Hawks. He stepped out for a smoke, he's all grimy. Looks like Sam."

Sam was my father's right hand. He was old school with long greasy hair and jeans with holes in the knees. Rumor had it he took a guy's head off with a machete back in the eighties.

"Are you telling me that bastard lied to me?" God dammit, could nothing go right anymore?! I'm not sure why I was even surprised at this point. Fucking Hawks.

"Looks that way, Mick. You want me to hold tight or do some investigating?" Such a good kid to offer help all the time. However, I wasn't risking his life.

"Hold tight. Keep me posted if anything changes. I'll be heading that way soon."

"Noted."

I disconnected the call, flexing my fingers over the steering wheel.

"I don't like this," Claire said, finally looking at me.

My jaw clenched. I didn't either. "It's fine. I'll handle it." I took a cleansing breath, trying to release some of the tension from my body. Her head fell back against the seat and she closed her eyes. "I was thinking I'd get you a ticket to Denver," I said, attempting to distract her from worrying.

"Fine," she said, still not looking at me.

The silence from her was seriously breaking my heart. After another five minutes, I couldn't take it any longer. "Fuck it," I muttered, sliding my hand across the console to her thigh. Her head whipped in my direction. "This isn't how I wanted things to end."

She chewed on her bottom lip before giving me a slight nod. "I know I said that I hated you before, I don't. Not at all." Her voice was quiet as she held my gaze, making her words mean that much more. "I'm sorry for not telling you the truth sooner."

My lips tilted up on one side as I studied her briefly. "Well I never hated you. Although I didn't expect you to get under my skin the way you have. I have another confession ... " I trailed off, sliding my hand to hers, interlocking our fingers. "I'm going to miss you."

Several things happened at once. Shifting my attention back to the road ahead, I was blinded by the bright blue/white headlight of a motorcycle gunning straight for me. My foot stomped the brake pedal, bringing the SUV to a screeching halt. Claire's scream reverberated in my head, the sound like a punch to my chest along with the seat-belt that tightened as it strained against me with the sudden stop.

I frantically turned to Claire, my hands flying over her body to ensure she was good. "You okay?" My fingers trembled against her soft skin.

Her violet eyes were wide, her chest heaving as she gulped in air. "Yeah, are you?"

"Yeah," A single gunshot fired before the windshield shattered in front of us, spraying glass in every direction. I grabbed Claire's head to push her body to the floor as I curled over her.

It was eerily silent after that for several long minutes. I slowly raised up at the sound of boots crunching toward us in the gravel. With one hand resting on Claire's head, I twisted the other behind my back to pull out the 9mm I'd tucked in the waistband of my jeans.

"Stay down, don't move," I murmured to her shaking form. She nodded as a soft sob escaped.

I remained still, waiting for another shot to be fired. When nothing happened, I cautiously sat up to look out at the dark road ahead. There was a man standing in front of the vehicle now. Even with the helmet on, it only took me a second to recognize him as outrage consumed me. My chest rumbled in a growl. Seconds later, I was out of the car with the gun cocked and aimed as I advanced on him.

"What the *fuck* are you doing?"

He lifted his hands for a moment, holding a pistol in his right before removing the helmet. A slow grin formed on his face. I glared at him.

"Evenin', Mick." He set the helmet on the hood, still holding the pistol casually at his side. I didn't lower my weapon.

"I asked you a goddamn question, Hawks!"

He chuckled. "That's cute, but I'll be the one asking the questions. Where is she?"

I tensed. "She stays out of it. You lied to me." He turned away from me, heading for the passenger door. "I'll paint your back with bullets!" He ignored me.

He yanked the door open before pulling Claire out while holding the gun to her cheek. Tears streamed down her face as she gaped at me in horror. He tugged her with him until he was standing in front of me again. I couldn't stop looking at her as he began speaking. "Jack knows you've got a hit out on him."

I glanced at him, frowning. "Where did you hear that?"

His grin widened. "Lorenzo doesn't work for *you*. You really think he wouldn't tell him?"

I released a breath. "Fuck."

He snorted. "Yeah. You're so predictable, Mick." His gaze swept over Claire as his hand on her arm slid down to her waist where he pulled her closer.

I saw red. The barrel of my gun was against his forehead before he could blink. Claire whimpered. "Let. Her. Go," I warned in a snarl.

He laughed and ice flooded my veins. "She's a weakness to you." He batted my hand away. "Typical, Mick, desperately seeking a wet hole to put it in." My eyes slid to Claire. "You couldn't leave well enough alone, couldn't go quietly. Instead, you had to seek revenge first. Then it became more than Delgado, didn't it? Now you know the truth about your mother because of this *whore.*"

"Call her a name again and I'll blow your brains out. What does he want?"

"Jack? He wants to teach you a lesson. You were supposed to be gone by now. You couldn't just play your little game of avenging your brother then disappear. We don't care about Delgado; he was always collateral damage."

My chest deflated. "What are you saying?"

"I'm the one that killed him and I've been trying to take you out since last year. Watson had to get greedy which led to him outing me. Then Delgado had *one* job which he fucked up so I found Wilson. Promised him a cut of the business. Of course, once I realized who he was, I decided to use that to my advantage. After we visited *Rosie's,* I filled Jack in on your plans. He didn't want you finding out the truth. Now you have, so we have a problem. You stepped in something you can't get out of."

I lowered my gun, keeping my gaze on him. "You've had him at that warehouse this whole time."

Hawks winked at me. "That a kid. You're pretty bright for a bastard."

"What do you want?" I asked, my voice thick.

"I'm taking everything. I've got Jack wrapped around my finger now thanks to you. Once he learned you were trying to have him killed, you became a liability which won't do. You're just as bad if not worse than Wilson. You know too much. *She* knows too much."

My nostrils flared in irritation as I tried to plan a scenario in my mind where I could grab Claire and shoot him before he'd react. It wasn't looking good. He was good with a firearm. It's one of the reasons he was brought on to take over for me. Which was now confirmed to be a ploy to take over entirely. He made me a fool by earning my trust, by lying about wanting to work *with* me instead of against me. I fell for it hook, line, and sinker. That pissed me off.

"I'm not going to tell anyone!" Claire cried out as she fought in his grasp.

He latched onto her tighter while moving the gun to the front of her chest. His free arm wound around her stomach.

Bile rose in my throat at how close he was holding her. I tried to swallow it back while racking my brain for an out as I met her frightened stare. "You'll be okay," I said, struggling to keep my voice even. "They're not going to hurt you. It's me they want." My gaze hardened as I pinned Hawks with a dark look. "If you leave her alone, I'll go with you."

"Mick, no!" Claire argued.

He lifted a brow, examining me before tipping his head back in laughter. The sound had my heart sinking to my gut. My free hand tightened to a fist as I aimed the gun at him again. "Take. Me," I ordered.

He sobered, his eyes narrowing at me. "You shoot me and she'll be dead in seconds."

"Drop the weapon! Hands in the air." A deep voice said from behind me. Of course, he'd have backup. My nostrils flared in irritation as I clenched my jaw so tight, I was afraid it would break. "I don't want to have to shoot you, Mick."

I lowered my gun, bending to set it down on the ground near my foot. Jeremy approached me from behind, grabbing my arm. So he was a no good piece of shit, too. That brought on a new kind of indignation that had me questioning everything except for the woman I could no longer protect. I continued looking at her.

"I'm so sorry." My voice came out gravelly as a tear slid down her cheek.

"The bitch is coming with me," Hawks said, tugging Claire around me. "She gets to have a little reunion with her boyfriend before they both take a dirt nap."

Claire fought against him, screaming my name between sobs. I shrugged away from Jeremy to go after them. He stuck his gun to my back. "Stay put, Mick."

"I'm going to fucking kill you!" I shouted as Hawks pulled her to a sedan parked just off the road, hidden behind the trees. "You touch her, and I'll blow you into so many pieces they won't be able to identify your worthless body!"

"Mick, please!" Claire sobbed when he shoved her into the passenger seat before slamming the door. It was then I noticed someone else was in the back seat of the car.

He wrapped his arms around her front to hold her in place as Hawks slid into the driver's seat. I couldn't see who it was but it didn't matter. I was going to get her back. Every single one of them would be dead.

Sliding my hand into my front pocket, I grabbed the small pistol I had tucked away. I was nothing if not resourceful and while I'd been led into their trap, they underestimated me. Mickey fucking Silver always got what he wanted, he was always prepared. People were going to die tonight, starting with Jeremy. The minute the sedan drove out of sight, he released me. Whirling on him, I pulled the trigger.

Chapter 15

Claire

"Don't be afraid, *sweet* Claire. We'll keep our hands to ourselves ... for the most part." Hawks chuckled as he sped down the winding road toward the freeway.

The man sitting in the back seat behind me secured a zip tie to my wrists, tightening until the material dug into my skin painfully. I bit down on the inside of my cheek. I couldn't appear weak in front of them. Now that I was on my own, I needed to find a way out of this situation. The last few weeks, as well as the last year with Cory, trained me to be tougher than I ever thought possible. It was time to put what I'd learned into action.

I lowered my hands to my lap, keeping my fingers interlocked. I needed to maintain a level head and pay attention to any clues they might offer up. The man I didn't know leaned forward between the two front seats.

"You think he'll follow?" he asked Hawks, who sped around a large truck before cutting in front of it and merging onto the freeway entrance.

"Of course he will. He's hungry for information so Cory is at the top of his list now. I don't know what he sees in this bitch." He gave me a sidelong glance. "If anything, he'll come for *her*."

The guy snorted. "She's the bait." He shook his head. "That's genius, boss."

I resisted the urge to make a smartass retort. Mick was already planning to go to Cory anyway. Not that brilliant of a plan from my side of things but whatever.

"I know it's genius, which is why I came up with it. Mick thinks I'm in his daddy's pocket while Jack thinks I'm team Silver."

My spine straightened as I turned my head slowly in Hawks' direction. "You're playing them both," I muttered quietly.

"Sure am, doll face. You wouldn't be in this situation if you'd havé let *me* take you to that VIP room."

I snorted. "Still pining for a lap dance?"

"You would have given me anything I wanted," he promised with a dark look.

"Keep dreaming prick," I growled. "Where are you taking me?"

"You're a foolish woman if you think I'd tell you."

"They'll figure it out, you know," I said. "One of them will kill you."

Hawks clucked his tongue. "You don't know them like I do. They're two sides of the same coin. When they put their mind to something, it's all they focus on. Jack thinks Mickey's coming for Cory and he'll be there waiting when he does. When Mick realizes Cory's dead they'll have a father son shoot out. Meanwhile, I'll be sipping a margarita at my estate in California while all this blows over and my minions clean the mess."

I felt like I was going to be sick. I leaned my head against the seat, shaking my head. That couldn't happen. "You're going to kill me." It wasn't a question, more of a realization spoken aloud. He answered anyway.

He chuckled while increasing his speed. "Oh, *sweet* Claire, you've been dead since the day you agreed to help Mickey Silver."

The rest of the drive was silent. No music playing, no phone calls made, no more conversation. The boredom almost outweighed the fear as we continued on the highway heading south. I could have dozed off if not for the fact that whatever plan this lunatic had involved my death.

Two hours later, I began to see the bright lights of downtown Portland come into view. I knew it because of the roadside signs. Hawks took an exit before navigating through the near empty streets in a sketchy part of town. We passed several abandoned buildings and overgrown parking lots before he turned down a dark alley. A set of headlights flashed as he pulled in front of the waiting vehicle. He got out, leaving me with Steven, who's name I'd learned when Hawks told him to call Jack ten minutes ago.

A man stepped out from the passenger side and my heart dropped to my stomach when he came into view from the headlights. That had to be Jack Silver. He had eyes like Mick and while his cheekbones were slightly higher, his square jaw and severe scowl looked every bit like his son's. Jack's gaze shifted to mine through the windshield, narrowing as he took me in. I glared right back at him. I had to assert whatever dominance I could. Knowing the truth about Mick and Cory's mother helped fuel the disdain I had for the man.

The two men chatted for a while before Hawks clapped Jack's shoulder and came back to the car to open my door.

"Get out," he demanded.

I did as he said, keeping my head low as he grabbed my elbow to lead me to the awaiting vehicle. After opening the back door, he shoved me inside, closing me in without another word. The driver turned in his seat, giving me a speculative glance.

"You Mick's girl?" He raised a brow.

"She's no one. Just another toy for him to play with," Jack said as he slid into the passenger seat. I risked a glance at him as he tilted his head. "You know he doesn't care about you, right? The only woman he ever loved was that whore who's marrying his brother."

"She's no whore," I gritted out, feeling the need to defend a woman I'd never met. Female empowerment, baby. Plus, from what I knew of Mackaela, she had a tough life and was better off now without the influence of their business. It was interesting that he referred to Simon as Mick's brother, not his own son. Heartless bastard.

Jack lifted a brow, giving me a once over before looking at the driver. "Get to the warehouse."

With that, we were off again on another misadventure I didn't want to be a part of. During the trip, I tried to get an idea of where we were in case I'd have the opportunity to share my location or run. I looked for significant landmarks or businesses that might be open late. I honestly didn't know if I was going to make it out alive at this point. However, if the opportunity presented itself, I planned to run as fast and far as I could or fight back if necessary.

We pulled into another alley before the driver cut the engine, stepping out and opening my door. He forced me out, walking me to the back door of some sort of dilapidated warehouse. I glanced back to see Jack still sitting in the passenger seat. He placed his phone to his ear as he stared at me. I lifted my bound hands, sticking my middle finger up at him with a smirk.

"Get inside!" the driver growled, shoving me over the threshold.

It was dark inside, and I could hear the sound of voices in the distance as well as faint rock music playing. I was escorted down a dimly lit hallway that felt like it stretched on forever. With every step I took, my heart beat faster as I wondered if this was the end for me. I thought about Mick while trying to remind myself that I was tough enough to endure this. Had he escaped the other guy that showed up? Was he on his way here now or had there been others waiting for him?

As we reached the end of the hall, a door swung open. We were met by a man who looked like he was in desperate need of a shower. His gray eyes scanned the length of me with a predatory gleam. I scowled at him as he gawked at me.

"She's a looker."

The driver shoved me toward the guy, causing me to stumble. "Sorry, Sam, boss's orders are not to touch. Put her with the traitor."

Just like that, I was left alone with this Sam. He took a step closer to me, flaring his nostrils. "You a prostitute?"

My jaw locked tight. "No."

"Shame." He shrugged before turning away. "Follow me, princess."

I had no choice but to do what he said as he turned down another short hall before stopping at an elevator. When the door slid open, he angled his head for me to step in ahead of him. I pressed myself against the far corner hoping the ride wouldn't last long.

The elevator stopped at the sixth floor before Sam ushered me out to the left where we stopped in front of a black door. When he pulled it open, I was hit with the smell of stale cigarette smoke. My eyes watered as he grabbed my forearm, tugging me into the dark room. He flicked on a light and I gasped when I saw Cory slumped against the far wall with his right hand chained to a radiator.

He looked like crap. His face was bruised and stained with dried blood. The t-shirt he wore was torn at the collar. He blinked up at us with swollen eyes that focused on mine.

"Holy shit, Claire!" He attempted to stand, falling to his knees before he could get upright. It was then I noticed his left ankle bent in an unnatural way. They hadn't killed him yet, though he may as well be dead.

"Don't speak, traitor," Sam said, guiding me to the opposite wall where a plastic chair sat. "Have a seat." He pushed me down before producing a rope from his back pocket.

"What are you doing?" I tensed, tucking my legs under the chair. Sam knelt before me, grabbing both my feet to tie them together.

"You aren't going anywhere, so get comfortable. The boss will be in to talk to you soon." With that, he left and I swore I heard the sound of a lock clicking into place once the door was shut.

Cory coughed as he leaned back against the wall carefully. "Man, they got you too, huh?"

"What are you doing here?"

His split lip tilted up slightly. "When Jack discovered who I was he wanted me dead. Couldn't risk spilling his deep dark secret."

"How long have you been here?"

"Nearly a month, I think. They took me the day after Mick visited you at *Rosie's*. Randall Hawks is the one who offered me the job down here if you hadn't figured that out yet. After he did some research and found out who I was, who my mother was, he knew it was only a matter of time before Mick found out. He turned me over to Jack Silver who offered me a deal I couldn't refuse. If I could steer Mick away from the truth, I would be a free man. If he found out the truth, we were all as good as dead."

Tears burned as I shook my head. "That's why you told him you were working with Ricky."

"Yeah." He nodded. "I made it sound like Ricky was looking for him so he'd go find him. Once he had whatever revenge he was seeking, Jack thought he'd walk away. But then he didn't get Ricky. I lied about Bianca, too. She didn't tell anyone anything. Hawks was behind all of it."

Everything Mick did was for nothing. They'd used his need for vengeance against him. I couldn't believe it. If he hadn't sought out this Ricky Delgado, if he would have quit without that desperate need to redeem what happened to his brother, all this wouldn't be happening. I couldn't bring myself to blame him though because I knew where his head was. After listening to how he felt, to what he wanted out of life, I wished I could tell him to run now. He was as good as dead if he came here. I was going to be his demise. That knowledge broke my already fragile heart.

"All Mick had to do was walk away. Instead he went after you and well, sorry sweetheart, but you're the black widow in this narrative."

"No," I choked out, shaking my head against the words I'd been thinking being voiced aloud. "He only approached me because of you!" I argued.

"Hawks planned it perfectly. He's truly brilliant. From the junkie kid to going to your work." He chuckled. "That guy is good."

Staring at him in shock, I said, "What is wrong with you? He's going to kill you!"

Cory glanced up at me with a shrug. "I told you, I've been here awhile, Claire. I've made peace with it. He wanted to take the Silver territory and he's done it. It was easy, like taking candy from a baby."

"I don't understand. If Mick was going to leave anyway, why create this web of lies?"

"If all Hawks did was find a way to get rid of Jack Silver, do you really think Mick would still walk away? You spent the last few weeks with him. He's a workaholic who puts business before everything. He would have come running back, no doubt fighting to turn Hawks in afterward."

"So the only way for Hawks to get what he wanted was to kill them both? That's what Ricky was trying to do last year when he'd shot Mick's brother, wasn't it? He was there to kill Mick for him?"

"Yeah, obviously he failed miserably."

"Why are you telling me all of this?" I wondered. "If I get out of here, I'll know too much. I'll turn him in."

A sad look crossed his face as he stared down at the linoleum floor below my bound feet. "I'm telling you because you deserve to know what you're dying for. We're not getting out of here alive, Claire."

I refused to believe I'd die here in some warehouse with a man who valued himself above all others. A man who clearly never loved me. It was evident in his lack of remorse as he explained why things had happened the way they did. It was a shame that Cory chose this path. I regretted wholeheartedly ever being involved with him. Although there was nothing I could do about it now. We might both be dead soon.

"How did they know I'd tell him about his mother?" I asked.

Cory pinned me with a dark look. "They didn't. The only reason you were supposed to be here was because I told them you knew my secret." I bristled. He'd outed me knowing the consequences. "Turns out you went and fell into something with Silver which merely thickens the plot but it wasn't expected. They had visual on you guys the entire time. There's a camera system in that house."

My stomach twisted into knots. I doubled over, wheezing out a breath. Oh my god, Hawks had been watching us. He saw *everything*. Revulsion ran through me. I vowed that if I ever got the opportunity, I'd kill that guy myself. That's how he knew I was Mick's weakness, that he'd come for me. Steven was right, I was the bait.

I tried to take a deep breath but couldn't seem to get enough air to my lungs. I was on the verge of a panic attack. When the door swung open, I jerked upright, the movement made me dizzy.

Jack Silver stood in the doorway with his arms loosely at his sides, watching me. "Have a nice reunion?" he asked with a wicked grin. When I didn't respond he shook his head, stepping further into the room. "No need to be shy, girl. Tell me, do you honestly think he was worth it?"

I bit back on my molars. "Fuck you!"

A wolfish grin formed as his eyes sparkled in the fluorescent light of the room. "What a harsh mouth for such a pretty girl. I can see why my son was enamored with you." He gave me a brief once over. "I bet you'd like to say goodbye to him?"

I glared at him, remaining silent. I wasn't in the mood to play whatever game he had arranged. I wouldn't give him the satisfaction of speaking any further. Jack still wore the grin as he slipped a hand into the inside pocket of his suit jacket, producing a cell phone. He hit two buttons before holding it up as the line rang. The minute I heard Mick's voice, my breath caught.

"Hey, *Dad*." His voice was full of hostility. I couldn't blame him for that.

"Son," Jack lifted a brow, "I have something you want here. She's quite beautiful and charming."

"I'm going to fucking *end* you." Mick growled. His words held a certainty that frightened even me.

Jack chuckled. "You'll have to find me first. Have you arrived in Portland yet?"

"I don't know, maybe you should ask Sam." There was a shuffling sound before another voice came on the line.

"Sir, he's got a gun. I—,"

Pop! Pop! Pop!

The gunshots were deafening even through the phone. Cory whipped his head up at Jack with his mouth hanging open. I'm fairly sure my face looked the same. Mick had to be here if he'd just shot the man who brought me into this room.

Jack's lips formed a thin line and I swear I saw him roll his eyes. "That was hardly necessary. He's harmless." The fact that he'd shrugged off the incident made my blood run cold.

"Well he's dead now." Mick said. "You're next, asshole." The line disconnected.

I screamed when Jack threw the phone at Cory, smacking him in the chest with enough force that I heard it connect.

He lunged for him with a roar while grabbing him by the scruff of his neck and lifting him to his knees. Turning his attention to me, he pulled a gun from the back of his slacks, pushing it into Cory's mouth.

"No, no, no ... " I breathed, squeezing my eyes shut. "Please, don't," I begged, recoiling when the hammer cocked.

The next noise I heard was Cory's muffled sob. The last was the blast of a single gunshot. My ears rang and my throat burned as I screamed in pure terror. Jack shouldered my waist, lifting me. I shouldn't have opened my eyes because I caught the sight of a crimson puddle forming on the linoleum as he hauled me out of the room. That's when stars danced in my vision and everything went black.

Chapter 16

Mick

"Put his body with the other one," I said to Kyle who grabbed Sam's lifeless leg before dragging him toward the open door.

If he hadn't been casing the place the last twenty-four hours, I would have wasted a lot of time driving around Portland trying to find the right location. So far, everything had gone surprisingly smooth. Knowing my father, it was too good to be true. Kyle had only seen Jack and his driver pull up with Claire. Hawks was still MIA. It wasn't difficult to sneak up on Levi while he waited in the car for my father. He'd been distracted on his cell phone so he didn't realize he had a gun to his head until it was too late.

With Sam, I had to bide my time until he decided to come out for a smoke. I'd been crouched behind the vehicle Levi was in for thirty minutes before he emerged. Kyle and I ambushed him quickly before cuffing him to the passenger door until Jack called. I knew he would call, too. Like me, he got off on the show. I wasn't too proud to admit it. I was a sucker for some good theatrical flair when exacting revenge, like the Freddie Mercury of the underground drug world. Hence, the situation I was in.

Now that I'd blasted two of his men, I waited outside the warehouse for anyone else that may be lurking around. Once Kyle had Sam tucked in the back, he closed the door and came to stand beside me.

"Got a call from Dom. He should be here soon."

Crossing my arms, I tipped my head back against the side of the vehicle. "Good."

Kyle nodded.

I wish I knew where Hawks was. The only reason I hadn't left to go find him myself was because Claire was here. I wasn't leaving her alone. Dom arrived in town with James a little while ago to search for the bastard. They were among the few that I trusted right now. I only allowed James to come, too, because Dom corroborated his alibi the last few weeks.

They'd actually been together doing family shit. Both of them had women with young kids. I hated pulling them away from their families, but I didn't have a lot of options. I needed some sort of coverage here in case this ended with a bullet through my heart. If I couldn't get Claire out of here, Dom and James would have to do it.

Dragging a hand through my hair, I stepped away from the vehicle, heading for the door that was propped open. I couldn't just stand here like a chump when my girl was inside. "I'm going in."

I grabbed the gun I'd swiped from Sam, tucking it into the waistband of my jeans in the back. I held mine in my hands, ready to use it should anyone come up on me.

"You want me to follow, boss?"

I glanced back at Kyle. "Stay here, out of sight. Give Dom a heads up. If they catch up to that spineless bastard, tell him to stand down on my orders. I don't want him in danger, understand?"

He nodded, giving me a quick salute before jogging away toward the back of the building. With a deep breath, I stepped over the threshold into the warehouse.

The place was sparse, damn near empty with crumbling drywall in most places. *Classy.* I stayed in the shadows which wasn't difficult considering the terrible lighting. I made my way down a long narrow hall. At the end, I hung a right finding an elevator. I continued beyond it to the stairwell. I took each flight slowly while listening for any sounds of life. I'd made it up eight flights before I heard my father's voice. I froze in place.

"She's not waking up yet,." he growled.

"Did you kill her?" Hawks laughed. "Damn, you're good." I gripped the handrail, clenching my teeth.

"She's alive. I think she's in shock. She probably saw his head blown off."

Fuck! They'd killed Cory in front of her. How was Hawks here if I hadn't seen him come or go from the building this entire time? The man was a goddamn enigma. I cautiously stepped up to the landing before sliding against the wall near the door.

"Anyone left?" Jack asked.

"Only the stripper and that prick son of yours."

"I can handle Mickey. You're certain you reviewed the footage to see if anyone else is implicated?"

Footage?

"Nothing I could hear. His burner phones were destroyed which doesn't surprise me. I don't think anyone else knows what you did."

"Good."

"You think he's in love with her? They were cuddled up a lot the last week. Never seen him so infatuated with a female before."

A wave of nausea rolled through me as my blood turned molten. There were cameras in the house? They had to have been placed there before we arrived. I should have never told Hawks my plan. How degrading and downright disgusting. Clenching my free hand into a fist, I counted to twenty while willing myself to calm down. I needed to know what they were planning with Claire before I reacted.

"I'll go see if she's alert yet. If not, I know how to wake her up," Hawks said. I heard his footsteps retreating.

He was not going to touch her. Before I realized what I was doing, I flung the door open, heading barrel first into the hallway. My father whipped around with his gun raised at my face while Hawks stilled, turning around with a wide grin.

"Got you, bitch," he snarled.

"Where the fuck is she?" I demanded. "Tell me now!"

"You think I didn't know you'd be casing the place? That you don't have a kid hiding in the bushes down there staked out like some 70's cop?" Hawks scoffed. "You're a fucking joke."

God dammit! This guy was always ten steps ahead of me. He reached into the back pocket of his jeans. I turned my gun on him instead, cocking the hammer. He produced a walkie-talkie, pressing a button on the side as he held it up to his face.

"Steven, bring the kid up."

"You're a dead man!" I marched toward him, pulling the trigger.

He flew to the floor before the bullet connected so I aimed again. Before I could fire off another round, I was grabbed from behind around the shoulders and my gun was knocked away. I was then pushed to the floor with a knee in my back.

"I was going to let you say goodbye to the girl. However, you're not being very compliant," Jack growled as he pressed his knee in harder.

Hawks picked himself up from the floor and seconds later the elevator down the hall dinged before the doors slid open. I lifted my head to see one of his men holding Kyle by the arm with a gun pointed to his head.

"Jesus," I breathed. "Let him go, he's just a kid."

"Take him to the room," Jack ordered. He eased off of me slowly, grabbing my gun from the floor. "Stand up!" he barked.

I did as he said, glaring at him. Hawks brushed past me, clapping me on the shoulder. "Let's take a walk, Silver."

Having no other choice, I walked beside him to a room down the hall that Steven and Kyle entered moments before. Steven left before we entered. He was probably heading back downstairs to keep watch. I'd have to take care of him later if Dom or James didn't first.

I wasn't sure what I expected, but it definitely wasn't the girl before me with blood dried on the corner of her beautiful lips and cuts on her wrists from where she'd been zip tied. She was loose now and hopefully uninjured otherwise.

I'd said before that I didn't have a heart. That if I did, it was buried deep. I'd been lying. Every ounce of anything that made me good within my body belonged to Claire Evans. As I took in the way she was curled into herself in the corner of the empty room, that heart I'd denied so long splintered into fragments.

An involuntary groan ripped from my throat as I stared upon her lifeless body. I was moving toward her automatically before falling to my knees in front of her. "What did you do to her?" I growled, placing my hands on either side of her head to tilt it up, getting a better look at her.

"She wouldn't stop screaming after I killed Wilson. Had to shut her up somehow," Jack explained.

My eyes drifted closed, my nostrils flaring. "You laid your filthy hands on her?" I could feel my heart-rate increasing with every intake of breath. Releasing her, I rocked back. "You *hit* her."

Claire's brows rose slightly as her eyes opened, widening at me. I blocked her face with my body. They wouldn't go for her unconscious. I hoped she'd understand. I pinned her with a warning look before shaking my head. Her eyes fell closed again as I stood on trembling legs, turning to face the man who raised me. He was no longer my father.

"Look at you," he said as he glowered at me in judgment. "You're weak over a female. A woman who's as insignificant as the dirt on your shoes."

It was difficult to ignore the unbridled rage that swept through me with his words. This woman was the best damn thing that ever happened to me. Instead, I asked the one question that had been plaguing me since I found out the truth. "Why did you do it?"

He quirked a brow. "I just told you she wouldn't stop screaming."

"Not *her*, you waste of life. My mother. Why did you kill her?"

"She was a no good whore who was looking for an escape in a loveless marriage. I entertained her until she ended up pregnant."

"Why didn't she keep me? Why did you take me away from her?" I could feel that now familiar sting of tears but I didn't care. I'd cry in front of this monster while taking him out with a single blow once I got the answers I needed.

"She didn't want you, didn't want her husband to know. Kind of a moron if you ask me to not even notice her pregnancy. Although you were a small baby. I had you for nearly two years before she came back saying she'd changed her mind. She threatened to take you away. I wasn't going to let her do that."

"So you killed her?" I snapped. "Murdered her in front of her other child, my *brother*, and left him there with her?"

Jack scoffed. "Please, don't tell me you feel sorry for that kid. He was out to get you, Mick."

"Like Simon was? You said he was better off without us. You claimed he didn't give a shit about me. You were wrong about that! Cory may have hated me, wanted to take whatever he thought I had, but that was only because of what *you* did."

The fact that I stood in front of him lashing out verbally and all he did was stare back at me with no sign of remorse, told me everything I needed to know about the last twenty-four years of my life. I had my closure so now it was time to end him.

This business and the things I strived for once upon a time didn't fucking matter anymore. *He* didn't matter and he sure as hell didn't love me. It was no wonder I was a failure when it came to real relationships. I never had a chance.

Turning back to Claire, I knelt down again before covertly pulling a blade from my boot. I wrapped my arms around her while tucking the handle in her palm behind her back. Tilting my head slightly, I placed my lips at her ear. I would have preferred to look her in the eyes but if they saw that she was awake, she'd be dead, too. I'd go out in a blaze of glory and Dom would get her to safety. There was one last thing she needed to know before this was over and I refused to let Jack Silver or Randall Hawks take that away from me.

"I have one last confession," I whispered low so they wouldn't hear my words. Her throat rolled in a swallow as I palmed her cheek, brushing my thumb against her lower lip. A tear rolled down her cheek and I rested my forehead against hers. "I. Love. You."

Standing, I spun as I tugged the gun from the back of my jeans, firing at Jack's chest. Another blast sounded and my head snapped to the right just as Kyle's body hit the floor. My gaze locked with Hawks who smirked at me. In a fit of rage, I fired off several rounds in his direction. I felt a bullet sink into my flesh but I didn't care at the moment. I remained standing to watch as surprise etched into his features. He gasped for air, clutching his chest.

I zeroed in on his hand, waiting for the blood to trickle out where his heart was. My brow crumpled in confusion. I winced as I pressed my palm against the hole on the left side of my upper rib cage. Kicking his head back, he let out a thunderous laugh while tugging at the buttons of his shirt. He opened it to reveal a bulletproof vest. I hissed out a mangled breath. Flames licked up my torso toward my throat as I choked out a cough that felt wet. The gun slipped from my hands as I backed against the wall, sliding down when my legs gave out.

"Mick, no! Mickey." Claire crawled over to me, pressing her hands against the wound when mine fell away. My vision blurred as I tried to get one last look at her gorgeous face.

"Claire," I breathed.

"You're going to be okay. Stay with me," she cried.

"He's as good as dead," Hawks said in a steely voice. Anger etched into her faded features as she turned to look at him.

"You got what you wanted," she growled. "If you're not taking my life, get out of here."

"Babe, no ... " I attempted to lift my hand but it wouldn't move. She gripped it as she shook her head at me.

"Hold on, Mick. You have to hold on."

"Oh I'm taking your life, just not the same way. You're coming with me."

The room went dark as I felt my head sag to the side.

"Mick! Mick!" Claire slapped my face. I opened my eyes in time to see him yank her away from me.

A surge of energy sprang to life and I leaned forward, reaching for my gun. He was hauling her out of the room as I lifted my arm. I wasn't quick enough, the bullet hit the wall. I moaned and coughed again. This time, I could taste blood at the back of my throat.

I didn't protect the woman I loved. I'd failed miserably and now time was up to make it right.

"Mick, stay alive!" I could hear her sobs though they were muffled by the rushing sound in my ears.

Lying face down on blood stained linoleum, I closed my eyes and took my final breath before slipping into oblivion with hope of forgiveness.

Claire

I lifted the knife Mick had given me, swiping at Hawks. I managed to slice through the sleeve of his shirt as he dragged me into the hallway. He howled at the sting of the blade, loosening his hold. Scrambling free, I darted back to the room to see Mick lying face down in a pool of blood. There was so much of it that I had no way of knowing who it belonged to. A sob rocked my body as my legs gave out. Before I could fall to my knees, I was yanked back by my hair. Hawks grabbed my wrist with his free hand, pinching it tight until the blade fell from my grasp. I grappled with him, trying to fight him off, but he was so much stronger than I was. I screamed as loud as I could, begging Mick to hold on. He couldn't be dead. I couldn't lose him this way.

As we reached the elevator, the doors swung open. I gasped as I took in the dark wild eyes that landed on me. Dom stepped out with his gun drawn, targeting Hawks.

"Let her go!" he demanded.

Hawks had his own gun aimed. His chest rumbled against my back when he spoke. "She's coming with me." He pressed the gun against my temple and I flinched.

With a pleading look at Dom, I said, "Mick's shot. Go ... Save him."

For a six foot something body builder looking guy, the look of sorrow in his stare both surprised and gutted me. He glanced down the hall then back to me. Was he seriously weighing which option was best?

"Save. Him," I gritted out. "I'll be fine." Tears clogged my throat as he nodded before taking off down the hall. I was terrified for my life, but Mick was more important right now. I still had the opportunity to get out of this, he may already be gone.

Hawks kept his gun directed at me as we stepped onto the elevator. "If he lives, I'll know." His voice was cold. "There is no scenario where I won't win. I've worked far too long and hard to get to this point. The West coast is *mine*." He shoved me away and I clambered to the other side of the small space.

"If he lives, he'll end you!" I spat. "If he doesn't, then I will." I met his dark stare, unblinking. I refused to let him intimidate me.

All I cared about right now was that Mick lived, that he'd be okay. He told me he loved me and I didn't have the chance to say it back. The words I hadn't said still lodged in my throat and I felt like I was suffocating on them. I should have told him how I felt.

Now, I'd never get the chance.

Chapter 17

Claire

Six Months Later ...

Whoever said time heals all wounds didn't know what they were talking about. It's been half a year since I last saw Mickey Silver and the agony that tightened my chest while creating nightmares had yet to subside. I could still hear his voice, so soft and smooth like honey in the midst of chaos.

"I. Love. You."

I could still smell the blood permeating throughout that room in the warehouse, making me nauseous even now as tears threatened to escape. Sometimes instead of violence, I'd have dreams of the two of us together. He'd hold me as I lay there stroking his chest while memorizing his handsome face. I'd feel his lips against my skin, the weight of his body above mine.

I didn't know which was worse, the fact that he may be dead or that he may be alive and I'd never have the chance to tell him how I feel. To say that I loved him, too, that I was sorry for not saying it back before he took that bullet.

I was a different person now than I had been. I'd been seasoned and groomed to be Hawks' pet. His spoil of war against Jack Silver. My skin was tanner, my body now stronger due to taking advantage of a workout room. I wasn't allowed many places other than my bedroom, so I spent time exercising when I could. It was one of my only moments of reprieve in the midst of despair.

I had a room of my own in Randall Hawks' sprawling mansion on the Northern California coast. It overlooked the ocean while sitting on fourteen acres. In any other life, I'd be in heaven, waking up to the salty brine of the water every morning. I had an entire wall of windows with a view of nothing except the ocean. The weather was mild for mid-October which helped ease my depression.

Sometimes I'd sit out on my private balcony to read as I listened to the waves crashing against the rocks below. Other times I'd lie in bed with the curtains open, imagining what life would be like if I didn't end up in hell with a man I couldn't stand. A man that murdered the one who owned my heart.

When we left the warehouse that night, I'd gone quietly in hopes of saving Mick. Dom had showed up to save the day only he was minutes too late. The fact that Hawks didn't go after him surprised me. When I questioned him after we were on the highway heading south, he'd said it wasn't worth it. He was certain that Mickey Silver was dead. If he weren't, he still held the promise that he would be eventually.

During the first month, I fought back as much as possible. I even attempted to run away. Unfortunately, my efforts were wasted. He had a lot of men around that made it impossible to go to the bathroom, let alone escape. He'd beaten me. Slapped me in the face and upside the head when I talked back or battled him. At one point, he'd grabbed my arm so hard I had a purple hand print for weeks.

I was constantly under surveillance by his men after my first attempt to break free. It hadn't let up since. I'd grown oddly used to it after all this time. The only thing I'd never grow accustom to was the way I was treated by Randall Hawks.

He never touched me in a sexual way which I was grateful for, even though I wasn't sure why. He'd make comments about my body or stare at me in a way that made me want to vomit, yet he never acted on it. The only time he was physical with me was when he struck me. That didn't bother me as bad as the not knowing when or if he might do something different. It was like he got off on degrading and belittling me.

He'd even gone as far as telling his men I was to be seen only. While I wasn't ever touched by those men, I definitely was *seen*. Several times over the summer, he'd thrown large parties where I was expected to remain at his side in whatever barely there evening gown he'd picked out for me. I'd stand there not saying anything because I was told not to speak. It was maddening to be his trophy. I absolutely hated it.

I was allowed to call my family upon our arrival here, however I had to read a script that had been prepared. I was to tell them I met a man and decided to travel to Europe through Christmas. My mother didn't believe it so I tried to be as convincing as possible for her safety. He'd held a gun to my head while I spoke with her. When the call ended, he'd told me he'd hunt my parents down and kill them if I ever told them the truth.

Some days I wished he'd just kill me and get it over with. I had no idea what he had planned for me. I was left feeling reticent, on the verge of breaking down frequently because I had no one to speak with that I trusted. I was allowed to text my mother once a week to let her know I was okay. Once a month, I got a ten-minute phone call with her where I lied through my teeth.

There was a time I thought I'd like solitude in a pretty place. I had been so wrong. Being alone meant louder thoughts, most of which were the negative memories that haunted me. Hawks also seemed to be playing some sort of mental game with me by keeping me in isolation. My only other source of communication was with his right hand, Steven. The same guy who'd restrained me in the car that night when they took me away from Mick. The same one that led Kyle into that room to be slaughtered right alongside his boss. However, he'd been unnaturally protective of me while I'd been here. If one of Hawks' other men were caught gawking too long or made a nasty comment, Steven would put them in their place. He'd appointed himself my personal guard, escorting me to meals and holing up outside the gym while I worked out.

How sad that I now found Steven my closest friend. He was younger like me and supposedly new to the business. I'd found out that Hawks was in his early forties. He had been aiming to take over Silver territory for a long time before ever meeting up with them. He'd been far more prepared than Mick had given him credit for.

Steven was nice enough and respectful. Although I wouldn't say that I trusted him as far as I could throw him. I didn't have faith in a single person at this house. He was teaching me to shoot a gun though and when I asked about it, he'd simply said it was a skill everyone should learn. Oddly enough, he only trained me on days when Hawks was out of the house or the guards were minimal. Sometimes I wondered if he were setting me up to either get out or get caught. I gave up caring a while ago, so I absorbed what I could of the training. I wasn't a bad shot now. Although every time I held a gun in my hands, I was filled with sorrow because it made me think of Mick.

That might sound messed up, but there were a few occasions during our time together that he'd offered to teach me how to shoot at some point. That time would never come now. I wasn't sure if my wounds would ever heal without closure. Not when I could still feel the slowing of his heart against my palms that soaked in his blood.

I mourned the loss of him every single day. I felt like he'd have come for me by now if he were still alive. Love wasn't something he gave freely so I knew he meant it when he said it. Just like I knew he'd do anything to make sure I was safe. The fact that he hadn't shown up, that not a single person mentioned him this entire time, solidified my fear that he was gone forever.

I stared out at the setting sun on my balcony as the warm breeze lifted the hair around my face. When I closed my eyes, a single tear rolled down my cheek and my breath hitched. "I miss you,." I whispered into the air.

The sound of approaching steps made me turn. Steven stood at the threshold of the glass door. "Boss wants you in his office."

Releasing a breath, I followed him back into my room. "Did he say what it was about?" I pulled a light cardigan on over my tank top. I tried to stay covered as much as possible when wandering the house.

"There's talk of a Halloween party. I hear he's inviting members of other outfits from the northern states."

I raised a brow at him while toeing on my flip-flops. "Is that information you're allowed to tell me."

He glanced down at the pale carpet. "Dammit."

My lips tilted up slightly. Steven kind of reminded me of Mick's guy Kyle, only a few years older. Poor Kyle never got a chance to be anything thanks to the bastard who currently held me captive. I swallowed the bile that rose in my throat as images of his poor lifeless body drowned in blood crept in.

"I won't say anything. Have you heard anything from the North?" I asked hopeful.

He continued staring at the carpet, his jaw tight. "Your boy's dead, Claire. He ain't coming back from what the boss did to him."

His words were like a hot knife twisting in my chest. I grimaced. It didn't matter that all signs pointed to him being gone, there would always be a small part of me that refused to believe it. Not until I saw his headstone or spoke with someone I could trust.

I didn't respond as he walked ahead of me into the marble-floored hallway. I followed him down the wide hall as we passed by two other rooms before heading down the stairs into the foyer. This place was so large that half the time it felt more like a hotel. There were random marble statues throughout the expansive main floor with rectangular beams on the ceilings.

Off the front entry foyer was one of Hawks' offices. Apparently, he had two of them, though I'd only ever been in this one. The other was reserved for official business or something else I didn't care about. Along with the gym, he also had a billiard room, a pool, and probably a dungeon in the basement. However, I wasn't about to go scoping that out to prove it.

Steven gave two solid knocks on the dark mahogany door before pushing it open. I stepped in ahead of him, glaring at the man I'd grown to hate even more over time.

He sat behind his ostentatious wood desk while reclined in the black leather chair with his hands behind his head. His lips tilted up on one side as he stalked me with his gaze. I took a seat in the matching leather chair in front of him, crossing my arms.

"To what do I owe the pleasure today?" I asked in a sardonic voice. I heard Steven close the door as he left.

Hawks grinned fully then, lowering his hands to the top of the desk. "It's been a few days since I've seen you. Thought we could catch up."

Snorting, I said, "Why don't you just ask one of your men what I've been up to? Better yet, don't you have a control room or something where you can watch your *footage*? Pervert."

He glowered at me across his desk, jaw ticking. "Watch it. Those cameras are just as much for your safety as they are for mine."

"Whatever," I muttered, rolling my eyes. "I haven't been up to anything because there's nothing for me to do. Where were you anyway?" I didn't really care. I found that he enjoyed talking for the sake of simply being heard. He was a total narcissist so I felt like at some point he might slip up in his need to speak and divulge important information.

"Went to pay Simon Silver a visit." My heart leapt to my throat. "Him and his woman disappeared shortly after I killed his brother. It's strange that I can't seem to find them or Dominic Deluca and his family."

"Good."

"The weirdest thing is that all of the men that worked for Silver Enterprises are now on my payroll except for three people. Dom, Simon, and a guy named James Hightower. It's like they just evaporated into thin air."

"You got what you wanted, *Randall*. Clearly they aren't invested anymore in the business, me, or you because you're still here running the show." I'd decided about a month ago to lose the filter with him. He didn't always hit me and sadly, I'd grown used to the pain he inflicted. I refused to be a damsel in distress which is why I chose to work out, as well as learn gun safety. If he didn't kill me first, I'd take a page out of Mickey Silver's book and get revenge one day. "Why do you care where they are? Haven't you done enough damage by not only killing Jack, but Mick, too?"

He leaned forward, pinning me with a glare. "We don't know they aren't planning retaliation. Maybe they're stupid enough to come after me."

I couldn't help the giggle that escaped. "You're afraid of them. What's the matter, Randall, guilty conscience?"

"Shut your mouth now, *whore,* or I'll shut it for you." I bit down on the inside of my cheek, wishing I had the balls to shoot back a retort right now. I wasn't that confident. "Now, back to the point of our meeting. It's time you started fulfilling your purpose here. Starting tomorrow, you'll be working for me by playing the role of a lifetime."

Ice flooded my veins as my eyes drifted shut. Here it was, the reason he'd been keeping me alive. Opening my eyes, I tried to keep my voice even as I spoke. "Isn't that a little redundant? You think you'll lure them out using me as bait, right? Kind of like what Mick did to take out Delgado and Cory six months ago."

"That's the difference between me and that piece of shit that's burning in hell." Pain sliced through me as I exhaled a shaky breath. He knew he was cutting me deep. The satisfied smile said it all. "I won't fall for you like he did. I won't soften or lose focus. Once word gets out that I have you here alive, they'll come looking for you."

My brow crumpled. "No one knows I'm alive?" I hadn't thought that he'd make it out like he'd killed me. Is that why no one had come for me?

Hawks chuckled. "Let's just say I found a pretty little decoy that worked out nicely to fake your death. You didn't think I'd have contingency plans in place in the event one of Mick's people grew a set to come to your rescue?" He clucked his tongue, shaking his head. "I've been in this business a long time, sweetheart. I haven't lost yet."

Clenching my teeth, I uncrossed my arms and fisted my hands in my lap. "There's a first time for everything."

"I took the liberty of leaving the body in Mick's office so they'd find you. Burned her just enough that they wouldn't be able to deny it was you. Now it's time for you to be resurrected."

"You're a sick fuck!" I seethed.

"Do not raise your voice to me!" he roared. I scowled at the vein in his forehead that popped. "Since we can't locate this crew, I have to find a way to get their attention by unconventional means."

My stomach twisted into knots. Pulling open the top drawer of his desk, he produced a piece of paper before sliding it toward me. I gasped at the image, feeling like I was going to puke. It was a photo of me that had been used for promotions at *Rosie's*. There was a tagline across the top that read, *Marvelous Masquerade: featuring Harlow the dominant damsel.* Lifting my wary gaze to his, I began shaking my head.

"What are you doing?"

"Sending out invitations to an exclusive party on Halloween night where you'll be the star. Even if they are out of the business, no one ever loses connections. I'm not naïve enough to think my team is free of rats. The minute someone sings like a canary, they'll come for you, and I'll be waiting to pick them off."

"Why are you doing this?" I asked in a breathless whisper.

"One of the first rules of business, *sweet* Claire, no loose ends." I wanted to punch that cocky smirk from his face. "You'd better go get some rest. Tomorrow's a big day and I want you looking impeccable on camera."

Chapter 18

Simon

We were staying in a house near the Oregon coast that was off the grid. It was one of Mick's old safe houses he'd used a couple of times that Hawks didn't know about. I don't think our father even knew about it. Not that his knowing mattered anymore because he was dead. I'd spent my entire life hating him. Just when I thought we were making progress toward a real relationship the rug was pulled out from under me. The things he'd done to Mick, along with the lies he'd told all came to light and it hurt more than I thought possible.

I'd only had the chance to spend time with my half-brother for less than a year before he was shot. I wished he were here with us now as we prepared the ambush on Hawks' compound in California. We were flying under the radar while still maintaining connections that kept us in the loop. Like the contact we'd just scored a stash of weapons from or the other that informed us of exactly where Claire was as of yesterday.

"Did you run into any trouble?" Mackaela asked while holding the back door open for me and Dom as we brought in the stash. I huffed out a breath as I carried the box to the small dining table.

"No. I think we're still in the clear. Hawks is searching though." Setting the box down, I turned back to her before pulling her into my arms. "We received word that he was in Seattle last week for a few days."

"Do you think anyone said anything?" she asked, lifting her head to look at me. I slid my thumb along her bottom lip.

"The only person in Seattle that knows anything is Dom's uncle on the police force. He won't talk. Hawks doesn't even know who he is." I leaned down to kiss her and she immediately relaxed against me.

"This is a lot of hardware," Dom grunted as he brought the last box into the house.

"Our inside man says we'll need it. There could be hundreds of guys at this compound. The more ammunition, the better."

"I don't like this one bit," Sadie said as she came down the stairs. "You're flying blind. We don't even know if that girl is there."

Dom slipped his arm around her waist, kissing her forehead. "He wanted us to think she's dead. The chances she's with him are pretty high. He wouldn't trust anyone else to keep that secret."

When we found the body at Mick's office, we assumed the worst. The girl looked enough like Claire that we figured Hawks had done her in after leaving Mick to die. Fortunately, for us, Sadie's good friend runs the morgue at the county hospital so we were able to do a DNA test to be sure. When we discovered it wasn't Claire, our plans began to take shape. That was just over five months ago, so to say we'd had some time to exhaust every effort and avenue would be an understatement.

"What do you think he has planned?" Mackaela asked.

I shrugged. "I'm thinking he's holding her until he can ensure every last one of us is gone."

"He knows we'll come for her," Dom said.

I nodded. "According to James, there's talk of a party at Hawks' compound on Halloween night. There was a text chain invitation sent out. He's baiting us." I pulled my phone out of my pocket, holding it up so they could see the screen.

"What is that?" Sadie asked.

"She's the model for his invitations? God, he's sick!" Mackaelea growled. She shook her head, muttering a curse. "If he knows we're coming, he'll be ready. It's a death sentence."

Dom spoke up then. "We're not leaving her there. The plan has always been to get her out. If Mick were here, he'd say the same thing."

Mackaela's face fell at the mention of his name and my chest grew tight. She'd been taking his absence the hardest. It killed me that I couldn't alleviate the pain.

"We've got enough weapons to get her out. Plus there's the C-4 to ensure this ends for good. We just have to make sure our plan is solid," I said. "Mick underestimated Hawks last time. That won't happen again."

"You're damn right," Dom said with a proud smile. "We've got a secret weapon that'll blow whatever that bastard's planning out of the water."

Claire

The last two weeks had probably been the worst of the entire time I'd spent here. Hawks hadn't hit me in the last fourteen days which was nice. The alternative was being forced to parade around in a skimpy outfit while Steven took photos of me as Hawks and his cronies looked on.

The photos were going to be used as some sort of media blast for this stupid masquerade party he was having.

It was finally the day of the event and I grew more anxious with each passing minute.

Mick's people might try to come for me once they found out I was alive. Even if they were able to find a way to get me out of here or get in the house, it would only be a matter of time before we were all massacred. Hawks would always be paranoid. He'd always be watching his back as long as we were breathing. It didn't matter if I promised never to say anything to anyone, I was a liability just like the others. The only way to ensure I made it out alive would be to kill him. I'd been working on a plan, though I wasn't entirely sure I could pull it off.

Steven seemed distracted lately so I took advantage of it. I asked him to take me shooting again yesterday when Hawks was away at some meeting. I'd been able to slip the gun I was practicing with beneath my shirt. I decided to stow it away in a drawer in my bathroom which was the one place Hawks didn't have cameras. If anyone knew, they hadn't let on yet.

All I had left to do was make sure I could handle fighting when the time came. I'd been working out a lot since I'd been brought here which improved my stamina significantly. I'd always been somewhat athletic because of my dancing, so I focused more on weights now to gain some muscle.

I didn't know for certain if anyone would come for me. Even if they didn't, I felt it was as good a time as any to try making a final break for it. I couldn't shake the feeling that this may be my last chance. I longed to see my mother again, to go back to a place I'd always wanted to leave before. Winthrop didn't seem as bad as it once had after everything I'd been through. If I never would have left, I wouldn't be in this situation. Although I never would have met Mick, either. That eased the disappointment because I was grateful to have him, if only for a little while.

I hoped that Hawks would be more focused on looking out for enemies to show up so I could slip under the radar this time. He'd frequently drink at his events and never missed a chance to put himself on display in front of everyone. Like I said before, he was a total narcissist. I would use that to my advantage if I could. Although me being a part of the invitations as well as the media blasts he put out meant I'd likely be on display, too. I'd have to find a window of opportunity to disappear.

My driving force was the desperation that heightened once I found out he was luring Mick's people. I still didn't know if he was alive or dead, but that small pang of hope I'd been holding onto grew at the thought of potentially seeing him again. If I managed my escape to find he was in fact gone, I'd go back home. I'd live a mediocre life in my small town. There was nothing left in the world for me without him. As pessimistic as that sounded, it was the truth.

I loved Mickey Silver despite the fact that we fought constantly, that he grated on my nerves at any given moment. The first time in my life that I felt content was during those few weeks I spent with him. Even under the circumstances, I'd felt a peace I'd never known. I didn't want more of the world or adventures if he wasn't by my side. No one would ever touch my soul the way he had. I'd continue to live for him because I didn't want him to have died in vain. However, I wouldn't be the same person I was before. He'd taken a part of me when we separated that night.

Hawks had ordered a woman by the name of Cynthia to come take care of my hair and makeup for the party tonight. Every time he had some sort of event at the house, she would make me over into the perfect specimen. Cynthia was a kind woman in her thirties who never really said much. She simply did her job before leaving with little to no conversation. I tried asking her once why she worked for him. All I got out of her was that she owed him a debt because he saved her life. I wondered if she was like me, stolen from another person while being forced to do his bidding or risk death.

Because this was a masquerade party, I would be wearing a mask so she spent a great deal of time on my eyes. They were lined in black with charcoal shadow to accentuate the unique color of my irises. The mask I wore was matte black with long bunny ears lined in rhinestones that only covered part of my nose and under my eyes. Cynthia lined my lips and painted them a dark red to add a dramatic effect. My hair was left down and curled intricately. It fell almost to my waist now.

Once she left me alone, I got dressed.

In typical fashion like his other parties, Hawks had chosen a black floor length gown with a high slit on both sides that started near the tops of my thighs. The neckline was cut low while draped with loose fabric. I put on a strapless bra before sticking the gun on the left side. I was right handed, so I figured if I needed to draw it quick that was the best way to go.

I smiled to myself as I took in my appearance in the long mirror. Beautiful yet deadly. Mick would be proud of me. Inhaling a deep breath, I ran my palms over the velvet material on my stomach. I wished I didn't have to wear these stupid five-inch heels. The only other option would be sneakers or flip-flops which wouldn't work because Hawks would notice. My saving grace was that they slid on without buckling or anything so I could kick them off to run if needed.

There was a knock on my bedroom door at five after seven. I took another deep cleansing breath. It was time to put on my game face to prepare for battle. I was as ready as I'd ever be even if my stomach twisted painfully when nerves sprouted like thorny vines. Steven stood before me in a white tux with a simple golden mask that only covered his eyes.

"You look good, Claire. The boss is ready for you to make your entrance."

My face fell. "Entrance?"

His lips tilted up. "Yeah, you're the star of the show tonight. Everyone is dying to see you."

Of course they were. With all their focus on me, this would be harder than I anticipated. As I followed him through the hall, I glanced down at the main area and halted. There were a lot of people here. Far more than any of Hawks' other parties. I couldn't even begin to try counting the number. It had to top out at close to one hundred. Placing my hands at my sides, I flexed my fingers as I sent up a prayer to whoever was listening. I needed to stay calm, stay focused.

Please let me out of this place tonight.

Steven turned back to me, grasping my elbow at the edge of the long black gloves I wore. "You can do this," he said quietly.

I fell into step beside him again as he let go of me. "There's so many people here."

"That's because the boss invited more than *his* people. There's definitely outsiders in attendance." My heart leapt to my throat and I attempted to swallow it down. "Hawks has extra security manning the door in case your friends show up."

"I doubt they'd come for me," I said as fear swirled with the unease that was steadily building.

"I don't know about that. You're pretty important to Mickey Silver." He shrugged.

"He's dead." My heart pinched at the words. Speaking them aloud made it all the more real.

"Is he?" Steven mused as we stepped to the top of the stairs.

I gaped at him. "Isn't he?" The beat of my heart increased as a warmth spread through me. A slow grin formed on his face.

"Maybe you have a friend on the inside. Maybe he knows more than he's told you in order to keep you safe." Before I could respond, he lightly gripped my bicep, forcing me to descend the steps.

Mick

Randall Hawks was going to die tonight. There was nothing or no one getting in my way this time. I'd be ready for whatever he tried to throw at me. Getting my girl back was priority number one. Priority number two was demonstrating my promise to him if he'd touched her. I'd blow him into so many pieces they wouldn't be able to identify his worthless body.

Death didn't scare me anymore after being on the brink six months ago. If it hadn't been for Dom's quick response and my driving force to rescue Claire, I wouldn't be here. That bastard's bullet hit me in the lung, puncturing before embedding within. It took an operation on top of nearly three months of recovery before I was back on my feet. Now that I was back, it was with a vengeance stronger than any I'd ever had in the past.

We were prepared for every possible scenario thanks to my inside man who happened to be the one closest to Hawks. Steven Cline. James had taken him by surprise after he'd gone downstairs at the warehouse that night. With a gun to his head, he threatened his life. However, he ended up not pulling the trigger because Steven revealed a secret that no one was ready for.

The guy was a mole from another crew on the East Coast that had been following Hawks for years. It wasn't just any crew, either. It was the actual mafia. He was ready to take him out when I'd reached out to Hawks last year. After hours of discussing things, I'd decided he would make a good partner. I'd thought he'd be perfect to take over for me since I intended to get out. I was totally off base with that judgement call which I'd probably never forgive myself for. Steven kept up the façade in order to check out Silver Enterprises as well.

When it was discovered that everything might sort itself out with Hawks wanting to end my father, the powers that be decided to let us all just kill each other off if we could. We all know how that worked out.

Agreeing to give them the territory because I couldn't care less anymore, I went from being one of the greatest drug lords to ever run the West Coast, to an informant. My debt would be paid. I'd be a free man if I helped take out as many members of Hawks' crew as I could, including the man himself.

So with the help of a far larger entity than I'd ever been a part of, I was en route with my brother and Dom to a sprawling California estate. We wouldn't be alone either. A group of about twenty-five men from the East Coast were joining us there to help carry out the plan.

"She misses you," Simon said as he navigated through traffic.

"I know," I said, lifting my hand to my head before dropping it. I was incognito tonight which meant I had to change my appearance. A simple mask wouldn't work so I'd cut my hair short and colored it black. "I had to be as far off the radar as possible if they were able to sniff you guys out."

Simon nodded. "She understands that. She's more worried about tonight. If this doesn't go well—"

"It's going to be fine," I growled. "The East guys are already on the property setting up. You two are to stay outside." I wasn't risking either of them for this. They'd help set the explosives once I gave the signal.

"Yeah, you're going into the lion's den though. It's dangerous."

"Claire's in there, I don't have a choice. You'd do the same thing if Mackaela were taken."

"Of course I would," he said. "But it hasn't been that long since you came back from death." While I appreciated the sentiment, I was in no mood for it right now.

"It's been *months* and I feel great. Better than before even. Come on, man, you've been through the same thing."

He shook his head. "I didn't lose a part of a major organ."

Shrugging, I said, "Technicality. I'm good, I swear. Hawks won't even recognize me. Besides, he still thinks I'm six feet under."

There could be no trace of me after that night at the warehouse. Thanks to Steven's quick thinking before Hawks had come down with Claire, he'd alerted some men in the area to prepare for emergency. I was admitted into the hospital under a false name. I didn't know about the body in my office until a month later when Sadie confirmed it wasn't Claire.

I'd been sick to death over her well-being this entire time, so Steven kept me informed as much as he could. She'd probably be pissed to know that I was getting updates on her and even a few pictures he'd taken, when for all she knew I was dead. It had to be that way though. I needed her to stay in the dark because it was safer for her. I wouldn't jeopardize her life again.

I loved her more than I'd ever loved anyone. I was so proud of how strong she'd been throughout this entire nightmare. Even on the verge of death, my mind was wrapped up in her, wanting to know where she was and whether or not she was safe. I couldn't lose her even if she didn't love me back. I'd never leave her alone again. She'd have to be the one to pull the trigger.

"Just got a text from Steven. He said they're bringing her down in ten minutes," Dom said from the back seat.

My chest tightened at the prospect of seeing her again. I pulled my mask from the glove compartment as Simon rounded the corner toward the gate of Hawks' compound. I tugged it over my head before adjusting it to make sure it sat properly. It was a charcoal color with spikes strategically placed around the upper face of a dragon. The detailing made it look extra ominous which worked well for me. I was all about that flair I loved tonight.

The car stopped at the edge of the rounded driveway. I straightened my red tie before stepping out. "The guns will be outside the pool gate," Dom reminded me before I closed the door.

They'd pat me down because they had to. Hawks was expecting us tonight, which based on the information from Steven, they'd be incredibly thorough. That didn't matter to me because I already had a layout of the place. I knew damn near every room in that house including the square footage. I even had intel on the specific entries Hawks' men would be focusing on.

I headed for the front doors of the mansion, blending in with the other party goers. Loosening a breath, I stuck my hands in my pockets while waiting patiently to be let in. Anticipation crawled up my spine the closer I got to the entrance. In a matter of minutes, I'd see the woman I loved after months apart. I needed to get this over with so I could whisk her away and show her just how much I missed her.

Chapter 19

Claire

I tried to keep myself calm as Steven led me down the stairs to the main area where everyone waited. I scanned the crowd, taking in women and men all done up in formal attire with different masks covering their faces. I was met at the bottom step by an awaiting Hawks who wore a devil mask that matched his crimson suit. How fitting for him.

He held his hand out to me which I reluctantly took while meeting his steely gaze. "You look beautiful, *Harlow*." His lips tilted up slightly.

"Thank you, *Randall*." I replied with a curt smile.

He straightened, glowering at me. Clutching my hand tightly, he guided me to the edge of the main room toward a small stage with a microphone. I was definitely on display. I bit down on the inside of my cheek, scanning the room once again. There were two men standing toward the back. One of them was leaning against the wall casually with his arms crossed as if he were bored, while the other skimmed the room persistently. He was taller than his friend, built well though menacing despite the flashy gold mask he wore.

When his dark eyes collided with mine, he tipped his head slightly and shifted his gaze toward the man beside him. I glanced back at the man with the charcoal colored dragon mask. He had jet-black hair that was cropped close on the sides and slightly longer on top. The blood red tie he wore stood out against the black shirt and suit jacket. His hazel eyes glimmered in the dimly lit room. My heart plummeted to the pit of my stomach when they flicked to mine.

I blinked at him. I could feel tears forming as I tried to hold myself together. My legs nearly buckled with the weight of relief that spread through me. I had the strongest urge to run to him but remained still.

Mick.

He'd colored his hair, but I'd know those eyes and that jawline anywhere. He was alive! He was here to rescue me. Slowly, he lifted his hand, placing his index finger to his lips. With a single nod, I shifted my attention back to Hawks who began addressing his visitors.

"Welcome to the party ladies and gentlemen. Happy Halloween!" he began. "Thank you for coming tonight. It will definitely be one to remember." He had no idea how true that was. His lips spread in a wolfish grin as he looked me up and down. "Let's hear it for the one and only Harlow, who's graced us with her presence this evening."

A series of applause sounded around the room as I looked back to where Mick had been standing. He was now slowly moving through the crowd, closer to the stage. He didn't look at me as he approached, keeping his focus locked on Hawks who continued speaking.

"We have a special surprise later tonight. She'll be entertaining us with one of her signature dances." There were catcalls at that announcement and my free hand clenched tightly into a fist. He still held the other firmly while maintaining an evil smile that I was just itching to knock from his face. "Enjoy your evening, my friends!" he added before raising a glass of alcohol in the air.

After taking a sip of the drink, he tugged me into his side, placing his lips at my ear. "Behave yourself tonight," he snarled before lightly shoving me away.

Typically, I'd end up at the edge of the room, sinking into the shadows while waiting for permission to go back upstairs. Mick was at the edge of the stage as Hawks joined the crowd. I gracefully stepped down, heading for the back hall that led toward the kitchen. I knew Mick would follow. Steven was standing at the mouth of the entry and as I slipped by, he motioned to the watch on his wrist before holding up two fingers. I had two minutes of freedom. I could work with that.

I stopped at the pantry door, glancing back to see Mick clap Steven on the shoulder. I couldn't believe they were working together. After entering the small room, I spun around as Mick closed the door. Before I could even speak, his hands were on me. He clutched my waist with one hand while cupping my face with the other as he lowered his head toward mine.

"Jesus, I missed the fuck out of you," he rumbled before smashing his lips to mine.

I drank him in, unable to hold back the tears as he ran his tongue along the seam of my lips before invading my mouth. With a groan, his hand slid from my waist to the back of my thigh where he lifted my leg. I wrapped it around him easily as he pushed me into the wall. I moaned when I felt his hard length between my legs. I urged him closer with my hand on the middle of his back. A series of emotions overwhelmed me and I couldn't breathe, but I didn't care. I'd missed him more than I could ever express in words or actions. The grief was completely obliterated in those few seconds we connected.

All too soon, he lifted his head. Our breaths mingled as I tried to steady my racing heart.

"I thought you were dead," I cried.

Nodding, he lowered my leg before sliding his hands to either side of my face. "I know, darlin'. I'm so sorry." He kissed my chin. "I'm getting you out of here, okay? We have a plan and a lot more firepower. I need you to play along for just a while longer."

Releasing a breath, I said, "Okay. I can do that."

His lips kicked up. "You're so brave, so strong to keep your head up during all this. I'm so proud of you."

My heart squeezed at his words. I tried to blink away the tears in fear that I'd ruin my makeup. "I had to keep going for you," I said. "Steven is really working with you?"

"Yeah, he's part of the mafia."

I gasped. "What?" I hadn't expected that at all. He didn't strike me as mafia with his baby face and willingness to kiss Hawks' butt every chance he got. He deserved an Academy Award for his acting.

Mick chuckled. "Yeah, long story. You're safe with him though. Simon and Dom are outside setting up our ticket out. There's other guys like Steven here, too."

"I can't believe it. You've been planning this entire time?"

His lips turned down. "Most of the time, after ... recovery."

"I told him to save you," I murmured, shaking my head. Meeting his gaze I added, "Dom came off the elevator when Hawks was taking me. I told him to go to you instead."

He searched my face in the darkness with a look of reverence. "You sacrificed yourself for me. I'll never forget that."

I rested my palm against his heart. "I love you."

His lips were on mine again, devouring me hungrily before taking several steps back. "As much as I'd love to rip that dress off you, we've got to go." He turned to grab the door handle. Glancing back at me, he said, "We're going to get out of here together, Claire. After tonight I'm going to spend the rest of my life with you."

Wrought with emotion, I couldn't speak as he slipped out the door. I counted to thirty before entering the hall to find Steven standing against the opposite wall.

"Boss is in the bathroom right now. You need to go mingle. Anyone with a golden mask is safe."

Glancing around, I lowered my voice. "Why do you call him *boss* still?"

He winked before heading to the end of the hall. "Force of habit. It's best to keep up appearances anyway. I can't go around calling him *asshole*."

Smiling, I shook my head. "No, I guess you're right."

Mick

"Independence day is set and ready to go." Simon's voice came through the small earpiece I was wearing.

I made my way toward the back of the house, glancing out the window to the pool in back. This place was way too fucking big for my liking which further added to my hatred of Randall Hawks. He was more than just a cocky bastard with too much money. He was also a complete show off. It seriously amazed me that it'd taken this long for him to go down. Of the party goers, about a quarter of them were enemies and he was none the wiser. It felt good to know I'd be rocking his world before ending him tonight.

"Glocks stocked near the back entry," Dom said.

I glanced back at the main room where everyone mingled while drinking like their life depended on it. "Retrieving now," I said before slipping out the back door.

"Johnny's got visual on the door. No new guests since twenty hundred," Steven's voice. He was methodical, precise, and downright brilliant.

"Whereabouts of Violet?" I asked, hiding in the shadows at the edge of the yard as I made my way to the guns they'd stowed.

"She's talking to a guest. *Shit*." I froze where I stood, scowling at the house. Steven huffed out a laugh. "All right, this guy went to touch her. She nearly broke his fingers. He's walking away."

Grinning, I continued toward the weapons. "My girl."

"Violet's headed to the bathroom now. Angel, that's your move."

"On it," the female said. I think her real name was Rosa. We had code names for the women for discretion.

There were two of them besides Claire, who I deemed Violet because of her beautiful eyes. The women were tough, if not more so than the men. They were cunning, quick, and totally willing to participate in bringing Hawks down.

Bending down at the side gate near the pool, I slid my hand outside the wrought iron before plucking three guns from beneath a shrub. I tucked one behind me in my pants, the other in the pocket of my suit jacket and the third I held as I made my way back to the house. A guy named Heath met me on the patio. I handed him the gun.

"When's the party over, El Diablo?" he asked.

It'd become my nickname since we'd started planning and was based on a comic book vigilante. I welcomed the name because the whole back-story was kind of on point. Being offed by an enemy before being brought back to life to seek justice, fit with what I'd been through. Although I had zero plans to maintain this profession after tonight.

"Twenty-two hundred," I said. "We'll have seven minutes before Independence Day goes off." I checked my watch. Fifty-two minutes until all of this was over.

I headed back in the house, wandering toward another long hallway. Rosa stood against the wall, scrolling through her phone. She glanced up at me as I walked by and I gave her a small nod. I was heading for the billiard room where Hawks was. I wanted to be near him when the diversion tactic we'd set up happened.

Claire stepped out of the bathroom then, nearly colliding with me. I caught her by the waist to steady her. I'd been trying to keep my distance from her until the right moment and it had worked the last few hours. Being near her after all this time was like quenching my thirst after being lost in the desert.

"Hey stranger," I murmured.

"Hey," she breathed, biting her bottom lip.

God it was tough not allowing myself to take her away this second. My hands slid up her ribs, stopping beside her chest. I frowned. "What do you think you're doing?" I growled, curling my fingers around the handle of a gun she was hiding.

"Shit."

"Yeah, shit, hand it over." Turning to Rosa, I said, "Cover me." She nodded as I grabbed Claire's arm, yanking her back into the bathroom. I closed the door quietly before whirling on her. "If someone notices that, you'll ruin the plan or worse, you'll end up dead."

Crossing her arms, she said, "I know that, which is why it's in a place no one will be touching me."

My mouth popped open. "Are you honestly going to tell me that's a risk worth taking? You were already pawed at several times tonight."

She frowned at me. "I can handle myself."

Nostrils flaring, I backed her against the vanity, caging her in with my arms. Her breath caught and my gaze flicked to her lips briefly before meeting her eyes. "You're quite the little badass now, aren't you? Packing heat, nearly breaking fingers, all while walking around this place like you could fucking own it."

"I could if I wanted to. I'm stronger now, Mick. I've been training with Steven and I work out more."

I gave her body a careful perusal.

"Yeah, I can tell. Trust me, you're my ideal bad girl and I would love to test just how bad you can be later. Right now, this is my show."

Before she had time to register what I was doing, I flipped her around so her back was to my chest. Pressing into her, I ran my hand up the front of her dress before dipping into her bra. I slid my fingers along her tight nipple, earning a moan. It took everything in me to stick to the task at hand. I grabbed the handle of the gun, removing it from the hiding spot before releasing her.

"You can have this back when the time is right. Now, get your sexy ass back out there before my restraint snaps and I risk everything by bending you over this counter."

She opened her mouth to argue but thought better of it. Huffing out a breath, she exited the bathroom. Rosa walked with her to the main room as I continued toward Hawks, tucking her gun next to the other one behind me. I glanced down at my watch again.

"Rapture in fifteen minutes. Dom, are you ready?" I asked.

"Fuse is good. Just waiting to ignite."

"Johnny, are you prepared to usher people out?"

"Affirmative, El Diablo."

Smirking, I stepped in the doorway of the billiard room. "Time to raise Hell."

Chapter 20

Claire

I no longer had a weapon thanks to Mick's constant need for control. I understood he had a plan, but sometimes things didn't work out the way we wanted. If the last year had taught me anything it was that. He should know that, too. The gal who'd trailed me to the bathroom veered off to the left as I entered the main room again. She hadn't spoken to me, yet I knew she was with Mick and whoever else he had in here. They all had different variations of gold masks.

Hawks had been ever the host as usual. He mingled around the room while observing me every once in a while. He seemed pretty oblivious to the fact that his home had enemies in it, including one he thought was dead. I hadn't seen him the last hour and wondered if that's where Mick was headed.

I grew anxious at the thought of them being together even if Mick had disguised himself well. With his shorter dark hair and the mask that covered all except the lower part of his face and eyes, he was nearly unrecognizable. If it weren't for the fact that I'd so thoroughly memorized his features months ago, I wouldn't know it was him.

I caught movement to my left, shifting my concentration to Steven who was inching toward the front door. He murmured something as his gaze zeroed in on one of the doormen. Was he talking to himself? I scanned the other people in gold masks. Out of the guests in this room, almost half were my new saviors. I noticed a couple others mouthing something as well. It was then I realized they were all communicating covertly with earpieces.

Holy shit! It was straight up *Mission: Impossible* in here.

"Hey, beautiful, how are you doing tonight?" a deep voice said from behind me.

I spun around, taking in the man with a deep blue suit and a white mask. His thin lips tipped up as he gawked at me in a way that sent a ripple of revulsion through me.

"Hello," I replied, clasping my hands in front of me.

"Are you enjoying the party?"

I plastered a fake smile on my face. "Yes, Randall sure knows how to throw one."

"Indeed." He continued his shameless staring. "You look absolutely delectable this evening. I'm looking forward to your show." He winked and I bristled.

Right, Hawks had promised a performance. As if on cue, Steven appeared beside the man, his jaw tight. "You're needed, Harlow. The boss would like a word with you."

"Excuse me," I said to the stranger who bowed slightly as we walked away from him. "Am I performing before this ends?" I dipped my chin, speaking quietly.

"Negative. Mick's in the billiard room currently. The real show is about to start so I need you next to me until he gives the word."

"What are you guys up to?" I asked as I followed him through the crowd. He stopped in front of a window that overlooked the side courtyard near the pool house.

"You'll see." He smirked.

I was grateful I wouldn't have to dance in front of the guests. Although I was still a bundle of nerves wondering when this would all be over. I was more than ready to kiss this place goodbye. I wanted to see my family again. I definitely had a new appreciation for those I cared about after what I'd been through. Some people would curl into themselves and fall into a pit of depression so strong that they'd never get out. While it would have been incredibly easy to do that, I chose to stay strong and persevere.

Steven placed a finger against his ear as if he were listening to whomever was speaking. His gaze shifted to mine. "Things are about to get chaotic. Stay close to me."

I was about to ask him what was happening when a loud explosion sounded from outside. My head swung to the windows in time to see the pool house erupt into a cloud of flames and smoke.

"Oh my god!" I gasped.

The main room erupted in chaos as people shrieked while scrambling to take cover. I stood motionless in shock, watching as they scurried about. After a few minutes, Steven reached for my arm before leading me through the throng of people. We headed down the hall where I'd last seen Mick. I glanced back, noticing that most of the invited guests were now headed for the front door while the ones in gold masks remained calm.

"Where is she?!" Hawks bellowed from the billiard room right before we entered. His eyes landed on mine, narrowing to slits.

"She's here. She was talking with Brennon," Steven explained.

I shifted my gaze to Mick who blended in with two golden masked guys on one side of a billiard table. There were three of Hawks' men on the opposite side. The room was sort of like an upscale game room with leather couches and a small bar. Mick winked at me as he tucked his left arm behind him. Was he going to pull a gun?

"It's the pool house, boss." A man entered the room with his suit covered in ash.

"Looks like our guests of honor decided to show after all. Did you see anyone?"

"Not a soul. I've got Hammond and Taylor scoping the grounds. People are leaving ... "

"Let them leave." Hawks growled as he focused on me again. "Get over here, girl. Now." Steven turned me in the direction of Mick before releasing me, giving a single nod to obey.

I made my way around the pool table toward Hawks in trepidation. I didn't want him touching me ever again. I took the route that had me walking by both the golden masked men and Mick. As I approached them, I was suddenly grabbed from behind before being pushed against the wall. Shouting ensued until there was the click of a gun cocking and Hawks' voice boomed out. My eyes widened as I realized I was being blocked by one of the men in a gold mask. He stood with his back to me while pressing me into the wall. I had to stand on my tiptoes to see beyond him.

Mick was to our right, blocking my side while his gun aimed at Hawks who was now flanked by two of his own men. The other one stood near the man that had entered, closer to the door with Steven.

Ripping off his mask, Hawks glared at Mick. "You're a fool for pulling such a stunt. I knew you people would show up to avenge Silver. Sorry to say, you're outnumbered." His voice was clear and deep, although I didn't miss the look of shock he was trying to mask.

Mick's lips tilted up slowly, forming a mischievous grin. He kept his gun trained on Hawks without speaking. His free hand slid behind his back, lifting his suit jacket to show the gun he'd taken from me. Carefully, I reached out to grip the handle before tucking the gun behind me. He let his jacket fall again, placing his hand at his side.

Hawks turned his attention to Steven and the other men beside him. "Go see if there's any sign of more." He looked Mick and the two guys up and down. "We can handle these ones."

A dark chuckle spilled from Mick as he shook his head. Hawks glared at him, jaw muscle clenching.

"We'll secure the house," Steven said before leaving with the other two men. That left Hawks with his two guards and the four of us.

"Did you really think you could walk into my home and take her without incident? Cute party trick with the little light show out back. However, you're going to have to do better than that if you expect to leave here alive."

"It's really not that difficult to acquire some dynamite when you need." The man flanking the other side of Mick said. "Creating a diversion was necessary for what we have planned."

"Graves, Finley take care of them," Hawks said, dismissively waving his hand.

He'd barely finished his sentence when the man in front of me and the one beside Mick fired off two shots, putting a bullet in each leg of Graves and Finley. They both collapsed to the ground, crying out in agony.

A series of gunfire sounded from the main room, along with hollering before it went eerily silent. Hawks pulled his own gun, squeezing the trigger. Nothing happened. Mick lowered his gun before crossing his arms.

"How careless of you to bring fuck all to a gun fight." Hawks' face turned ashen as he blinked at him in confusion. "You see, *Randall*, you're the one who's outnumbered. We didn't come to avenge the death of Mickey Silver."

"Who are you exactly?" he demanded in a gravelly voice. Of course, he wouldn't recognize Mick by now. He was too full of himself to realize who he was dealing with even in perilous times.

Mick's shoulders tightened as he dropped his hands to his sides. Even though I couldn't see his face, I knew he was angry. Fury rolled off of him in waves.

"I'm the darkness you have nightmares about. The one single entity in this world sent back from below to destroy you. The motherfucking reckoning, you arrogant piece of shit!" Ripping his mask off, he aimed the gun again. "*I'm* Mickey fucking Silver and the devil sent me back to collect for your sins." Cocking back the hammer, he pulled the trigger, hitting Hawks in the hand that held his gun.

"Ahhhh!" he screamed, lifting his hand up to inspect it. He peered down at his now mangled and bloodied fingers. His eyes were full of panic and rage.

Mick stepped toward Hawks who was clutching his right elbow with his still intact left hand to keep the injured one raised. "I'm sure you're wondering why you have no bullets." He nodded his head to the two men who'd been shot in the legs. The guys in the golden masks went to them before taking their weapons and dragging them out of the room. "Your number two isn't who you thought he was. You've had a target on your back for a long time and it all ends now."

A loud guttural growl roared from Hawks' mouth as he charged toward Mick who lifted his free arm, elbowing him in the chest. Hawks stumbled back.

"I'm going to make it count this time. You're a dead man, Silver."

Ignoring him, Mick glanced at me over his shoulder. "Lose the mask, darlin'. I want him to get a good long look at your face before you put a bullet between his eyes."

I pulled my mask off, scowling at Hawks who blinked at me while shaking his head. "I should have killed you!"

"Yet you didn't," I said. "You had to play with me instead, *beat* me, and use me to stroke your filthy ego. You probably should have quit while you were ahead." Mick growled beside me.

"You don't have the guts," Hawks spat.

Quirking a brow, I raised my gun as I aimed for his face. "Don't I?"

Mick bit down on his bottom lip, pinning me with a hungry look. "Damn, I like that," he murmured huskily and my blood warmed. "Let's not kill him just yet though, babe. He needs to suffer." Nodding, I lowered my gun. "Now here's the deal, *Randall*. I've got several men clearing this house, taking out your team, and fixing to literally blow the roof off this place." He glanced down at his watch. "We have about ten more minutes until the neighbors get a show that will put 4th of July fireworks to shame."

"With your dynamite?" Hawks released a bitter laugh, ripping a piece of his shirt to wrap it around his hand.

"Actually, the dynamite was for that *cute* little diversion. The party has been going for a few hours now. That's plenty of time to lay C-4 around the perimeter."

Hawks' chest rumbled as he glowered at Mick. "Fuck you. You're bluffing."

Mick shrugged. "Maybe, although I wouldn't bet against me. Now, you're going to walk out of here or I'll let my woman end your miserable life in this room."

He had no choice but to do as Mick said. His men were obviously gone if no one had come to his rescue yet. Hawks headed for the doorway as Mick grabbed my free hand, leading me to follow. We wandered down the hall, back to the main room that was now empty except for Steven who stood near the stage area. He'd removed his mask and suit jacket. He waited there with his hands behind his back, a look of indifference on his face as we approached.

"Stupid traitor," Hawks spat at his feet. Steven didn't move.

Mick let go of my hand before grabbing him by the scruff of the neck, forcing him into a folding chair that had been set out on the stage. Steven produced a rope from behind his back before securing him to the chair while Mick held a gun against his forehead.

"If you move, I'll kill you, which I really want Claire to have the pleasure of doing. Don't disappoint me, asshole."

Hawks stayed perfectly still with his hands bound behind him and his thighs strapped to the seat of the chair.

Mick lowered the gun, cocking his head. "So you touched her then? Marked up her body with bruises and blood."

Hawks' jaw clenched, his eyes darkening as they pinned me. "She's mouthy."

Mick glanced back at me. "That she is. Turns me on. It's one of the reasons I fell in love with her," he replied before focusing back on him. Without warning, he connected a perfect upper-cut to Hawks' chin. His head fell back before sagging forward. "What did I tell you would happen if you touched her?" He struck another blow to his cheek. "They won't be able to iden-tify your body, you worthless bastard!"

Mick stepped back beside me, pulling his cell phone from the front pocket of his slacks. My body hummed at the raw ferocity emanating from him. Was it wrong that I was totally turned on by the way he'd defended me? Bringing the phone to his ear, he began speaking almost immediately.

"Be ready on my command. Is the road clear?" He listened for a moment. "Perfect. Any last words for the almighty Ran-dall Hawks who played with the wrong asshole?" A slow smile formed on his lips. "Yeah, he's not worth the breath. Hit the detonator when I signal."

He slid the phone back into his pocket after disconnecting the call. Steven stepped around Hawks to stand on the other side of Mick.

"By now I'm sure you know that I've never worked for you," he began. "Do you remember about five years ago when you visited New York and stole that woman? You know, the one you keep under wraps except to play dress up with your new doll." He shifted his gaze to me when I gasped.

Cynthia *was* like me. "You're a vile human," I fumed.

"He's not human," Mick muttered.

"She belonged to someone else like Claire did. You killed him so you could take her, then you brainwashed her into thinking you saved her. You may think you're hot on the West Coast but on the East, you're public enemy number one. I've been waiting to take you out for a long time."

"Fuck. You," Hawks gritted out, wincing when he tried to tug at the ropes around his wrists. Blood trickled out from behind him and my stomach wobbled.

Even after all I'd seen these last few months and before, I hated the sight of blood. It brought me back to that room where I'd thought I lost Mick forever. Where the floor pooled with the blood of two innocent men alongside Jack Silver. He got what was coming to him. Mick and Kyle didn't deserve it.

A new rush of anger swept through me as my fingers twitched against the cool steel of the gun in my hand. Randall Hawks had taken my life away for half a year. He'd tried to break me down, to bend me to his will. Instead of cowering, I grew stronger like a phoenix rising out of the ashes. Loving me the way he did, Mick was allowing me to be the one to end this. It was my turn to cast judgement.

"Claire," Steven said, turning his attention to me. I looked at him. "Remember when I took you shooting at the beach? What was it that I told you when you shot that conch shell?"

Despite the situation, I smiled fondly. Even when I thought Steven worked for Hawks, I'd enjoyed learning to shoot with him. He'd never been aggressive toward me or said cruel things.

Now I knew why. "Steady, aim, and picture the shell as *his* head," I replied.

Steven smiled as Mick chuckled beside me. "Do you remember what happened to that shell when you pulled the trigger?"

Focusing back on Hawks, I met his stare as I glowered at him. "I blew it to pieces."

I swore I heard Mick groan beside me but I didn't look at him. My attention was totally concentrated on Randall Hawks. The man who brought out a different side of me that I'd let lie dormant until now. I never considered myself capable of violence, let alone murder, before him. Yet here I was, so ready to end his life.

"You worthless bitch! You won't get away with this. Do you know who I am? Who I have in my corner. You people are nothing!" he hollered at us, looking demented on the brink of snapping.

"Isn't that adorable," Mick said. "You think you're actually bigger than who you've fucked over. Steven?"

"Yeah?" Steven crossed his arms with a slow grin.

"Aren't you a descendant of Gotti or something?"

"Capone," Steven said.

"Ah, my mistake. Would you like to tell Randall here who you really are before she caps him, or should we just let it remain a mystery?"

Hawks' eyes enlarged, darting between the three of us. His chest heaved as he worked out the conversation in his surely scattered mind. Once he realized it, his throat rolled in an audible swallow. "Mafia," he breathed.

"Steady, aim, Claire," Steven said. I lifted the gun in my right hand while using my left to stabilize the base of the handle.

Mick lifted his hand, sticking his middle finger up. "See you in Hell, bitch." He turned to me, resting his hand against my cheek. "Make it count, darlin', or don't. He'll be nothing but ash soon anyway."

Inhaling a deep breath, I took one last look at Hawks to make sure I had his undivided attention. His brow rose as if challenging me. After all this time, I was finally getting my revenge on this vicious man. He'd taken everything away from me for a power he no longer held. I searched within myself, trying to find a moment of weakness to stop me. I felt nothing, and while that should have scared me, it didn't. I now understood Mick's need to seek vengeance. The desire to right every wrong I'd been dealt kept my hands steady.

I watched Hawks suck in a ragged breath as his shoulders squared. He had no idea what I was capable of. Before he could exhale, I squeezed the trigger.

Mick

The second the gun went off, I grabbed Claire's hand before tossing it to the ground and pulling her with me to the front door with Steven on our heels. As soon as he stepped off the last stair outside, a series of clicks and pops sounded.

"Run," I said, pulling her with me. How she kept up with me while still wearing those stilettos, I'll never know. This girl was a certified badass and she was all mine.

Glancing back at the house as we hauled ass to the edge of the gate, I saw the first spark ignite then the next. Simon and Dom had laid the explosives strategically around the perimeter of the house before wiring up a mechanism where they could detonate. In seconds, we were encased with a blast of heat as the world erupted around us. Everything, including the house, was blown to smithereens.

Tightening my hold on Claire, I sprinted toward the road where the car was waiting.

Simon was leaning against the hood with Dom, both of them laughing about something. Steven's guys were long gone except for Johnny who was his ride. They'd taken out most of Hawks' men, leaving their bodies in the house to destroy the evidence. Anyone who had the decency to leave the party after the first explosion would live because no one still breathing had seen our faces. It was the perfect crime.

As I slowed to a walk, my chest tightened when I registered the feel of Claire's warm palm against mine. Stopping suddenly, I spun on my heels, catching her by the waist before she collided into me. We were both breathless and I knew there would come a time in the near future that she'd likely go into hysterics because of her first and hopefully last kill, but right now that didn't matter. We were alive. More importantly, we were together.

Palming her cheek, I tilted my head down before crushing my lips to hers. Her mouth parted in a gasp so I used that to my advantage. I slipped my tongue into her mouth, earning a moan that sent a jolt of awareness straight to my cock. Dropping my free hand over her ass, I pressed her into me as she bit down on my bottom lip.

"Fuck, I love you," I said, claiming her mouth again.

"Listen, as great as it is that you're both out and alive, we don't need a show," Simon hollered from the car.

Claire pulled back from me, inhaling a sharp breath. I smirked at her as I responded to Simon. "Give us ten minutes. Take a walk or something." I kissed her again, loving the way she immediately melted against me without hesitation.

"Mick ... " Dom said in warning. I reluctantly released my girl.

"Buzz kills," I muttered as I slipped her hand in mine again before heading for the car. Claire laughed and that was probably one of the best sounds I'd ever heard in my life. She was my kind of crazy to be laughing after what just happened.

I opened the back door for her, leaning in as she slid to the opposite side. "Stay right there. I'll be back in a second." She nodded as I closed the door.

"How long until the fire department shows up?" Simon asked Steven who was texting on his phone.

"ETA is about five minutes so we gotta roll out. You sure you aren't looking for work?"

My brother smiled, shaking his head. "This was fun and all but it isn't really my style. Plus, I'm sure my fiancée would break a few of my bones if I even joked about taking you up on that."

Steven chuckled before shaking his hand then Dom's. He faced me with a smile. "You're a fucking marvel to be on the brink of death and get the justice you were seeking, El Diablo."

I cleared my throat. "Yeah, thanks for all the help. I couldn't have gotten her back without you. I wouldn't be here if you hadn't taken up for her or for me." I owed this man my life. Steven was the main reason I was still here. I got lucky, which was a word that didn't normally hang out in my vocabulary. The adrenaline coursing through me had me feeling a little erratic and emotional.

Steven clapped my shoulder. "Your girl's a good egg. She's smart as hell and tough as nails, too. If you guys ever need anything, you know where to find me."

"Thanks, same here." He gave a final salute as Johnny waved before getting into a car parked across the street.

"Let's get out of here," I said, slipping by Dom to crawl in the back seat.

I grabbed Claire by the waist, pulling her between my legs as I rested my back against the closed door. Wrapping my arms around her, I kissed her temple as she relaxed against me, folding her arms over mine.

"I keep feeling like this is a dream," she said softly as Simon turned the car around, heading down the road toward town. "I can't believe you're here."

Hugging her tight, I said, "I promise this is real. I'm not going anywhere, darlin'. It's you and me."

She tilted her head back to look at me in the dark cab with tears pooling in those violet eyes. I slid my thumb over her cheek, brushing a few that escaped. "I love you, Mickey Silver."

I swear to God as long as I lived, those words would break my heart a little more every time she said them. I didn't deserve this woman. I coveted her when I had no right. I put her through hell. I was no better than Randall Hawks, yet by some miracle, she gave me her heart. "I love you more, my sweet Claire."

Her lips tipped up in the corner as she nestled against my chest again, resting her head over my heart. "How long will you love me?"

I ran my fingers through her silky hair, responding without an ounce of hesitation. "Forever."

Chapter 21

Claire

After a few days of lying low in a hotel, we went back to Seattle so that Mick could take care of closing down the business for good. During our time apart, he'd allowed Steven and the, I can't believe I'm saying this, mafia to take over. It wasn't only the business that needed sorted. He also had to make sure that Simon would be able to run their shop on his own with the handful of employees they'd hired. Mick and I weren't staying in Seattle. At least not for a while, which had everything to do with all that happened in the last year. There were so many bad memories that I just couldn't stomach the thought of continuing to live there at the moment. Mick felt the same way. Even if he hadn't, he would go anywhere with me. He'd said as much.

We were currently on our way for me to officially meet Simon's fiancée, Mackaela, at their house in the Alki Beach area. I was a little nervous because she was the only other woman he'd confided in, the one he'd grown up with that was his best friend. It wasn't due to jealousy or anything like that. I simply wanted her to like me.

Mick slid his hand to my denim-clad thigh, squeezing just above my knee. He was driving his classic Camaro which was the only vehicle he had now.

"She's going to love you like I do," he assured.

I tucked my hair behind my ear, chewing on my bottom lip. "I've heard so much about her and I already like her. I just want to make sure she knows how I feel about you. That I'm not like the girls from your past."

Mick's brow crumpled. "Trust me, she knows that. In fact, the first time you came to one of my parties, she knew you were different. She caught me watching you and called me out on it."

My lips tipped up. "Really?"

He chuckled, pulling into the narrow driveway. "Yeah." He killed the engine before turning in his seat to place a hand under my chin, drawing my lips to his. I instantly moved closer to him. A warmth flowed through me that put me at ease as he kissed me. Pulling back, his forehead rested against mine. "You ready?" Nodding, I released a breath before reaching for the door handle.

Mick held my hand as we approached the front door, continuing to hold it as he rang the doorbell. After a few beats, Simon answered the door. He gave his brother a hug and smiled at me. They didn't look a lot alike, but there were certain similarities. Simon was leaner and taller by a few inches with nearly black hair and emerald green eyes, whereas Mick had hazel ones and his hair was more of a dirty blond. Although right now, his hair matched his brothers since he'd colored it to go undercover at Hawks' estate.

"Hey, guys, come on in." Simon stepped back, allowing us to enter before closing the door. "Mackaela's just washing up. She's working on an art project for school. She's been painting like crazy this past week."

"Has she calmed down any?" Mick asked, tugging me along with him to the open living room. He sat down on a black couch before pulling me into his lap.

He'd been incredibly touchy-feely the last few days. I didn't mind. We went from being near each other every day to being apart for six months. After thinking he was gone forever, I couldn't bear being separated. His arm curled around my waist as he absently swirled his thumb along my hip.

Simon sat in one of the adjacent armchairs, smirking at his brother. "Maybe a little. She still wants to kick your ass."

Mick laughed. "That's nothing new."

Just then, footsteps sounded from behind us as Mackaela began speaking. "Actually, I don't want to kick your ass anymore. Although the urge to slap you is still pretty strong."

I turned to look at her, taking in her long dark hair that was pulled up high on top of her head. She was wearing a baggy t-shirt with leggings. I noticed the skin along her neck looked pinker than the rest, almost puckered. I wondered if the scar was partial evidence of the rough life Mick said she'd had. My gaze drifted to hers. She smiled at me as she entered the living room.

"Claire, a woman I envy," she said. My brows lifted. "You're a freaking saint to put up with Mickey Silver."

I smiled. "It's nice to meet you," I said. "Although you've been dealing with him much longer. That takes a special kind of patience I'm not sure I've mastered yet." Mick pinched my waist and I giggled.

"True, though I have the luxury of ignoring him and not having to see him every day. I'd run the other way if I were you."

Mick growled. "Easy."

Rolling her eyes, she punched his arm. "Calm down, Mickey, she's not going anywhere." She looked at me again. "I'm so glad you're okay. I'm sorry about what happened to you."

"Thanks," I said. "I'm so grateful for your guys' help. Honestly, you put your lives at risk for me. I'm not sure saying thank you is enough."

Mackaela moved to sit on the arm of the chair Simon was in. "Mickey would move the earth for you if he had to. We'd do the same because you're important to him."

Simon nodded. "We're family, it's what we do."

"All right, it's getting too deep in here," Mick grumbled.

I was only now learning how difficult it was for him to show emotion in front of others. He'd spent so long living a life where he was expected to be fierce and ruthless. I felt kind of special that I was one of the few who'd seen a softer side of him.

"So what's the plan?" Mackaela asked. "I hear you're intending to leave Seattle."

"Yeah," Mick said, sliding the hand at my waist to my thigh. "We can't really be here right now after everything. There's too many bad memories."

Mackaela nodded. "I get it. Where are you going to go?"

Mick glanced at me, the corners of his mouth tilting up slightly. "Colorado." I gave him a smile. "We're thinking Boulder, right, babe?"

"Yeah." I turned to Simon and Mackaela. "I wanted to be somewhere smaller than here, but not totally remote like my hometown."

"When are you planning on leaving?" Simon asked.

I bit down on my bottom lip. "We're leaving tomorrow."

Mackaela's eyes widened as they flew to Mick's. "You just got back."

"Mack," his voice was soft, "I'm sorry to leave again so soon. It's just too difficult. We also haven't had a lot of time together just the two of us. After everything ... " He shook his head, clearing his throat. "I just want to try normal for a while."

Her lips turned down. "I understand."

"We'll come back for the wedding next summer though. I promised to walk you down the aisle." He smiled at her and I didn't miss the flash of emotion in her eyes.

Simon wrapped his arm around her waist before kissing her arm. "I honestly think it'll be good for you, bro." He looked at me. "You, too. Besides, we can always come visit."

"We'd like that," I said. Mick agreed.

Mackaela ran a hand through her hair. "I'm so happy for you both. I can't believe you found someone, Mickey. It's just ... " Her eyes welled with tears. "It's just that I could have lost you for good six months ago. That pain was worse than anything I'd ever felt. You're my best friend and all I've ever wanted was for you to find something meaningful. I just wish I had more time with you, both of you." Her gaze slid to mine. "I know you don't know me that well, Claire, but you should know I think you're really amazing. Trust me when I say I didn't expect him to ever settle down. Knowing now that he's ready for that means the world to me."

"I promise to take care of him," I said, my voice thick with emotion.

It was true that I didn't know her well. Yet the way she spoke, the look in her eyes, told me everything I needed about the relationship between her and Mick. From what I'd learned through him, he was like a brother to her for so long. They were family. To have her blessing meant the world to me. It further solidified my love for him. Despite his cocky attitude when we first met and his denials, he had a heart. If I'd ever doubted that before I certainly didn't now.

"Can you make me another promise?" she asked, swiping at the tears as she sniffled.

"Of course," I said as Mick frowned at her.

Smirking, she said, "Please don't be afraid to put him in his place from time to time. You can always call me if you need tips."

The three of us laughed while Mick muttered something un-intelligible. "You don't have to worry about that."

Mick

After the heart to heart, I decided I needed a drink. Simon and I disappeared to the upstairs deck that provided a clear view of Seattle's skyline across the water. The sky was a gloomy gray, and I could smell the hint of rain and seawater in the air.

I stared out at the choppy water, taking a sip of my beer. Simon stood beside me at the railing, leaning against it with his own beer in hand.

"Do you miss him?" I asked.

He was quiet for a full minute before answering. "No. Do you?"

Lifting my shoulder in a slight shrug, I said, "I know it probably doesn't make sense, but yeah. I do miss him. Not who he was the last ten years or so, just who he was before."

Jack Silver was a vile human for doing what he had to my mother, to Cory's mother. He spent my entire life lying to me, so that was something difficult to forgive. At the end of the day though, he was still my father. He was the only parent I'd ever had.

"I always looked up to him growing up. He obviously wasn't Dad of the Year or anything in hindsight, but when I was a kid I loved him. All I ever wanted for so long was to be just like him, to impress him. When he'd mention how proud he was of me or task me with new responsibilities, I'd felt like I was on top of the world."

Simon nodded while frowning at the water. "It bothers me that I started to open up to him knowing what I do now. When we met up last year to talk, he'd acted genuinely sorry for not being involved in my life. He claimed that my mother made it out like I was fine with her and that asshole Todd. He said until I found you, he didn't know what was going on in my life. After hearing what he did to your mom, I feel like it was all a lie." His gaze slid to mine. "I won't miss him. I stand behind that because I never knew him like you did. However, I'd be lying if I said I wasn't upset he's gone now. I didn't really get a chance with him you know?"

"Yeah, maybe that's for the best." I ran a hand through my hair. "It hurts more than I thought it would. Claire was right."

Simon lifted a brow as I smiled tightly. "When I made the call to Lorenzo after I found out Cory's secret, she told me I'd regret wanting Jack gone forever. She thought I'd change my mind. At the time I thought she was crazy." I shook my head with a sigh. "I pulled the trigger though, Simon. I'm the one that ended his life when he showed no remorse for what he'd done." The images I had from that night still burned in the back of my mind. "He might have ended up dying at Hawks' hands anyway but being the one to take out the man that brought me into this world hurts a lot fucking more than I thought it would."

He placed a hand on my shoulder. "I can't begin to imagine what that feels like. I'm sorry that you have to bear that burden now."

I took a healthy drink of my beer. "Out of all the things that have happened in the last year and a half, that will haunt me the most. It's why I want to get out of this town for a while. I need to separate myself from the memories that I can't shake. Claire wants that, too."

He released my shoulder, staring back out at the view. "She's good for you."

"She's too good for me," I corrected and he chuckled.

"That's probably true."

"How did you know Mackaela was the one?" I asked.

His lips tilted up on one side as he looked at me. "There was just something about her that I couldn't help be drawn to. When I first met her, she was harsh, yet her eyes didn't match the rest of her tough exterior. Initially she intrigued me. I knew she was broken and I hated myself for thinking about her as *more* when I was there for her after her mom died. She was mending a broken heart. While I wanted to help her, I also wanted to pull her into my arms and never let go. Mackaela may have been lost when we met, but I swear she's the one that saved *me*."

"She's never loved anyone as much as she loves you, Simon. You helped her when I couldn't. While it kills me that I was a horrible friend to her, I'm glad she had you. That she still has you."

"She's everything to me. I can't imagine my life without her. After I was shot, I realized that life is too short. I don't think either of us expected to fall in love. It just kind of happened. You know what she's been through, so for her to trust me, to give herself to me, I knew right then and there that I'd love her the rest of my life."

"You're the only person in this world I'd want her with," I said.

He grinned. "I know. I also know that even if you don't see it or feel it, you're worthy of Claire. You cheated death to get back to her. That's not something many have the opportunity to do."

"I never thought there'd be a day that I'd love someone more than myself," I admitted with a wry grin. Simon laughed. "She's everything I could have ever wanted without even knowing exactly what that was. She confronts me without fear and when she loves, it's like the purest form of pleasure I've ever felt. I never really believed in fate or luck before her. I want her by my side for the rest of my life even though the thought of it scares the shit out of me."

Simon held his beer bottle up in my direction. "To the women who made men out of the Silver brothers." I clinked my bottle against his.

We each took a drink and I focused back on the skyline, inhaling another deep breath. It was a long brutal road to get to where I was now, but I'd do it all over again if I had to. I'd take another bullet. I'd welcome the heartbreak of my father's betrayal. I'd even make the same mistakes if it meant discovering what I hadn't realized I needed. To have something to hold onto made it all worth it.

Epilogue - Claire

"You're literally fucking killing me," Mick groaned as I made up our new bed.

We'd been in Boulder for a week now and just had the last of our new furniture delivered. I was eager to sleep on a real mattress finally instead of the blow up one. The minute the king-sized bed was assembled, I began making it up with the new sheets and comforter. I'd just placed the pillows when he'd said that. I glanced over my shoulder at him.

"How?" I asked, narrowing my eyes when I caught him checking out my ass.

"You're all bent over in those leggings. I'm having a really hard time concentrating," he grumbled, setting the power drill in his hand on the nightstand.

Rolling my eyes, I turned around to face him. "You're supposed to be mounting the TV."

He stepped closer, placing his hands on my hips. "I'd rather mount you." His eyes darkened as he bent his head to kiss the corner of my mouth. "We need to make sure the mattress is comfortable," he added, trailing a path with his lips to my neck.

A flood of warmth spread through me as a familiar ache formed between my legs. Wrapping my arms around his neck, I let my head fall back while he continued nibbling my skin. "That's sound logic." I gasped when he pulled me against him. I bit down on my bottom lip, so easily distracted by him every single time.

He lifted his head, lips hovering over mine now. "I'm a logical man, sweet Claire." He kissed me then and it was game over after that.

I opened for him, gliding my tongue against his while tugging at his shorter hair. He groaned as he lowered his hands to my thighs before lifting me in his arms. He guided me backward until I was lying on the bed. Settling between my legs, he slid his left hand up my ribs to my chest, making me cry out as he swept his thumb along my hardened peak. I lifted my hips, rocking against him and he shuddered.

"God, you feel good," he murmured against my lips.

I lifted the hem of his t-shirt, running my hands up his smooth, firm stomach. He sat up slightly to remove the shirt. My focus shifted to his jeans. He stared down at me as I undid the button before pulling the zipper down and fisting his cock. He grew even harder as I stroked him slowly.

His chest rumbled. "I don't think I'll ever get over what your touch does to me."

"Good." I released him before tugging his jeans down further.

He stood unexpectedly, chest heaving as he pinned me with a hungry look. He removed the jeans completely before his hands flew to my waist, tugging down my leggings and panties. After that, he reached in the drawer of the nightstand for a condom as I yanked my shirt over my head, grateful that I wasn't wearing a bra right now. He inhaled a sharp breath as he hovered over me again, running his length against my wet center. My eyes closed and I wrapped my legs around his waist.

"Look at me, darlin'." he whispered. My gaze lifted to his. "I don't deserve you and I question your sanity for staying with me." He put his weight on one hand, holding his body above me as he used the other to position himself at my entrance. "But I love you so fucking much and I'm so grateful you're mine."

My heart constricted as I cried out when he slipped inside, gliding in and out slowly as he peered down at me.

"I love you." I curled my fingers around his tattooed muscles when he lowered his lips to mine again.

He kissed me deep and slow, igniting a fire in my blood. It didn't take long for me to cry out as euphoria took over. Before

I could come down, he rolled so that I was now on top of him, straddling his hips. I gave him full access to my chest and he cupped each breast while gazing up at me with his lips parted. I leaned back, bracing my hands on his thighs as his attention drifted to where we were joined.

"God damn, I love watching myself move in and out of you," he confessed on a groan.

I rode him hard and fast, climbing toward another orgasm as he grabbed my hips, pumping into me. I felt myself tighten around him as my body trembled with another powerful climax. He followed right behind me and I collapsed against his chest, lying my cheek above his racing heart.

Mick tangled his fingers in the hair at the back of my head, holding me tight against him as our breathing slowed. My index finger slid along his shoulder absently.

He rolled me to his side before sitting up. "I'll be right back, don't move," he said before brushing his lips against mine and sliding off the bed. He wandered to the master bathroom, closing the door.

He was only gone a few moments before crawling next to me again. I lifted up to position myself so that I rested my head on his chest again. He curled his arm around my shoulder before running his fingers through the ends of my hair.

We were quiet for a while and when Mick finally spoke, his voice came out gruff. "Growing up, I was always striving for excellence, trying to gain my father's attention so that he'd be proud of me. All that time I'd thought he cared about me, that he *wanted* me." His hand ran from my hair, over my arm that rested on his waist. He interlaced our fingers, moving his thumb over mine.

I nodded against him. "I'm sorry he made you feel like you had to be perfect to be accepted," I said.

"Me too. I hate that I'll never get a chance to find out if he ever really loved me." He inhaled a deep breath before releasing it slowly. "Actually I don't think he ever did because he never would have given himself up for me. Not the way you did, Claire." He lifted his head. I pulled back slightly to look at him.

His eyes were misted with unshed tears, his brow crinkled slightly. "It was instinctual," I said. "In the moment I didn't know what Hawks was planning or what he would do to me. I didn't know if I'd make it out alive. When I saw Dom, I couldn't risk being rescued if it ended up being too late for you. I didn't want to live in a world where you didn't exist. Even if we didn't end up together or even if you'd have sent me off on a flight that night and things happened differently, I would have come back to you, I think."

He shook his head. "You're so much better off without me. I was an asshole to you, I *used* you. Sometimes I'm afraid that you're going to realize you made a mistake. That I'm not the man you want me to be because I won't be able to take care of you properly or give you all you want."

His vulnerability sent a pang of sorrow to my chest. He thought he wouldn't be able to give me what I wanted, yet he was so wrong. I found a peace in him that I'd never known before. I felt like I'd been searching my whole life to be content, to be satisfied. Mickey Silver gave that to me. When I was with him, no matter where it was, I felt ... home.

"I thought I could have grown to love Cory at some point the first few months we were together," I admitted. "There was this guy in high school who was a total jock that you probably would've hated. I thought the same thing about him, but just couldn't bring myself to develop the feelings. My parents have only been married for ten years. They were both with other people previously. My real dad died when I was ten."

"Claire ... "

I shook my head.

"I've never mentioned it because I don't like to think about it. He was a total nomad, a restless soul that was constantly bouncing from job to job. He couldn't sit still exceptionally long. Him and my mom never married even though they stayed together until I was around seven. He wanted to get out of Winthrop, wanted to see other places. He'd only stuck it out as long as he had because of me."

"I'm so sorry," he murmured, releasing my hand to cup my cheek. "How did he die?"

"He had a degenerative lung disease that eventually killed him. He'd ended up moving to the East Coast and I'd visited once or twice before he got sick. I miss him despite the fact we weren't incredibly close. I was used to him being gone so I was able to cope. I'm a lot like him though. I crave adventure, I'm restless and I want to see the world. That's why I came to Seattle." I bit down on my bottom lip, lifting my hand to rest against his heart.

"Mick, all I've ever wanted out of life was to explore. I never felt like love was that important. It might seem strange because I'm a young woman and most at my age are falling in love, dreaming about weddings or babies. That's just not me. I've never felt like I needed anyone, until you."

"Babe." He brushed his lips against mine before pulling back.

"I know we really haven't spent a lot of time together in the grand scheme of things. It's just that when I'm with you, it feels right. I'm comfortable around you. I'm not afraid to be myself. I don't know what I want out of life yet. I only know I want you by my side. When I thought I lost you, those six months apart were a nightmare for me. I didn't care that Hawks beat me." I frowned when he winced at the thought. "Sometimes I'd mouth off to him on purpose because I wanted to feel something, anything other than the pain of losing you. That's how I know what I feel for you is real. Because losing you affected me more than my other losses. Then when I saw you again, it's like my heart healed itself with that first glance. I instantly felt whole."

"You're the strongest person I've ever met to go through being held captive like that for so long. You were in isolation, yet here you are having made it out without being overwhelmed or completely broken. I hate that I'm the reason that happened to you, that I couldn't get to you sooner."

"I don't blame you."

"I know, because you're a beautiful soul and that makes me feel even more like a bastard. I swear to you I've never felt the way I do about you with anyone before. I love you more than anything in this world. When I think about my future, you're in it. I've felt that way since the day I took you to the waterfall."

I swiped at my cheeks as tears spilled out. "The same day you told me you were an asshole and didn't need me." I smirked at him, earning a chuckle.

"Yeah, well, I didn't want to admit it. I was trying so hard to resist the pull you have on me because I knew you'd be better off without me. I held on to you longer than I should have because I was selfish. It led us down a road where I almost lost you."

"It led me to you," I said. "We're together and everything is okay now. That's what's important."

He licked his lips, nodding. "Forever, okay?" His brows rose. "I don't want to scare you off or anything but I'm serious when I say I want to spend the rest of my life with you. Whether that involves marriage or simply proving my love to every single day, I'll do it."

My lips tipped up. "Who would have known that Mickey fucking Silver was such a sweetheart," I teased.

He kissed me soundly before moving until he was settled between my legs again. "Only for you, sweet Claire. As far as anyone else is concerned, I'm still a cocky prick with no morals." He tugged my bottom lip between his teeth.

I moaned as he bit down on the side of my neck before soothing it with his tongue. "I don't mind the lack of morals right now," I admitted in a breathy voice.

He placed his lips at my ear, releasing a low growl that sent a flood of heat straight to my core. "I love you so much my sexy as hell, badass partner in crime."

The End

Acknowledgements

I would like to start off by thanking all of the readers for once again taking a chance on me and reading my stories! It means the world to me that you are entertained by what I write. Thank you!

Next, I'd like to thank my incredible team of amazing women at Aurora Publicity for believing in me and helping me make this series better than I ever could have imagined. Cam, I love that you love this story as much as I do! You've changed my life for the better and I am so grateful for your hard work and feedback on this series. Also to Samantha, Laura, and Melody for helping me blossom into a real life author with your encouragement and help. I am so incredibly grateful to be working with you all.

To my husband, Jeff, you're my biggest fan and constant supporter. I love you so much.

To my mother for encouraging me, my best friend Liz for believing in me, and the rest of you that do the same; you're appreciated more than you know.

Here's to creating more stories in the future!

~ Melissa

Contact

K. MORGAN

www.melissakmorgan.com
Facebook: @AuthorMelissaKMorgan
Facebook Group: M.K.'s Book Babes
Instagram: @author_melissa_k_morgan
Email: authormelissakmorgan@gmail.com

Silver Series

Two brothers. Two Women. One dangerous world.

SOMETHING TO BELIEVE IN, BOOK #1

She's nothing he expected. He's nothing she wanted.
Mackaela Stone is damaged. Haunted by her past, she's worked
hard to wall herself off from ever repeating the mistakes that left
her feeling too filthy for love. But meeting Simon Silver might be
enough to crack those fortifications—if he can overcome his own
turbulent history.
Trusting one another is hard enough, but finding faith, hope
and love may be more than they can manage. Is their connection
enough to give them something to believe in? Or is the damage
done too great to overcome?

SOMETHING TO HOLD ONTO, BOOK #2

She was supposed to be the key to everything he ever wanted.
He was the shadow of a past she swore she'd leave behind.
Claire Evan's is risking it all. She knew her new job—working for
the golden boy of Seattle, Mickey Silver—might be too good to be
true. But the perks of playing his game were more than she could
resist, even if the price included being dragged deeper into his

cruel, dark world. Now his game of revenge may take them both down a path of mutual destruction.

Can working together finally open their eyes to what matters most? Or will the cost of cold ambition leave them both broken and alone?

STANDALONE CONTEMPORARY ROMANCES BY MELISSA K. MORGAN

Always Beautiful

Sometimes fate doesn't just throw you a curve ball, it hits you in the face. Breaking your nose, blackening your eyes, and making you second guess everything you've spent your entire life working toward. Do you ignore that ball and continue in the direction of security and stability? Or do you throw caution to the wind, follow your heart, and potentially become so damaged that you'll never recover?

Experiencing an intensity she's never known, a passion she's never felt, and a way to escape the mundane has Lucky changing her once solid foundation. But seasons change and so do people. When she discovers Zeppelin is hiding something from her, those walls she let fall so easily begin to build back up. Zeppelin finally reveals his devastating secret and Lucky is left with two choices. Walk away and forget him entirely or take his hand and follow him into the darkness and sorrow.

(Available in eBook on Amazon.com and Free in Kindle Unlimited)

Let Me Down

Maria Fredericks is starting over. After nearly a decade of living in the shadows of a deep depression and losing herself, she is finally moving on.

Nothing matters anymore as long as her and her six year old daughter are happy and safe.

As a result of the many years being broken down, Maria is strug-

gling to figure out who she is after everything she was made to believe.

Knox Allen is no stranger to pain. Though he was able to obtain a second chance at life, not a day goes by that he doesn't remember what it was like to feel like nothing.

Knox and Maria find solace in each other, but the temporary respite is not as serene as they thought it would be. Maria can't trust him or herself for that matter. Knox fears their unexpected bond will end up hurting him in the end.

Can two broken people survive the modern world and all the drama that goes along with it? Or will their fears get the best of them and leave them crashing and burning at the end of it all?

(Available in eBook on Amazon.com and Free in Kindle Unlimited)